This book is dedicated
to the memory of

*Colin Coffey*
&
*Donal Bolton*

Lives should not be measured in years
but by the quality of the memories
left behind.

To
PAULINE,

My 'MISTRESS OF CEREMONY'

MANY thANks

Hugh

1

# Hiding Ugly Children

## By

## Hugh Flanagan

# HIDING UGLY CHILDREN

## Prologue.

The talking was over. He had tried everything to buy time and to reason, but quickly found there was no changing a twisted mind bent on murder. Lying chest down on the top of a narrow block wall and with his hands tied to his legs behind his back, he grimaced as he strained hard to break the restraints, his feet and hands pulling strenuously in opposite directions, but they would not budge.

His tormentor yanked on the restraints. "Are you ready to take your last breath, Joggy?"

He winced as a bolt of pain seared through his joints and muscles. It felt as if his arms were being torn out of their sockets.

"Fuck you, you miserable piece of shit."

"Joggy, such language, I'm surprised at you, and you about to meet your maker!"

"They'll find me and they'll know it was you," he shouted.

"You'll never be found," he said with sadistic joy.

"I guarantee it. Take your last breath it has to last you a lifetime."

In the past, Joggy had mused on the nature of his death several times. Occasionally during his walks and at other times at mass while enduring a lengthy boring sermon, and always he dreamed of old age, a short illness, during which he would get the chance to say goodbye, and then a quick death. The reality however was going to be very different. He was, at forty two, going to die young. He would not get the chance to say goodbye and his death would be quick --- and horrible; he was about to drown in a slurry pit. Joggy took one last look into the slimy green piss pond that was to be his final resting place. He turned his head to the left away from the methane vapours he could not smell, but knew to be there. He filled his lungs to bursting, clamped his lips and eyelids tightly, gritted his teeth and then began to top it up with a series of short sharp nasal breaths.

As he waited for the final push, desperation drove his thoughts into overdrive and a great sadness came over him. For the first time, he thought about his family. He had been too pre-occupied arguing his case to think of them before this. Alice, his wife of twenty years, he tried to recall the last time he had looked into those beautiful hazel eyes and said I love you…. but couldn't remember. He thought about his son Daniel, now eighteen, and how he would miss him becoming a man. He thought about Helen, vivacious like her mother, just into her teenage years; he would miss that sharp mind and equally sharp tongue. He thought of Katie, only six, with a head of auburn curls, and as cute as a puppy. It would be harder for her; she would grow up with only vague memories of him. He could feel the emotion building; tears rising. He breathed faster and choked them back. With his heart thumping and pulse racing, he thought of begging for his life, then instantly dismissed it. No way was he going to show weakness and give the bastard even a morsel of morbid satisfaction to feed on. Anyway, he knew, he would only be wasting his breath: his fate was sealed.

 Suddenly, his restraints tightened and his head rose up. He felt the warmth of moist breath on his ear. "Goodbye Joggy," the man whispered. "Be sure to pass on my regards to Luke."

Then with a rough push, he was rolled off the narrow wall and fell, right side first. It was a short fall, and even though he was prepared, the warm acrid water very nearly made him gasp some of his precious breath. He sank quickly for the first couple of feet through the top layer until he hit the solids and his descent became more gradual, like being sucked into quicksand. He writhed and wriggled in the desperate hope of freeing his hands from the bonds, but they would not budge. His descent came to a halt. To preserve what air he had in his lungs, he ceased wriggling. As he lay at the bottom of his viscous tomb, a curse played on his tongue while a prayer echoed clearly in his head. "O my God, I am heartily sorry for having offended thee."
He cursed his stupidity; chasing after a madman and not telling anyone where he was going. He had allowed blind rage to consume him and now nobody knew where he was and nobody was going to save him.

The pressure on his ribcage was almost unbearable. With only seconds left before his air and life expired -- he wondered if his body would ever be found. His final thoughts turned to the letter and the last time he saw his old friend Luke. Never in his wildest dreams did he imagine he might be greeting him again so soon.

# Chapter 1

The letter had arrived by post a few months earlier. It was a Wednesday. He had come home that evening from his work as a freelance gardener to be greeted at the front door by his wife Alice. She held the letter in her hand. Normally she opened all the post. However this one was different. She knew who it was from and did not feel it was her right to open it. Imprinted in the top left-hand corner was the official stamp of Portmand Prison and his name, Joggy Jackson, written in clean black letters. "What's for dinner?" He pushed the letter deep into the back pocket of his faded blue dungarees. "I'm starving."

"Aren't you going to open it first?" Alice was anxious to know its contents.

"Later, after I've had me dinner." He squeezed passed her in the doorway. "The contents of that envelope could spoil me appetite." He removed his black donkey jacket and hung it on the back of the kitchen door.

He sat at the end of the kitchen table, retrieved the letter from his back pocket, ran his thumb slowly across the handwriting and then propped it against the ornate glass sugar bowl in the centre of the table for everyone to see. He was as eager and as curious to know what the letter had to say as his wife, but he liked to play the game: drawing the inquisitive tension out until someone snapped; usually it was Alice. But it also made him a little uneasy; Luke had never written to him before.

Alice called the three children in for dinner. Daniel burst in through the doorway. Being eighteen his long legs easily out-sprinted his two younger squealing siblings. Helen was fourteen and Katie was six. They all spotted the letter but it was Katie who asked. "Who's that from, Da?"

"I think it's from Luke Baker."

"Who's he?"

"A friend of mine who got into trouble and is now in Portmand Prison."

"Was he bold, Da? Is that why he's in prison?"

"Yes pet." He would have preferred to answer her truthfully, but it would have prompted too many questions. "It's because he was very bold," He could not meet her inquisitive eyes.

Alice glared across at Joggy as she placed a plate of mashed potato, sausage and a fried egg in front of Katie. "Put that in your mouth. It'll stop ya asking so many questions." She frowned on talk of Luke Baker at the dinner table: murderers were not welcome in her kitchen, not even in conversation.

When dinner was over she and a reluctant Helen cleared away the dishes. Helen grumbled and complained to her Mother. "Why don't you ask Daniel to help clear away? Why do you always ask me?"

It was part of Alice's upbringing, for the women folk to wait on the men and so she had no answer for her daughter or at least one she could understand, so she resorted to her stock answer. "Because that's the why."

"That's a stupid answer," Helen said sharply.

"Don't be so cheeky," her mother retorted.

"I'm telling you now, mum, whoever I marry will starve before I'll wait on him."

Alice poured out the tea and then seated herself on the sofa by the window. Rays of evening sunlight transformed her auburn tresses into rich copper. She glanced at her husband, who was nonchalantly leaning back in his chair at the end of the table savouring his tea. "Are you going to open that letter?" She had finally lost her patience. "Because if you don't, I will."

"Lord, aren't you an impatient woman." He cracked a smile and reached for the envelope, slipped the handle of a teaspoon into the corner of the fold and sliced open the top. He extracted a single sheet of white note paper and -- after quickly scanning it for anything that might upset Alice or the children -- he read it aloud.

It was dated Tuesday 20/03/1973.

*Dear Joggy,*
*I hope this letter finds you, Alice and the children in good health. I know I asked you and several other friends not to visit me again, but this is different. Joggy I'm dying. The rats, (the actual word was bastards) they'll no longer be able to keep me locked up. I'll shortly walk my land again as a free man. But before I go, I would like to see you one last time.*

*Please, for old time sake, don't let me down. Make it as soon as possible.*

*Your friend always*
*Luke.*

"What do you think of that?" He searched Alice's face for a reaction; she looked worried.

"Are they letting your friend out of prison Daddy?" Katie asked.

"Yes pet." His voice was almost a whisper, as he absorbed the implication in Luke's letter. "In a manner of speaking they are."

"Can ye all go out and play," said Alice. "I want to talk to your father."

The children left reluctantly. Alice waited until they were well gone before she spoke again. "What are you going to do?"

"I'll have to go and see him."

"When?"

"Saturday."

"You'll do no such thing, you'll go tomorrow."

"But tomorrow's a work day."

"I'm quite aware of that," she said, in mild frustration. "By the sound of his letter, Saturday might be too late. Besides, he wouldn't ask unless it was important."

"I thought you didn't believe in his innocence?"

"I don't. I still think he did it. But it's for your sake, that I think you should go. After all, it may be the last chance you get to repay your debt."

He jumped up from his chair. "You don't need to remind me of my debt." he snatched his black donkey jacket from the back of the kitchen door.

Alice knew where he was going. "Tell Tom I was asking for him," she said to her husbands retreating back as he shrugged himself into his Jacket and went out the door.

He sauntered down the footpath to his front gate with Alice's words still echoing loudly in his head. At the gate he stopped and reached into the left-hand pocket of his bibbed overalls and took out a packet of Sweet Afton cigarettes. With the cigarette between his lips he patted his other pockets in search of matches. He cupped his hands to protect the flame from the breeze, a couple of quick pulls and the flame gripped the tobacco. He latched the gate behind him, shoved his left hand into his Jacket pocket, withdrew the cigarette from his lips and started walking. It was a ten minute walk, down the hill, under the dark grey stone railway bridge, where a sign painted on one wall in bold black capitals warned, POST NO BILLS. He then climbed to the top of the opposite incline and crossed a small bridge fording a rippling stream. The road levelled out and he made his way the short distance to Baker's. Theirs was the last in a line of four cottages that skirted the left-hand side of the road. The yard was another fifty yards up the road on the right-hand side. The ruins of the Baker ancestral two-story home stood on one side of the yard: No glass remained in the windows and the roof had fallen in.  The yard was a scrap yard of old cars, shelled, which doubled as housing for Tom's numerous sows. At the far end of the yard was a stone outhouse with a low wall on one end, encircling an open space. Leaning on the wall, enraptured, was Tom Baker - a small man, wearing oversized top boots and a grimy beige cloth cap.

Joggy halted beside him. "I see Winter's boar has arrived."

"Gawnee, gawnee, Joggy," said Tom, not taking his eyes of the boar as it mounted a young sow. "Isn't he a fine specimen?" A lascivious smile hung about his lips as the boar got into his stride. "Gawnee, gawnee, Joggy," Tom said excitedly. "With every jig a little pig and sometimes three and four."

Joggy laughed and then accompanied Tom back to the house.


* * * *

Tuesday morning, shortly after he had driven away from the house, Joggy, dressed in his best Sunday suit, opened the top button of his shirt and loosened the tie. He had argued with Alice that morning on what to wear. He wanted to wear casual; trousers, shirt and jumper, but Alice insisted he look his best.

His chat with Tom, Luke's brother, the previous evening shed no light on what his brother wanted. If Tom knew, and he was pretty sure he did, he wasn't saying. Probably under orders not to talk, he thought.

Black rain clouds lurked ominously on the horizon as he manoeuvred his pride and joy; a two-year-old slate grey Morris Traveller, around the grey twisted roads that led to Portmand Prison. He was still in the habit of chastising his children, shouting at them to keep their feet off the leather seats, as they climbed with abandon into the back. He had recently bought it and the newness of it had not worn off him yet. Its highly varnished wooden frame gleamed in the rain-cloud broken sunlight. The nicotine-stained fingers of his right hand gripped both the steering wheel and a Sweet Afton cigarette. The smoke drifted out through the top of the partially opened window. The overcast sky matched his gloomy mood.

Joggy parked the car in the visitors' section of Portmand Prison and, with the help of the rear view mirror, re-adjusted his shirt and tie. Twice that morning as he progressed through the security check points he was asked," Are you a solicitor?"

He felt chuffed and at the same time worried. While he waited in the reception area for Luke, he could not help noticing that the only men in suits were solicitors. He suddenly felt self-conscious and overdressed.

For Luke Baker, prison was hell on earth. Gone was everything he cherished…. the carefree lifestyle…..the open countryside…..walking the land and counting his stock. Gone was the chorus of birdsong that woke him each morning. Gone was the friendly banter that prevailed while supping a few creamy pints of an evening in O Meara's. Gone was his friend John Canavan. He awoke now to an incessant wall of sound, metal doors clanging and banging and harsh grating voices telling him what to do. Daily meals were served with hundreds of strangers, people he had no desire to meet or get to know. The injustice of his situation tore at his soul, depressed him and made him ill.

A door opened at the far end of the reception area and Joggy was taken aback when Luke entered in a wheelchair. The once-healthy forty-four-year-old was thin and emaciated. His cheek bones were sharply defined beneath sallow, blotched skin. His clothes hung from his shoulders as if they were suspended on a wire coat hanger and in his lap his skeletal hands cradled a white handkerchief with tiny specks of blood on it.

The prison warder parked him so as to face Joggy across the table.

"You look good in your Sunday best, Joggy," Luke gasped. "But you didn't need to get all dressed up for me." He lifted the handkerchief and coughed a long, wheezy, dry cough into it.

Joggy tried to smile but pity overcame him. "Lord, Luke, I was going bullshit you and say how well you looked, but you and I know that'd be a lie. What on earth has happened to you? I mean, Jaysus, are they not feeding ya?"

"Food is not a problem Joggy. But you've got to have an appetite for it. There are people in here who have the appetite for the food and for the place, and it doesn't bother them. They've been in and out of here so often it now feels like a second home to them. They belong here. I don't."

"I agree, you don't belong here, but you can't give up either. You can't lose hope."

"Hope," Luke sneered. "Hope is for the guilty. Those who believe they'll one day be free. But I am innocent, and so Joggy that day will never come for me."

"What do you mean? Sure they'll have to let you out sometime."

"Only if I express remorse, and I can't be remorseful for something I didn't do."

He took another fit of coughing. Joggy could only look on, not knowing what to say. Luke stopped and wiped his mouth.

"Thanks for coming at such short notice, Joggy. I really appreciate it."

"I'm just sorry it's not under better circumstances, like over a game of twenty-five."

"So do I, so do I." He glanced over Joggy's shoulder at a warder who was watching them intently, then leaned a little closer.

"There's a screw behind you Joggy and he hasn't taken his eyes of me since I came in." He tried to laugh but coughed instead. "He must think I'm going to make a run for it."

Joggy looked over his shoulder at him and then back at Luke. "Don't worry about him; he's too far away to hear us."

"Still, I'd better tell you what I need, before time is up." Luke's sunken grey and bloodshot eyes pleaded with Joggy. "I want you to clear my name." He said no more, allowing it to sink in. "Wh..wh..what?" The word stumbled out. "Me? You want me to clear your name? But how on earth can I do that?"

"By finding the real murderer! You know I didn't kill John Canavan?"

"Yeah, I know that, but what makes you think I can find the killer?"

"The same way you found Missus Tynan's jewellery."

"A jaysus, Luke, there's a world of difference between working out that a magpie was thieving those baubles and catching a killer."

"Not really, it all boils down to logic and observation and you're the most logical and observant fella I know. I appreciate I'm asking a lot. But I don't want to die and have my name forever known as a murderer. I want to sleep in peace and all I'm asking is for you to try."

"But where on earth would I start to look?"

"The only good thing about being in here is it gives you time to think. I believe the person who killed the 'Horse' Canavan had to be local. Not alone that, but I think he held a grudge against both of us. He murdered John and set me up for it. John kept a small black notebook. I remember seeing it a couple of times on his kitchen table. Whenever he'd see me looking at it he'd pick it up and put it in his pocket. I'm thinking that something in that notebook got him killed. Why else would he be so secretive about it? The guards never found it: Which leads me to believe that the killer took it or more than likely it's hidden in the house; because I never saw it on him. The only book he carried around with him was a book of Robert Frost poems."

"I remember that little book," Joggy interjected. "He showed it to me once. It was a hard-back with gold lettering on the front and edge."

"The guards never found it either and neither did they find his bike. I think the killer has them both."

"That's all very fine, but even if I do find them there's no way of identifying them as Canavan's."

"Ah, but there is. John initialled everything of value he owned, in case they were stolen. I called one day when he had just bought the bike and found him scratching his initials into the handlebar and when he finished he replaced the right-hand rubber handgrip to hide it." Luke took another fit of coughing but when he finished he asked again, "Will you do it, Joggy?"

"I don't know if I'll be successful Luke. I wouldn't want you to pin all your hopes on me."

"I can understand that. But freedom is not just about the body, it also affects the mind. Right now I'm fettered to the memory of the 'Horse' Canavan's murder. Think about it. What's the first thought that comes into people's minds when my name is mentioned?"

"The 'Horse' Canavan murder," Joggy said hesitantly.

"Right. So you see what I mean. Just now I'm not free in people's minds to wander to places I was always associated with. They can't get past it. I'm there shackled to that memory." Once again his bloodshot eyes pleaded with Joggy. "Get me out of there Joggy, please."

Joggy stared unseeing at Luke's face for an indeterminable time. Alice's face had replaced it and she was saying over and over, it may be the last chance you get to repay your debt. "I don't know if I'll be able to do any good, but I'll give it a shot," he said eventually. "I'll make some enquires and see where that leads me."

Luke's face lit up. "That's all I can ask for Joggy. Knowing that someone cares and is carrying on the fight to clear my name will allow me to rest in peace. Thank you," he said warmly. "You're a true friend."

"It's the least I can do. You saved me once, now it's my turn."

"God, Joggy." Luke became visibly distressed and coughed. "I didn't ask you here to return a debt. That never entered my head. I asked because you're the only person I know capable of clearing my name. I don't want you to do it if you think you're under some sort of... obligation."

"I'm sorry Luke, I'm sorry, I shouldn't have said anything. I'm doing it because I believe you're innocent. Not for one minute have I ever thought you were otherwise. I have always defended you, in O' Meara's and out of it. So rest easy.... I'm doing it."

Luke relaxed. "I know how you defend me Joggy, Tom has told me several times."

The bell went for time up and the warder who had been watching them moved away from the wall and started towards Luke. "When you were doing all that thinking, Luke, about who would have held a grudge against both you and Canavan, you didn't by any chance come up with a likely suspect for me, did you?" He pushed his chair back and stood up.

Luke shook his head. "Afraid not, Joggy. I've stood on a few toes in my life, but I didn't hurt any of them badly enough for them to do this to me."

Joggy and Luke said their goodbyes and the warder wheeled Luke back to his cell. With sadness in his heart, Joggy watched him go and wondered if he would ever see his old friend again.

* * * *

Alice sat listening intently to her husband as he replayed his conversation with Luke.

"You're not seriously thinking of doing this, are you?"

Joggy ran a hand slowly across his mouth.

"You are," she said in astonishment. "You're going to do this. Have you thought it through?"

"I've done nothing else since I left the prison."

"No, I don't mean the fantasy: the one where you picture yourself as some sort of… caped crusader or private detective on the trail of the baddie. I mean the repercussions this could have on all of us. If you are to believe Luke, and if this person really exists, do you honestly think he is going to lie still and allow you to expose him? He's killed once. What's to stop him doing it again?"

"Because the last thing this person wants to do, is to let us know he exists. This person wants us all to continue believing that Luke is the killer. If he or she is as smart as I think they are, they'll not do anything to change that."

"Alright, so you have given it some thought," Alice conceded. She realised what this meant to Joggy. But she was still not happy. This was the last thing she expected. She did not want her husband involved, but for now she felt she had no choice other than to go along with it … after all, it was she who encouraged him to go in the first place. "Just, give yourself an extra day to think it over. Before that is," she tried to smile, "you turn into Sherlock Holmes."

* * * *

When Luke was first incarcerated, his niece brought him an oil painting to hang on his cell wall. She thought it would help cheer him up. It was a country scene with a stand of tall oak trees. Behind them a church spire stood stark against an azure sky. In the foreground beside a rippling stream, a herd of Friesians grazed freely on a rich green pasture. At first it cheered him, gave him hope, but gradually as time wore on and hope dwindled, it began to tease him ... mock him … even torment him. He took it down and pushed it under his cell cot.

But tonight he retrieved it and re-hung it. And now lying on his cot, he smiled at the scene, illuminated by the moonlight filtering through the high window of his cell. He closed his eyes and dreamed of walking his land again, of sitting on the tree stump by the river's edge, smoking his pipe and listening to the gentle trickle of the water and watching sandpipers and kingfishers at play.

* * * *

On Friday evening after work Joggy, head down, walked up the rough concrete path to his home. All that day and the previous night he had tossed and turned it over and over in his head. While he wanted to do the right thing by Luke, he could not risk putting his family in the line of fire of a killer he did not know. The inherent danger to his family was too strong.
Alice was standing in the doorway when he looked up, a solemn expression on her face.

"It's all right, it's all right, I've changed my mind. I'm going to write to Luke tonight and tell him I can't do it."

Alice stood her ground in the doorway.

"What? I thought you'd be happy?"

"I'm so sorry." She grasped his hand.

"He's dead, isn't he?" The answer was in her eyes.

## CHAPTER 2

Joggy sat on the top step of the front porch of his white pebble-dashed cottage and watched the sun go down. He had bought the cottage a few months before they were married. It had only three rooms then; a typical country cottage, two bedrooms, one each side of the kitchen. Shortly after they moved in, they built on a bathroom and as the years went by and the family expanded, they kept adding more rooms until finally Alice was satisfied with the finished product. It was now her castle, her pride and joy and it stood on the top of a hill. A concrete footpath, which today was lined on both sides with daffodils, crocuses and the last of the snowdrops, weaved its way up the incline to the front door. All around them lay unspoiled countryside … fields of green with spring lambs and grazing cattle. One of the fields had a small wood running parallel to it; that was the children's playground where eager, young, imaginative minds acted out their dramas and played their games. When it grew dark, the distant lights of Oldbridge were clearly visible from the front step. Above the town the night sky glowed a warm orange. Two hundred yards away lay the Galway-to-Dublin railway line, where late at night, while you lay in bed, half asleep, the last goods train passed and its whistle, an eerie shrill in the dead of night, would send shivers down your spine.

He sat there quiet, subdued. Ten days had passed since Luke's death and his mood had not changed. It bothered him deeply that he had reneged on the commitment he had given to his best friend. He knew Alice was right, family safety came first. But no matter how he justified it to himself, it still ate away at him like a cancer.

Alice placed her hand on his head and gently kneaded her fingers through his unruly hair, black and tousled and with the odd strand of steely grey. She sat down beside him. He turned slowly to her, gave a hint of a smile and then turned away again. She could see he was hurting. The pain was in those smoky-blue eyes of his.

She knew her husband almost as well as she knew herself, for there were no secrets between them. He held what some would regard as old-fashioned principles: honesty, integrity and above all, honour were hugely important to him. He was a man of his word. She understood that and the circumstances of his past that drove him forward and influenced the decisions he made in daily life. Burning brightly within her was the same powerful emotion she had felt the day she married him and it pained her to see him like this.

He took a drag from his cigarette. She never allowed him to smoke in the house, nor would she kiss him when the taste was on his breath. He now always carried a packet of silvermints and munched two every night before he went to bed.

"John Canavan's notebook," she said, after a few thoughtful seconds. "The one Luke said the guards never found!"

"Yeah!"

"I was just wondering if he had a hiding place in the house, one where no-one would think of looking."

"I'm sure he could have." He wondered why Alice had broached this up-to-now taboo subject.

"I suppose the only way to find out is to search the place."

"I suppose it is."

"I don't think it would do any harm to have a little look; do you? Especially now that the place has been empty this few years. I think it would satisfy our curiosity." Her eyes glowed with the warmth of her smile.

Excitedly, Joggy cupped her face in his large calloused hands. "Alice you gorgeous woman," he said and planted a big kiss on her lips.

"Stop that. What would the neighbours say if they saw us?" Feigning indignation, she slapped lightly the back of his hands.

"They'd say I was the luckiest man in the world." He jumped down off the step.

"Where are you going?"

"To search Canavan's. There's no time like the present, besides, if I don't do it now I won't be able to sleep tonight."

"Just be careful," she called after him, as he moved swiftly down the path to his car.

"I will," he shouted back over his shoulder.

A short distance from Canavan's, he parked the car down a bog lane in a field gateway. He plucked a silver torch from the boot and made a wide detour, approaching the house from the fields. The night was black save for brief glimpses of moonlight that penetrated through small tears in the blanket of cloud.

Canavan's was another old three-roomed-cottage, a bedroom on either side of the kitchen, an outside toilet opposite the back door and a fuel shed beside it. Ever since his mother died, John had lived alone with only a radio and his many books for company. Now, for the first time, Joggy switched on his torch and shone it on a large flat stone that John used for a step outside the timber fuel shed. He lifted it and to his relief found the backdoor spare key was still there. He let himself in. The place was a shell and smelt of damp. A backless chair sat among torn scraps of wallpaper and lumps of ceiling plaster were strewn across the grey concrete of the kitchen floor. The ceilings of all three rooms were pock-marked with holes, showing evidence of a previous search. Even the old Stanley range in the kitchen was gone, leaving only the painted red–brick surround. Joggy's heart sank. He had not expected the place to be in such disarray. After a quick search, there was nothing left for him to do, but go home. He locked the back door and placed the key back under the flat stone.

"Find what you were looking for," a voice asked.

Startled, Joggy turned around and was immediately blinded by torchlight. His hand shot up to shield his eyes from the glare.

"Joggy Jackson!" The voice sounded surprised. "I'd never have taken you for a burglar."

Despite his rapidly beating heart pounding loudly in his ears, Joggy recognised the voice as that of the local sergeant, Ed McNeill. "Lower your torch, Ed, you're blinding me."

Ed lowered his torch and after a few seconds, Joggy's eyes readjusted to the dark.

"What were you doing in there?" McNeill asked.

"Well I definitely wasn't robbing the place, because there's nothing in there to rob."

"That doesn't answer my question, Joggy."

"I was looking for something, but I didn't find it."

"And what would that be?"

"I can't say."

"Well whatever it was, it's probably gone. The knackers gave the place a good going over a while ago. The only thing left after Canavan's relatives cleaned it out was the old Stanley range, and the knackers helped themselves to that."

"So what do we do now?" Joggy enquired.

"We go our separate ways. But on your way home from work Monday evening, I would like you to call and see me at the station."

"What for?"

"To discuss this misadventure of yours, of course!"

"What's to discuss?" Joggy asked irritably. "I wasn't robbing the place and I certainly didn't break in."

"Well, in the eyes of the law you were trespassing and you didn't have permission to enter the premises, and, might I add suspicion of robbery to that. After all, you did not know there was nothing left to rob till you entered the house. So I think we do have something to talk about. Don't you?"

Joggy said nothing.

"So ... Monday evening." The Sergeant walked away with a smile of quiet satisfaction. But it was too dark for Joggy to notice that.

The encounter left him embarrassed and a little curious. He called after McNeill. "How did you know I was here?"

"Old Missus Quinn across the road saw the light of your torch in one of the windows and thought the knackers were back. I'll tell you one thing Joggy, you'd never make a living as a burglar."


When Ed returned, Mary McNeill was draining the last of her cocoa from her 'Greatest Mum in the world' mug.

"Any trouble?" she asked without turning around, her eyes firmly fixed on the T.V.

"Nah, just kids messing around."

"There's still hot milk in the saucepan if you want to make cocoa."

"Thanks, I think I will."

When Ed came into the living room, Mary had the T.V switched off and was preparing to go to bed.

"I'm going up," she said. "Are you coming?"

"In a few minutes, I've something to do first."

She knew better than to enquire further. Ed was never forthcoming about his work. The answer would have been vague at best and she would be left none the wiser.

Ed left the living room and entered the short front hall. It divided the main house from the Garda station. He turned right and then unlocked the station door on his left. Inside the door two tall slate grey filling cabinets stood with their backs against the wall. He unlocked the third drawer with the initials I. J. K. written in bold black marker on the front and extracted a manila file from the section marked J.

# Chapter 3

The angelus bells had just finished their chiming on the radio as Danny entered the kitchen in his stockinged feet. There was a spring in his step and the joy of life echoed in his voice. "Hi Dad!" He had removed his soiled rubber boots and left them sitting outside the back door.

Joggy was sitting at the end of the kitchen table perusing the Kilpatrick notes in the local weekly paper and worrying that his name might appear there shortly. He had not told Alice of his misadventure. He hoped he could sort it out Monday evening without her knowing. "Well someone's in a happy mood." He took off his reading glasses and smiled at his son. "What has you in such good form?"

"You won't believe it, Dad, but Mister Winter has asked me to work for a few hours tomorrow and as many Sundays as I want after that."

"I hope you turned him down," Joggy replied flatly.

"Why would I do that? Sure I'll be able to save what I earn for college. The more money I make the less of a burden it'll be on you."

"That's a very noble notion, Danny. But we do not work on Sundays."

"Loads of people work on Sundays; doctors, nurses, farmers!"

"None of which you are. The answer is still no."

"Come off it Dad, it's only a couple of hours and anyway he's paying me double money."

"That's very generous of him," Joggy said sarcastically. "But I don't care if he is paying you in gold, the answer is still the same, no, you are not working on a Sunday."

"I didn't ask you for permission. I'm old enough to make my own decisions and anyway, I've already said yes."

Joggy placed his reading glasses on the outstretched newspaper, rose and glared up at his son, who, at six foot two, was four inches taller than his father and sported the same head of black tousled hair.

Danny was not afraid of his dad. His father had never hit him. Nevertheless, this fierceness in his father unnerved him.

"Maybe you didn't hear me, Daniel." He spoke sharply, emphasising his son's full name. "So let me make it crystal clear to you. You are not working on Sundays, not for Fred Winter, not for anybody while you live under this roof."

Danny parted his lips as if to object but Joggy lifted a finger and stifled the words in his throat.

"And this time, it would be wise of you not to go against my wishes."

"You're unbelievable." Danny had fire in his eyes. "Here I have a chance to ease the burden of college on you and you just throw it back in my face."

"Some things are more important than money, Danny. Someday you'll understand that."

Right now Danny did not want to understand. A few minutes before, he was delirious with joy. He had it all worked out. The number of weeks, the money he would make and how much of it he would be able to save. In his mind it was perfect. He turned sharply away and slammed his bedroom door behind him.

Joggy sat back down, a little shaken. Alice came from outside and stood in the kitchen doorway, their eyes momentarily held each other. He guessed she had been listening. The loud strains of Danny's favourite group, Slade, suddenly started up in his room.

A short time later after Joggy left for a walk, Alice knocked and then paused for a few seconds. She was mindful that he was becoming a man and did not want to rush in and catch him in an embarrassing position. She opened the door slowly and entered the room.

Danny flicked a switch at the side of the record player, the arm lifted and the music stopped. "It's not fair Mum, he has no right to stop me making extra money."

Alice sat on the edge of Danny's bed. "Let me ask you something. Do you respect your Father?"

"Yes, of course I do."

"Good, I'm glad to hear that. Being a good parent is not easy, Danny. Sometimes we have to make unpopular decisions and sometimes the reasons for those decisions do not become clear 'till much later."

"Why can't he explain it to me now?"

"He's not ready, I guess. But he's not the only one who is against Sunday work. Would you like to hear my reason?"

"Go on."

"Sunday is God's and mans only day of rest. There are enough hours in the previous six days to get done whatever people need to do, without it spilling over into the only rest day we have. That's my reason. But as for your father and why he is dead set against Sunday work…well…his is a more personal reason. It's something that runs very deep in him and maybe soon, he'll tell you about it. Right now you've got to trust his judgement. And believe me when I say that you would do the same if you were in his position."

"I still don't understand why he can't tell it to me now?"

"Leave it with me and I'll talk to him…alright?"

"Alright… but it better be a damn good reason."

\* \* \* \*

Before it became dark, Danny cycled the half mile back to Winter's farm, down the gravelled and potholed laneway and around the back of the large two-storey farmhouse.
Fred Winter was in his mid-forties and a bachelor. He had nursed his ailing mother until her death, four years earlier. His father and younger sister had died years ago. The farm, one of the biggest in the district, was his passion, his life and he watched over it with pride. Fred was polite and well respected in the Kilpatrick area. When Fred came up in conversation in O' Meara's pub, someone always finished it off with, "he's alright for a prod."

Daniel knocked on the kitchen door and was pleasantly surprised when it was opened by a tall, beautiful girl with short, cropped blonde hair and the darkest brown eyes he had ever seen. He was momentarily rendered speechless.

"Who is it, Virginia?" Fred's voice boomed from the kitchen.

"I'm not sure." The girl replied in a Northern Ireland accent that Danny had heard only on T.V. "but I think he's a mute."

"It's, it's Danny Jackson, Mister Winter." He stuttered and reddened with embarrassment.

Fred Winter filled the doorway with the width of his shoulders. Virginia retreated back into the kitchen.

"Yes, Danny, is something the matter?"

"Yes sir, I'm afraid my parents won't allow me to work on Sundays."

"I'm sorry to hear that. When you live at home you have to abide by your parents rules, so I suppose it can't be helped. Thank you for letting me know."

"Will I call down next Saturday?" Danny asked tentatively.

"Of course, this doesn't change anything. It's no fault of yours."

"Thank you." He turned his bicycle around to cycle home.

"Let me guess," Fred said, with a thoughtful smile. "It was your father who said no?"

"Yeah." Danny was surprised. "How'd you know that?"

"History, Danny, history!" Fred closed the kitchen door.

\* \* \* \*

Later that night in the silence and privacy of their bedroom, Alice turned onto her side in the bed and faced her husband.

"Your spat with Danny still on your mind?" She whispered.

Joggy lay on his back. He turned his head and tried in the gloom of the room to find her eyes. "I didn't handle it very well, did I?"

"I've seen you handle things better. But, to be fair, it was a hard one. You should talk to him. Explain to him. He's old enough, he'll understand."

"Yeah… maybe."

He slid across his pillow, found her lips, kissed her, said goodnight and turned away.

# Chapter 4

Josie Tyrell turned the corner at O' Meara's pub and cycled up the hill, carrying in the front basket of her bicycle a bunch of brightly coloured flowers. From his perch on the window-sill of the pub, Squeak Malone watched with interest. His hawkish eyes followed her every movement, up the incline around a slow bend and in through the front gates of Kilpatrick graveyard. Squeak moved swiftly, almost running up the hill and over the stile in the wall beside the main gates. He kept out of sight and watched.

Josie stopped at the graveside, looked furtively around, placed the flowers, said a prayer, blessed herself and left. Josie Tyrell was a blow-in. She married a local. The child they had together was born mentally handicapped. After a period, the pressure got to the husband, who could not take the innuendo about his manhood. He packed his bags in the middle of the night and left a note saying he was sorry, but he was going to England and would not be back. So Josie had no one belonging to her in the graveyard.

Squeak stole out from behind an old ivy covered gravestone and made his way to where Josie had placed the flowers. He pushed his cloth cap back and scratched his head at the name on the headstone. He then licked his lips in anticipation He could almost taste his first pint of the day.

Spit Sweeney was sitting with two other men in front of an open fire playing cards when Squeak walked in. Spit hocked up a mouthful of saliva and spat it into the flames. It hissed as if in indignation. His salivary glands produced more saliva than he needed, necessitating him to spit or swallow the excess. He preferred to spit. He was a small round-headed man with black-framed glasses and a red sweeping-brush moustache. He lived in the village with his elderly mother, worked occasionally as a casual labourer and loved gossip.

"Morning Spit," Squeak said in his-high pitched choirboy voice.

"Don't tell me." Spit instantly deciphered the big stupid grin on Squeak's face. "You have something large and juicy for us?"

"I have, but it's hard to talk with a dry throat."

"Mick, a pint please." Spit shouted to the barman. "It'd better be worth it, Squeak, or it will be the last one I'll buy you."

"It is, it is." Squeak said excitedly. He downed half the pint in the first swallow and then wiped his mouth with the back of his jacket sleeve.

"Well come on." Spit was impatient for the news.

"You'll never guess whose grave Josie Tyrell has just put flowers on? The 'Horse' Canavan's, what do you think of that?"

Spit, who was about to hock another ball of unwanted saliva into the fire.... swallowed it instead.

* * * *

That evening Joggy pulled up in front of the Garda station. Squeak watched. Sergeant McNeill with the evening sunlight gleaming off his bald pate, pared a block of tobacco with his penknife, rolled the slivers between the palms of his hands and then packed them into his pipe. He didn't look up when Joggy entered and approached the open hatch on the wooden counter. He had already noticed through the half-frosted front window his car pull up and park in the church car park opposite the station.

"Evening, Joggy." McNeill sucked hard on his pipe to ignite the tobacco.

"Let's get on with this," Joggy replied irritably.

"What's your hurry?"

"Alice will have the dinner on the table and it'll be going cold."

"Keeping secrets from her are you?"

"I didn't tell her because there was nothing to tell.... anyway, it's none of your business what I tell my wife, so let's get on with this."

"No need to be so tetchy, it's only a friendly chat I want."

"I doubt that." He eyed the man with suspicion. McNeill was not liked in the village. He had an unsavoury reputation and Joggy had heard enough stories from people he knew, who were not liars, to suspect it was fully justified.

"Close the door behind you like a good man and push down the latch. I don't want the whole street to know our business."

The sound of the door closing carried all the way to Squeak's keen ears.

McNeill opened the door at the side of the counter and invited Joggy in.

"Have a seat." He pointed to a blue painted chair beside a neat tidy desk.

Joggy's eyes narrowed. "Are we still talking about the other night?"

"Yes and no."

"So, what is this about then?"

The Sergeant sat back on the warm heavy cast-iron radiator under the window, pulled twice on his pipe and exhaled. "A mutual interest: Luke Baker." The words floated out along with the cloud of hazy blue smoke.

Joggy stayed silent; his face inscrutable. Years of playing cards had taught him how not to give the game away. First to blink loses.

Learning nothing from Joggy's facial expression, McNeill continued. "I believe, like you, that Luke Baker was hard done by. I'm not altogether convinced of his guilt or innocence but something about the case smells."

"If I remember rightly, Ed, at the time you were taking up your new position here, Luke was taking up his in Portmand Prison. So you wouldn't have known him .... But, go on."

"I'd like to join you on your little crusade to clear Luke's name."

"Crusade? What crusade?"

"The one you agreed to take on, the day he died, when he asked you to help clear his name. He thought the notebook you were searching for the other night... just might help his cause."

"How'd you know about that?" Joggy was stunned. "We told nobody."

"I have my spies." McNeill winked, delighted to have penetrated Joggy's poker-face veneer.

Joggy extracted a packet of Sweet Afton cigarettes from the front pocket of his bibbed dungarees. He took one out, rewound his memory back to his last visit with Luke and with his minds eye went over what happened. Absentmindedly he twirled the cigarette between his fingers like a baton, stopping occasionally to tap one end on the box. Suddenly, he put it in his mouth, lit it, took a deep drag and announced, "It's that red haired gollywog of a prison warder, that's who your spy is. All the time we were there, the cunt never took his eyes off us."

The light dulled in the Sergeant's eyes and Joggy knew he had come up trumps.

"But…" Joggy then began to doubt his own conclusion. "He couldn't have heard us above the chatter, he was too far away."

"He can lip read." McNeill, realised he could deny it, but he needed Joggy as an ally and taking him into his confidence was the best way to do it.

"What, you're joking?"

"He has a deaf brother. He learnt how to lip read from him."

"How hard did you have to twist his arm to get him to do that?"

"Not too hard. I did him a favour once by keeping his alcoholic father out of jail."

"And how long will he be paying off that particular debt, I wonder!"

"When he leaves the job or when I retire, whichever comes first."

"Thank God I'm not in debt to you, the mafia give better terms than that."

"So, do you want my help or not?"

"Why would I want your help? And don't tell me your conscience is pricking you, because I know you don't have one."

"As a friend I can be very useful, as an enemy…let's just say you wouldn't want me to be your enemy."

"That doesn't answer my question. Why? What's in this for you?"

"So, is that a no?" He nonchalantly dragged on his pipe as if he had not got a care in the world.

"Not if you gave me all the gold in the world would I make you my partner." Joggy stood up to leave.

Unruffled, McNeill stayed sitting on the radiator. His attention was on his pipe. He pushed down some loose tobacco with his finger, sucked vigorously, and then exhaled a long cloud of sweet smelling smoke. "It seems we have a communication problem here, Joggy. I was just been polite when I asked. What I meant was, make me your partner or face Judge Griffiths and explain to him what you were doing in Canavan's the other night and then the following week all your neighbours can read your explanation in the local rag."

"You're a dirty bastard, McNeill."

"Is that a yes?" He asked, again undeterred by the insult.

Joggy weighted up his options and soon saw he had none. He cursed Mrs Quinn for ringing McNeill. He thought of Alice and instantly understood he could not tell her. The secrets were beginning to pile up. "I'll not work with anyone who holds anything over my head."

"Charge dropped and forgotten about… we have a deal?" McNeill stuck out a hand.

Joggy sighed heavily and ignored the outstretched hand. "My word is my bond."

McNeill stood up and started slowly pacing the floor, puffing earnestly.

"I've given this case a lot of careful thought. In my experience, nine times out of ten, the last words a condemned man says before he dies tend to be truthful. And if that is the way with Luke, then a grave injustice has been done. Because this case is closed and a positive result achieved, it would not do for me to be seen to be asking questions. My superiors would take a dim view and suspect I was trying to undermine the original investigation."

"Which you are of course… but…. for your own good reasons," Joggy mocked.

McNeill ignored him again and continued on undeterred. It had the desired effect. Joggy now knew that whatever reason McNeill had for muscling his way into the investigation, had to be a strong one. And nothing that he could say or do was going to shake him off. So he gave up and listened.

"So, I cannot be seen to be involved directly. What I can do is to pass on as much information as I can get my hands on. But I'm afraid you will have to do the leg work. Do you think you could handle that?"

"It's what I intended to do in the first place."

"Good. Now I think you should go, before Squeak becomes suspicious. Where are you working tomorrow?"

"Cashman's on Cherry Blossom lane."

"Will there be anyone about, say, lunchtime?"

"No. They're not usually back till after five."

"I'll call and see you tomorrow, then."

* * * *

"Have you spoken to Danny yet?" Alice asked as she wiped down the pink floral table oilcloth.

Joggy glanced out from behind the daily paper. "No, not yet."

"Well now is as good a time as any. He's in the tool shed, mending a puncture."

Alice stood looking at Joggy, a dishcloth in her hand and a determined look on her face.

"Right." Joggy got the message. He folded his paper. "I suppose I'd better talk to him then."

He leaned against the doorframe of the tool shed and watched as Danny, with his back turned to him, dunk part of the bicycle tube into a basin of water and then watch carefully for bubbles.

"Do you want a hand?"

Danny glanced back. "No thanks, I'm fine, it's a slow puncture." He rotated another piece of tube and again dunked it in the basin.

"How was school today?"

"Fine."

He cleared his throat. "Listen Danny, thanks for not working on Sundays."

"You didn't give me much of a choice, did you?"

"You went against my wishes once before"

"Yeah, well I thought twice might just be pushing it. Anyway I was right the last time; Mister Winter pays me well and treats me fine." He moved away from the bike and sat against the base of the stone shed wall. "The other evening when I told Mister Winter I couldn't work Sundays, he said, 'I know who stopped you, it was your father.' I asked him how he knew and all he said was, 'history Danny, history.' What did he mean by that?"

Joggy straightened up and folded his arms. He cleared his throat again. He looked down at his slippered feet and thought about how best to answer him. "Years ago…." He raised his head. "My father worked for a farmer by the name of Jeffrey Waller. He worked long hours including Sundays. Waller worked him so hard that one

Sunday my father had a heart attack while tossing hay into a hayloft and died."

"I didn't know that, you never said."

"I know, I probably should have told you before now."

A puzzled look grew slowly on Danny's face. "But, what's that got to do with Mr Winter?"

"Waller was Winter's uncle." He turned and was gone.

Chapter 5

\* \* \* \*

Three suspected U.V.F members were shot dead this morning, when the car in which they were travelling on their way to work, was targeted in an I.R.A ambush,' the radio announcer said grimly, as he read the one o' clock news.

"Afternoon, Joggy," said McNeill.

"Afternoon," Joggy mumbled, through a mouthful of egg, onion and bread. He was sitting on an old wooden chair in the tool shed, his feet resting on a concrete roller. Beside him on an upturned tea chest sat a thermal flask of tea, a well-worn Jacobs Christmas biscuit tin full of sandwiches and a small Phillips transistor radio, which he now switched off. He made no attempt to offer McNeill tea.

McNeill sat down on the other end of the stone roller. "You haven't had a change of heart, have you Joggy?" He extracted his pipe from an inside pocket and tapped it on the roller.

"No, I'm still in."

"Good." McNeill, filled his pipe with loose tobacco. "First things first then. A little background on Luke and John would be helpful. As you said yourself, they were gone by the time I came. So perhaps you'd fill me in on the type of people they were and in particular, this so called friendly feud of theirs." McNeill clenched the pipe between his teeth and lit it.

"Right, where do I start?" Joggy took a mouthful of tea and pondered his own question. "I'd known Luke and the 'Horse' since my school days. I use to live on the opposite side of Kilpatrick then. On the hurling field Luke, was a legend. He played in the backs while his younger brother Tom, played in the forwards. He was fiercely protective of Tom." Joggy smiled as the memories came flooding back. "When a skirmish broke out in the forwards involving Tom, and in those days there was always a skirmish. A war cry would rise up from the backs and there'd be Luke, galloping up the field to the side of his younger brother, waylaying any opposing player who was stupid enough to get in his way. It was a sight to see: After a brawl like that, it would take several days for Luke's temper to cool?"

"Did you ever see his temper boil over, other than on the field of battle?"

"No, not once. Away from it he was fine; easy going. He wouldn't hurt a fly. He was also a loyal and generous soul who'd give you anything that was in his cupboards. But when it came to money… anything that entered his wallet seldom came out again. You know, he was engaged to be married once but she took off with someone she was seeing behind his back. He never bothered with the fairer sex after that."

"And John Canavan, what was he like?"

"The 'Horse,' he was a bit of a slieveen, a sneak. He was the last born and only boy of four children; the runt of the litter you might say. The local lads, using reverse humour, gave him his father's nickname, who from all accounts was renowned for his strength. The opposite was the case with the 'Horse.' He was as thin as a whip. When he lifted anything heavy his legs wobbled and his knees knocked together."

"Did he play hurling with Luke?"

"God no, he didn't play sports. He never married either. But he was fond of chasing widows. He's was like the proverbial Cuckoo, always on the lookout for someone else's nest."

Joggy took a mouthful of tea and a bite from his sandwich and thought about what to say next. "When the 'Horse' was in his early twenties he took himself off for England. He came back about ten years later for his mother's funeral. After the will was read and he found the house was his, he stayed. He always seemed to have money though, which was peculiar, since he never worked. He had an aversion to work. Joggy smiled. "So much so, that if someone offered him a job, he'd report them to the guards for threatening behaviour."

Joggy's attempt at humour fell on deaf ears. McNeill looked blankly at him. He withdrew the pipe from his mouth. "From what you're telling me, they sound like the odd couple. Not the kind that would be friends."

"Well you know what they say; it takes all kinds to make a world. I suppose their friendship was a bit odd. I reckon myself it was mutual admiration. John admired Luke for his strength and quiet sense of humour. Luke, you know, was the undefeated bale tossing champion of Kilpatrick sports for twelve straight years. While on the other hand, John read a lot and was known for his intellect. Luke probably admired him for the way he could recite a Shakespeare sonnet or excerpts from his party piece; Martin Luther King's mountain top speech. I don't think Luke always understood what he was saying…it seemed he just liked the way it sounded.

"How did this so call friendly feud start?"

"Nobody knows. Maybe Luke wanted to prove an intellectual point, by trying to out- smart John."

"Do you recall any of the previous incidents?"

"Well, I can recall the last three. Luke opened the back door of his house one morning and found he was walled in by a two foot deep turf bank. He then went to the front door and found it also was blocked by turf. Then, just before Christmas, John had a good win on the horses. He wanted to celebrate by getting drunk out of his skull, so he hitched up the ass and cart. He spivied himself up, oiled the greying hair and drove into the village. The ass at least he figured would know the way home. Luke and a friend got him home that night and put him to bed. The next morning the 'Horse' was woken by an almighty racket. When he investigated, he found the Ass in the kitchen still hitched to the cart. The poor terrified animal had shit and pissed everywhere. Luke and his anonymous friend had dismantled the cart and reassembled it in the kitchen. The smell lingered for nearly a week." Joggy took another drink of tea and a bite from his sandwich.

"The incident that happened a few days before John Canavan's body was found, what was that about?"

"I was just getting to that," said Joggy, a little annoyed at McNeill's impatience.

"A few evenings before he died, John cycled into Kilpatrick for messages. After he bought what he wanted in Columns, he parked his bicycle beside Luke's, behind the shop. He then walked up the street to O' Meara's. Knowing Luke he would have saw him in the bar mirror and he'd then give the peak of his cap a couple of twists; it was a habit he had when he spotted the buyer of his next pint. They spent about an hour and a half before going home. When they reached Canavan's, John invited him in for a bite of supper. Luke never one to turn down a free meal, gratefully accepted. "The Horse" didn't skimp. He gave Luke a fine feed of rashers, sausages, eggs and fried bread, washed down by several mugs of strong sweet tea. Luke was well full by the time he left for home. When he walked into his own kitchen Tom was waiting; starving.

"Help yourself," said Luke. "I've already eaten."

When Tom queried the missing sausages and rashers, Luke exploded. The bellow could be heard by the last of his neighbours, four houses away. Canavan had fed him his own fry."

"Thank you," said McNeill. "Now the facts as I know them are these. Number one; Luke had motive: he was humiliated by Canavan. Number two; the murder weapon, a length of gun-barrel piping, had Luke's finger prints all over it. It also had Canavan's blood, hair and bone fragments stuck to it.
Number three; straw with Canavan's blood on it, was found by the pig sty in Luke's yard.
Number four; his own brother, testified that Luke had said, "He would kill John Canavan."
Those are the facts of the case as I have been told them. Ok? So let me play the devil's advocate here," he said, getting into his stride, "and then you tell me why I'm wrong."

"Fire away."

"Luke was still pissed, his temper as you said yourself, being slow to cool, when John Canavan suddenly turns up at his door. He sees an opportunity. He invites Canavan up to the yard to show him Winter's newly arrived boar in action.
With Canavan enthralled, he picks up the gun-barrel pipe and with one mighty blow crushes his skull. He then picks up Canavan and carries him across the field and throws him into the river; that done, he goes back picks up the gun-barrel pipe and tosses it onto a scrap heap of metal. Now Joggy, show me what's wrong with that story."

"Right, number one; there was no evidence of violence in any of their past pranks. Plus no one saw John Canavan in the area on the evening he died.

"Number two; the gun-barrel pipe was an alien metal in that yard. They searched the yard thoroughly and that was the only piece of gun-barrel pipe found. Luke said that when he entered the yard that evening, the pipe was lying on the gravelled surface so he picked it up and tossed it on the scrap heap and that is how his finger prints came to be on it.

"Number three is a difficult one. I have no explanation at the moment for how Canavan's blood came to be on straw in Luke's yard. Number four; what Luke said was in the heat of a moment. We all say things in the heat of the moment that we don't mean. So I would ignore that. As far as your story is concerned, it's total bullshit. Why, after killing John Canavan, would he leave the murder weapon in a place where it could be easily found? Why did he not clean up after him and dispose of the bloodied straw? And why would he bother carrying Canavan's body across a field, where anyone passing the road could have seen him. Not to mention the fact that there was no access to the bridge from that side of the field. He would have had to carry him the length of the field to a gap, to a low area in the river, then carry him up the other side and toss him over briers and furze bushes into the river. Other than that he'd have to travel down the road in front of his neighbours and toss him over the bridge wall. When, all along, in the yard, was a large heap of old tyres. All he had to do was place him in the middle and set fire to them and John Canavan would never have been found. Or he could have fed him to the pigs…they eat everything. The thing is, I know Luke was no genius, but he was not that stupid either. So what do you think? Have I punched enough holes in your story?"

"You've certainly given me something to chew on, that's for sure. It looks like I need more info. While I work on that, could you have a chat with John Canavan's sister and see if she'll let you have a poke through his things for that note book?"

"Yeah, I can do that. How are you going to get more info?"

"I know people!"

"I bet you do."

Joggy eyed McNeill, "Tell me the real reason you're interested in Luke?"

"To be honest Joggy, I abhor cases with untidy ends and this one is as scraggly as it gets."

Joggy didn't believe him, but for the time being he was willing to play along.

# CHAPTER 5

The wet clothes flapped and clapped in the wind as Alice and Helen hung them out on the line to dry.

"Mum, how did you meet dad?" Helen asked, as she handed her mother a faded brown tartan work shirt belonging to her father.

"Why do you ask?" Alice removed two clothes pegs from the pocket of her navy-blue apron

"I'm curious. You've never said how ye met. Was it love at first sight? Did he sweep you off your feet?"

Alice paused for a moment and smiled at the memory. "No, I'm afraid it was a lot slower than that."

She then tossed the shirt onto the line and pinned it down. "If I confide something personal to you, Helen, do you think you could keep it to yourself?"

"Of course." Helen suddenly felt grown up and chuffed at the thought of her mother taking her into her confidence. She handed her mother a blue pillow case. "I wouldn't breathe a word to another living soul, cross my heart and hope to die," She said, as she made the sign of the cross on her heart.

Alice smiled at her daughter's eager and expectant face. "Do you know that for the first three months of our courtship, your father never kissed me?"

"Did he not fancy you?"

"I was beginning to think that too, but as it turned out it was quite the opposite. In those days your dad was woman shy. Actually I think it's a trait that exists in all the Jackson men. Danny's shy and by all accounts your grandfather was a shy man. Your father and I knew one another for years. He was two years ahead of me in school. I always had an eye for him. One Friday night when I was eighteen, my sister Frances, and I went to a dance in Kilpatrick hall. Your father was there standing at the back of the hall watching the dancing and tapping his feet to the music. Then a Siege of Ennis started and your father was dragged unwillingly into it. We danced together a couple of times during the Siege. The dance finished and your father walked away. Then they announced that the next dance was to be a ladies choice. I chased after him and tapped him on the shoulder and asked him to be my partner. I made sure we stayed that way for the rest of the night. For the next three months we went to the cinema, dances and an occasional evening in the pub, but he never once came close to kissing me. I was getting really worried. Then one night after the cinema, he saw me to my gate. I said goodnight and turned to go in, but he grabbed my arm and turned me back to him." An involuntary smile lit up Alice's face as she relived the memory.

"I want to ask you something," he said, and for the first time I saw fear in his eyes. I didn't know what to expect, so I just said, 'yes?' 'I've falling in love with you,' he said. My heart jumped and just when I thought I couldn't be happier, he asked: 'Will you be my wife?' I jumped on top of him and kissed him. Then he asked, 'Is that a yes?' So I kissed him again. Come to think of it, I never did say yes. We kissed until my cheeks became wet and when I opened my eyes, tears were running down his face. He then explained why it took three months to kiss me. He had lost his mother when he was only five and his father when he was fifteen. These were huge emotional upheavals in his life. Then he fell in love with me. He thought by not kissing me he could somehow distance himself emotionally from me and if we broke up, he would not feel as bad. But it didn't work, because he fell for me anyway."

"Ah, that's so romantic," Helen gushed as she handed her mother the last item in the basket; a white t-shirt belonging to Danny. Helen felt she could ask her mother any question now that she was in her confidence. "Did you go to bed with dad before you were married?"

Alice glanced sharply at her. She snapped the empty wicker clothes basket from the ground. "Now you're asking questions you shouldn't be asking miss. It's time your mind was on something else. I believe you have homework to do."

* * * *

"Joggy," Nancy exclaimed cheerfully. "How nice to see you. Come in, come in." She held open the front door and stood to one side.

"You must have smelt the scones," she added, closing the door behind him.

"I've a tray of hot curny ones fresh from the oven sitting on the kitchen table. I was about to pour myself some tea, so your timing couldn't be better."

She bade Joggy sit at the table while she poured the tea. She wore Jasmine perfume. It was faint and pleasant. She then cut two scones in half and buttered them. The butter melted into the warm steamy centre. Joggy bit into the scone and drank a mouthful of tea hoping it would steady his nerves, but his nerve was sinking as fast as the rapidly melting butter. Nancy was a talker. She rattled on about the weather, her neighbours and the recently departed. Never once did she stop to ask Joggy the reason for his visit. It wasn't in her nature. She was sure he'd get to it in his own good time.

Noticing that Joggy's cup was half empty, Nancy retrieved the teapot from the cooker and topped it up. Beneath her new perm was a beaming face. He smiled uncomfortably back. He had known Nancy since he was a child. She was older by eight years. Time had been kind to her. Apart from the smiley lines around her eyes and mouth, her looks had altered little from when he was sixteen and she was his fantasy woman. While his friends slept in bedrooms filled with dreams of fighter planes and motorcycles, his, was filled with images of Nancy. The Nancy of his youth had small, but perfectly formed breasts, a pert round bottom, smiling teasing eyes, flowing chestnut hair and an infectious laugh. Though her figure was slender, she made it move in ways that girls with more ample proportions, could not.

He watched her now as she returned the teapot to the solid-fuel cooker. Her figure was still the same, probably because she never had any children to distort it all out of shape.

He watched her now like he had back then, at mass, when she sauntered up the centre aisle on a Sunday morning to communion: the rhythmic movement of her hips had filled his youthful eyes with delight. It was as if they moved to music; soothing classical music or maybe it was just the angelic tones of the choir acting as a soundtrack to his fantasy.

A sudden and embarrassing thought brought a rush of blood to his face. He felt it radiate and glow as he remembered how he had his first orgasm, masturbating to a fantasy of Nancy.

"And how are Alice and the children? I haven't set eyes on them in ages."

"Alice's in good form and the kids are growing faster than dandelions."

Nancy sat back down as Joggy took his courage in his hands.

"Nancy!" He paused and took a deep breath, "I've been placed in an awkward position and I need your help. It concerns your brother John."

"Well if it's legal and I can help you, I will."

He tried to swallow the lump in his throat, but it wouldn't go down.

"As you know Luke Baker died recently."

"May the devil have fun with his murderous black heart." Her gentle face clouded over with anger.

"Yes, well, mmm, before Luke died he asked me to call and see him. I actually was the last visitor he had."

"I don't like the way this is going Joggy. If it's anything to do with Luke Baker, don't ask," she warned.

"Please, Nancy?" Joggy, held up an open hand, keeping calm and speaking softly. "Let me finish what I have to say. I know it's upsetting for you but my sincere intention is not to upset you."

"Go on then," she said cautiously.

Joggy could hear his heart thumping faster than the tick-tock of the clock on the dresser as he blurted out the one sentence that could get him tossed out of the house. "Luke, before he died, asked me to clear his name."

"What?" Nancy exclaimed, "The sheer gall of him. He was as guilty as sin. I attended his trial. I heard all the evidence and there could be no doubt he did it."

"That may be so Nancy… but a lot of that evidence can be explained away."

"My god, you think he's innocent? You're on his side," she said, in disbelief.

"It's not about taking sides Nancy, it's about finding the truth. I believe Luke may have got a raw deal. He swore to me that day that he didn't do it and I don't believe any man wants to die with a lie on his lips. Think about it, Nancy, do you really believe Luke would have killed his good friend over a few rashers and sausages?"

Nancy pushed her chair back and with one hand brushed the crumbs from the lap of her red apron. She stood up and tottered to the kitchen window still holding her cup. In the distance, across the flat green fields, half shrouded in cloud was Slieve Cranoc,.

"I don't know what to believe now," she said eventually. "Before John was killed I certainly would not have picked Luke as a killer. But the evidence…."

"The evidence can be twisted to fit the case Nancy. It doesn't mean it's the truth. I've not been able to sleep properly since Luke asked me and if you're like me, you won't be able to lie comfortable in your bed 'till you know the truth either." He joined her at the window and keeping his voice soft almost hypnotic, he added, "You have every right to hate your brother's killer Nancy, but let's be certain that his name really is, Luke Baker."

Nancy looked hard at Joggy, a man she had a lot of respect for and the last person she would take for a fool. She then looked down into the soggy tea leaves on the bottom of her cup; wishing she could read them. Finally, she lifted her head. "What do you want from me?"

"I need to look through John's personal effects."

"What for?"

"I'm looking for some missing items; a book of Robert Frost poems and a small black notebook or diary."

"Why do you need them?"

"Because I think they may point to his real killer."

"You've got two hours," said Nancy, as she pulled open the double wooden doors and let in the light on her brother's personal effects. "Two hours and not a minute more. I don't want you here when Ted gets home. I don't want a scene." She left him and walked back into the house.

Ted was Nancy's husband. He and Joggy rubbed one another up the wrong way, always had; always would.

It was a large galvanised steel shed with an earthen floor. Stacked neatly along one wall were John's and his mother's furniture. The makings of two beds, two sets of drawers, two wardrobes, a kitchen dresser, several wooden chairs and a kitchen table upon which a selection of pots, pans, crockery and other household utensils sat. Joggy started with the mattresses, meticulously searching every inch. From there he moved on to the drawers and was more than a little surprised to find John's clothes still in one of them. He emptied each drawer until the cabinet was a skeleton, finding nothing, he returned it to the way it was.

Then it was the turn of the wardrobes. Again he found John's clothes still hanging up and again he searched every inch and again he found nothing. In the mothers wardrobe he found four large cardboard boxes of books and an Olivetti typewriter. He pulled these out onto the floor. The kitchen table and the other miscellaneous items also came up empty. He glanced at his watch and noted he had less than an hour left.

Conscious that the sands of time were running out, he raced through the boxes of books as quickly and as carefully as possible. In the four boxes he found everyone from Shakespeare to Ibsen in plays, from Dickens to Wolfe in novels and from Wordsworth to Plath in poetry.

"Time's up Joggy," said Nancy, "Ned will be home any minute now."

Her sudden appearance surprised him. He had been so absorbed he had not heard her leave the house or her approach on the gravel yard.

"Nearly finished." He picked up the last two books. He examined them, re-packed the box and placed all four boxes back in the wardrobe.

"Did you find what you were looking for?"

"No, but I found these." He lifted up a small bale of typed manuscripts tied together with butcher's string. "If you don't mind, I'd like to bring them with me and read them. They might be important. I'll return them to you when I'm finished."

Nancy glanced apprehensively over her shoulder at the side gate to the backyard. "Ok, ok." She hurriedly, closed the double doors. "But don't show them to anyone else."

"I won't, you have my word."

She rushed him through the house to the front door. Her hand was on the latch when she heard Ted's car pass the front and drive around the side of the house.

"Joggy." She held the door open, "I hope for your sake you're proved right, because if you're wrong, you're going to look very foolish."

# CHAPTER 6

Ed McNeill walked into Rooster's bar, stood at the entrance and looked around. The place was brightly lit but sparsely populated. There was a pool table at one end where two men were playing. He scanned for the one person he knew to be a regular Tuesday night patron. He grinned when he spotted him, all eighteen stone, sitting alone at the far end of the bar. "Charlie me auld flower." McNeill gave him a solid slap on the shoulder as he planted himself on the bar stool next to him. "I thought all that swearing under your breath when your numbers are not called, was what you lived for each week."

"No fucking way. This bar stool is as near to that bingo hall as I ever want to get. I let the wife do the swearing while I do the drinking. Two hours supping the black stuff." He held his pint aloft, as if it was a chalice. 'Heaven.'

"Excuse me!" McNeill called to the barman, who seemed more interested in watching the pool game than serving customers. "Two pints please."

Charlie raised a quizzical eyebrow. "What brings you here?"

"Same as you, wife wanted to go. Simple creatures really. It's amazing what keeps them happy."

A half-hour passed in friendly banter before a short lull developed in the conversation. McNeill lit his pipe and glanced casually around. The pub was quiet, no more than a dozen patrons. He was about to speak when the bar door opened and a small round man wearing a trilby hat entered. He sat two seats away from them. McNeill slid of the high stool and picked up his pint. "Let's move to the corner."

Reluctantly, Charlie followed him. "What was that for?"

"Two ears too many."

It was the first inclination Charlie had that McNeill wanted something.
McNeill settled into the seat, crossed his legs and extracted the pipe from between his teeth. "Been back to number 10 McKenna road recently have you?" He exhaled a cloud of smoke.

"Jesus no, one mistake was enough. If my wife ever found out I'd be a dead man." Charlie's chubby red cheeks rapidly lost all colour. "You swore you'd never say a word."

"And I haven't. But, what I said to you then was that my silence came at a price and now, it's due for repayment."

"I thought maybe you'd have forgotten about that."

A self satisfied smirk appeared on McNeill's lips. "I never forget."

"Obviously not. So what do I have to do?"

"I need a copy of John Canavan's case file, including scene photos."

Charlie stared at McNeill in disbelief. "You don't come cheap, do you? Here was I thinking you might want a blind eye turned or a summons quashed, but no, you want the file of the hottest murder case of the last decade. Do you know or do you even care....," Charlie stopped talking when he saw the look on McNeill's face. "You're enjoying this aren't you, watching me squirm. You're a bastard, McNeill. When this is done me and you are finished, you hear me, finished."

McNeill knew the consequences of what he was asking Charlie to do. If he was caught, the man could be fired and lose his pension. But he didn't care he had a bigger fish to fry. "Now, now, me auld flower, don't be rash. Just remember one thing Charlie, the debts in my hands and I'll tell you when it's finished."

McNeill drained the last of his pint and stood up. "You have two days my friend. Call me and I'll meet you." He turned and left the pub.

* * * *

Every Thursday morning, without fail, Squeak called into the Garda station with his dole slip. Normally the slips are handed in on a Tuesday morning, but Squeak fearing he would forget and not get paid, handed it in as soon as his post arrived.

On this Thursday he knocked on the service hatch and after a short delay, McNeill slid open the opaque glass panel. "Squeak, I'll be with you in a minute," he said, "I'm on a call."

He pushed the glass back again and returned to his phone-call, but the hatch did not close fully. Squeak leaned in as near to the opening as possible and listened intently.

"Sorry sir, you were saying?"

(inaudible)

"Yes sir, I do know Joggy Jackson."

(inaudible)

"No sir, he's not a trouble maker."

(inaudible)

"Well, he was the last visitor Baker had before he died and since then he's been making enquires into John Canavan's death."

(inaudible)

"It's either Baker asked him to clear his name or he believes that Baker was wrongly convicted. Nothing else makes any sense."

(inaudible)

"Yes sir, I'll keep you informed as soon as I know more." McNeill hung up the phone.

Squeak took a hasty step back. McNeill opened the hatch and received Squeaks dole slip. "Sorry for keeping you waiting," he said.

Squeak walked calmly past the Garda station window and then, like a slipped greyhound, took to running. He burst through the door of the bar wearing a smile that was doing its best to touch his ears. He was as excited as a child on Christmas morning.

"Whoa," said Spit, "I think world war three has broken out. Paddy," he shouted "a pint for Squeak, I think he's got something juicy."

Squeak vigorously shook his head from side to side as he tried to catch his breath. "No, no," panting, he raised his right hand and displayed two fingers, "two pints."

"Jesus, Mary and Joseph," said Spit. "Maybe world war three has broken out. Alright Squeak, two pints, but it had better be worth it."

* * * *

Know your man and you will know happiness, Alice's grandmother had said to her on her wedding day. It was advice Alice took to heart. But Alice also had her own philosophy on life and in Joggy she found a kindred spirit who shared it.

She was determined to turn out children who were decent upright people; respected, educated and spiritual.

It was Thursday evening and Alice was standing at the sink drying the dinner dishes. The day had been unseasonably warm and dry; a day borrowed from the summer yet to come. The children were on the road cycling. Since the road was usually quiet of traffic, she did not worry about them. But she was worried about her husband. Through the window above the sink she watched him prepare the earth. Digging the sod, turning and breaking it with a garden fork, at a rate a man half his age would have difficulty keeping pace with. Something was eating away at him.

Over the years she had worked out that her husband had two sets of moods. The first was the one he was in now. Something happens and it sends him into the pits of despair. In that mood he'd become quiet, almost withdrawn; prone to bursts of frenzied activity and tetchiness. Her way of handling it was to let him blow off steam for a couple of days and then gently talk him out of it.

The second mood overcomes him more gradually. A minor slight or injustice that at first seemed unimportant percolates deep inside, leaving a light despondency, like bubbles on the surface. He does not immediately recognise what it is that is bringing him down, but, over a few days, the answer usually becomes apparent. The mood would leave him distracted, quiet and restless, and given to long walks. In that situation, Alice would give him the time he needed and when she thought he'd had enough time, she would gentle pose the question. "Do you want to talk about it?"
He'd either talk or he'd say, "No, not yet." She had learned long ago, from her mother's mistakes, when not to push it.

Katie came running up the footpath, all smiles, all excited, and, turning the corner of the house, skipped over to her father.
"Daddy, Daddy, I can ride Helen's bike," She grabbed him by the finger of one hand. It was as much as her little hand could grip.
"Come on, I want to show you."

"Later pet, later, I'm busy."

"Now Daddy, now." She pulled him away. "I want to show you now."
He had no choice but to go with her. She dragged him down to the front gate. There Alice joined him. Katie straddled Helen's bicycle but, because it was several sizes too big, she was unable to reach

the saddle. She placed her left foot on the pedal and with her right foot, scooted the bike along the road, trying to build up enough speed to jump on the right pedal and cycle. This she did several times and each time she did it she lost her balance and toppled over.

"Katie!" Joggy, hollered. "Call me when you can really ride it." He walked back to the garden.

Katie was devastated. She cried quietly. She did not want her dad to hear her.

* * * *

Alice and Joggy rarely argued in front of their children. Whatever gripes they had with one another they had them out late at night in the privacy of their bedroom. That night in bed she tackled the problem. She sat up on one elbow and rested her head on her hand. "What's going on," she asked softly.

"There's nothing going on."

"Oh yes there is." She had a smile in her voice. "You've been in a bad mood ever since you came back from Nancy's. Did something happen there?"

"No, nothing."

"Well something's eating at you. Did you know that poor Katie had been practising for hours on Helen's bike, just for you? And, she was able to ride it. But in her excitement to impress you, she lost it. And then you snap at her. That wasn't very fair. You don't normally act that way with the kids, particularly Katie."

"I know, I know, I feel bad about it, I'll make it up to her."

"You'd better. Now tell me about the trouble maker in your head, what's he saying?"

He sat up and leaned back against the headboard. "I'm worried," he said, finally. "And I'm afraid."

Alice was taken aback. "Afraid?"

"It was something Nancy said the other evening. She said I would look very foolish if I failed to clear Luke's name, and you know, she's right; I am going to look foolish."

Reassuringly, Alice stroked his thigh. "Not in my eyes, you won't."

"Maybe not in yours, but in the eyes of a lot of people, I will. Do you know, this morning, before I went to work, I visited

Kilpatrick church. It's never bothered me before, Alice, whenever I've taken on a job; I've been happy knowing I'd make a success of it. But this…. this has me worried. I don't know if I can do this. I feel like a sham, pretending to be what I'm not. The other day in Nancy's, going through John's things, his furniture, his clothes….. it was eerie. It felt like I was robbing his grave." He sighed deeply. "I don't want to be seen as a failure, Alice!"

She stroked his thigh again. "You'll always be my hero."

He smiled at the corny line.

"It's not too late to stop you know. The word's not out. Very few people know you're doing this," she said, seizing the opportunity she had been waiting for since the day he had visited Portmand Prison.

"Do you think Luke would understand?"

"Of course he would. He wouldn't have wanted you to do something you weren't comfortable with. Besides, every chance you get you can still defend him and proclaim his innocence."

"Maybe you're right. Maybe I should stop before I get in over my head."

Just saying the words relieved him and for the first time in days he relaxed as the burden slipped off his shoulders. He slipped back down under the covers.

"Thanks." He slipped an arm around her and pulled her close to him.

"For what?"

"For being you." He planted a kiss on her lips.

She snuggled in closer. "Now tell me. How are you going to make it up to Katie?"

"You'll have to wait and see, other than that you can read my mind," he teased.

She reached down under the covers and purred, "I see you've read mine."

\* \* \* \*

Katie was not her normal chatty self on Friday evening. She had an inquisitive mind and was forever asking questions, usually of her father, but not this evening. This evening she ignored him.

"Cat got your tongue Katie," he asked, when dinner was over.

She turned her head away. "We're not talking."

"Pity, because I've got a present for you, but, if you don't want it, I'll have to give it to someone else."

Katie looked at him warily from beneath hooded eyes. "What is it?"

He reached into his jacket pocket and drew out a small cardboard box wrapped in bright coloured paper and gave it to her. Everyone gathered around to look. Katie enthusiastically ripped open the paper and opened the box. She turned it upside down and a bicycle bell dropped out.

"What am I going to do with this," she asked.

"Well you can ring it to let people know you're coming."

"But I don't have a bike to put it on," she cried.

"Are you sure? Have you looked outside the front door recently?"

Katie rushed to the door, knocking over her chair as he ran. She screamed in delight when she saw the pink and white bicycle with the word SORRY written on a piece of cardboard. She turned around and hugged her father and then spent the rest of the evening, riding up and down the road ringing her bell.

# CHAPTER 7

Victoria ran the carpet sweeper back and forth across the front-room carpet. She rapidly became bored with the chore and paused for a moment, folding her arms across the top of the handle and then resting her chin on them. The day was bright, dry and windy. She watched though the front window as a young chestnut sapling wrestled with a sudden gust. It was as if it had the plant by the throat and was shaking it violently.

A movement beyond the sapling caught her eye. A short, dark-haired girl was walking on the gravel road towards the house and looking nervously about her.

"Sandy, Sandy," the girl called out in a loud whisper as she rounded the back corner of Fred Winter's house. She had hoped to find her terrier where she always found him when he strayed -- eating from a pot of waste food. But this time he was not there. The girl stared down at the farmyard with its many large sheds and tried to muster the courage to go and search them for her dog.

"Hello, can I help you?" Victoria enquired.

The girl jumped. She had seen Fred leave and had not expected anyone else to be in the house. "Lord almighty," she said, with her hand over her chest, "you're after scaring me shitless."

"I'm sorry, I didn't mean to." She stepped out of the doorway and walked over to the girl. "I'm Victoria Parker, Fred's new housekeeper."

"I'm Louise. I live in the house across the road from the top of your lane."

"Oh right and who's Sandy?"

"Sandy's my dog, he's gone missing. You haven't seen him have you?"

"Is he a wee brown shaggy haired thing?"

"Yes, that's him, you saw him?"

"I have, but not today. If you'd like I'll give you a hand to look for him."

"I saw Mr Winter leave. Will he be back soon?"

"No, he's gone to Oldbridge. He'll be a couple of hours."

"That's a relief."

"Why do you say that?"

"The last time I was here, Mister Winter warned me that if he found Sandy down here again, there would be consequences." As Louise and Victoria started towards the sheds to begin their search, a disturbing thought hit her.

"You don't think that he… did…something to Sandy, do you?"

"No of course not; he's a farmer and farmers love all animals."

They called and searched for nearly an hour but to no avail. Sandy was nowhere to be seen.

"Don't worry," said Victoria, "It's likely he spotted a rabbit and went after it. I'm sure he'll turn up later."

"I hope you're right." Louise was not entirely convinced.

Victoria walked Louise back towards the head of the lane.

"What height are you," Louise asked, craning her short neck to look up; a deformity she had since birth. Her head practically sat on her shoulders. But God had compensated by giving her a sense of humour and a pretty face.

"Five feet ten….and you?"

"Four-foot-eleven on my tippy toes. Do you find being tall a disadvantage in getting fellas?"

"Sometimes it can be a problem. Can you recommend any good-looking tall guys?"

"How about Danny Jackson, have you met him? He works here every Saturday on the farm. He'd be ideal for you; tall, handsome and smart, but unfortunately, painfully shy. You'd probably have to ask him out"

"I've met him. He's cute. He wouldn't honestly expect me to ask him out. Would he?" Victoria asked doubtfully.

"No, but if you're interested, you might have to. Every Saturday night he goes to the Park ballroom and every Saturday night he stands in the shadows watching. Beats me why he doesn't summon up the courage and ask, because with his looks he could have any girl he wants."

"The Park Ballroom, where's that?"

"In Oldbridge. Why don't you come tomorrow night with Vinny, Danny and me. Danny usually has his dad's car."

"I'd love too." They reached the top of the lane. "Who's Vinny?"

"My boyfriend, he lives just down from Danny; they're best friends."

Victoria's smile turned to a frown. "Oh wait, I'll have to pass it in front of Fred first."

"Why? You only work here he's not your dad."

"No, but while I'm down here, he's acting as my guardian. But look, don't worry, I don't foresee a problem. I'd better get back before Fred comes home." She started walking backwards, "I'll talk to you tomorrow, Louise, and don't worry about Sandy, I'm sure he'll turn up."

* * * *

From Saturday to Saturday, only two tasks remained constant on Winter's farm for Danny -- to keep the turf basket full. When empty, it was left outside the back door... and to supply enough potatoes and vegetables for the week-end. To know precisely what vegetables were wanted, he had to knock.

"Hi," said Danny, when Victoria opened the back door.

"Hi." Victoria smiled.

"Do you know what vegetables you need?"

"Vegetables, oh right, amm." Victoria was caught off-guard. "I know I need a head of cabbage and a turnip and a...." The more Victoria looked into those deep blue eyes, the more confused she became.

"Listen." She tried to give herself space to think. "Will you fill the turf basket first and when you come back I'll have worked out what else I need from the garden."

Danny grabbed the wicker basket and disappeared into the turf shed. It was not long before he was back and this time Victoria was ready for him. "Danny," she said, as he placed the turf basket on the ground.

"Yes."

"The other evening when you called around -- I hope I didn't offend you ...you know, joking that you were a mute."

"Well, I would have found it funny, except... that..." He looked away slightly. "I've a brother who's deaf and dumb."

"Oh, God, I'm so sorry. Me and my big mouth. I shouldn't have said anything."

"It's alright, really, you weren't to know. Well...what other vegetables do you need?"

"Yes of course, I also need potatoes, carrots and a couple of parsnips."

* * * *

"I just met Danny on his way to the garden" said Fred, when he entered the kitchen, "He seemed very happy with himself."

"Probably amused at my discomfort."

"Discomfort?" He began to search the dresser, opening drawers and looking behind upright plates.

"Yeah, discomfort. What age is Danny's deaf-and-dumb brother?"

"Someone's pulling your leg Victoria," He moved his search to his jacket which hung off the back of a chair, "Danny doesn't have a brother, just two sisters."

"Wanker," she muttered.

"What did you say?"

"Nothing. What are you looking for?"

"My car keys, have you seen them?"

"They're hanging up on the side of the dresser."

"You're too organised, Victoria. I'm going into Kilpatrick, I won't be long."

Danny returned with the potatoes and vegetables and knocked on the open back door. He called out, "Hello."

Victoria came to the doorway. "You know…." She wore a deadpan expression. "It's bad luck to mock the afflicted."

"Who did I mock?" Danny tried hard to suppress a smile.

Victoria's deadpan expression melted. "Me, you mocked me, now were even. Can we call a ceasefire and start again, please?"

"I'd like that."

"I was talking to Louise yesterday, she told me you're going to the Park tonight; can I have a lift?"

"Sure, no problem, say, nine o' clock?"

"Thanks, that's great. I'll be at the head of the lane, waiting."

At nine o' clock that night, Danny, with Vinny in the passenger seat, parked at the head of Winter's lane. Vinny climbed out and collected Louise from her home across the road. They waited for half an hour, but Victoria never showed.

Situated on one corner of the junction that splits Kilpatrick in four, was the sole public house of the village, O Meara's. Through the front door, you entered into a narrow ceramic-tiled passageway. In front of you was the lounge, frequented mostly by passers-by and the few locals who thought of themselves as higher up the food chain than those who patronised the bar. To your right is the bar and to your left are the toilets. The odour is of stale beer and cigarette smoke and the pungent smell. The décor has not changed in years and there are few customers still alive who can still remember the original colour of the wallpaper.

On Sunday morning after mass, the Jackson family, as was customary, made their way to O Meara's. As they entered into the passageway they were met by Spit Sweeny coming from the bar.

"Well, well, well, if it isn't Joggy Jackson." Spit stopped abruptly, "or is Sherlock Holmes you're calling yourself these days?"

"What are talking about?" Joggy asked sharply.

"Did you not think I'd find out? By the way, I think it's admirable of you to try and clear Luke's name. I really do."

"Who told you that?"

"Now, now Joggy, you know I never reveal my sources. Let's just say I heard it from the trees."

"Have the trees got nothing better to do, than to be spreading malicious gossip?"

"Ah, but that's where you're wrong Joggy." Spit was clearly enjoying himself. "When it's true it's not malicious. Unearthing the secrets of the village is my role in life. You should look upon me, as a..." He paused, for a word.

"A scourge?" ventured Joggy.

He ignored Joggy's jibe "More, a sort of collector of local information -- a village historian if you will. The true history of a village is not what's on the surface, Joggy, but what lies hidden. I see it as my duty to tell and re-tell those elusive little stories, until they become folklore. Those dark little tales people like to hide, like ugly children, in the shadows, never to be paraded in daylight again. Now, if you'll excuse me Joggy, me bladder has an urgent appointment with a urinal."

Spit disappeared quickly into the toilets.

"Why did Spit call you Sherlock Holmes, dad?" Danny asked.

"I'll tell you when we get home." He raised a finger to his children. "Don't, pursue this in the pub," he warned.

"If Spit knows," said Alice, "the whole pub knows. We don't have to go in if you don't want to."

"Unfortunately we have to." He pushed open the bar door. "We might as well face it now as later."

Heads turned and conversations were altered or fell to whispers. They found a seat under the window and sat down. Joggy strolled to the bar.

"The usual Mick," he said to the barman.

Mick pulled the lever on the pump and slowly and expertly poured the pint. "Is it true what I'm hearing?"

"That depends on what you're hearing."

"That you're looking into the 'Horses' murder."

"Might be," Joggy replied warily.

"Luke and the 'Horse' were good customers of mine, and I have to say, I could never see one killing the other."

"Neither could I."

"I don't envy your task Joggy, but I wish you the best of luck with it."

"Thanks." He returned to his family.

"Are you still going to back out?" Alice whispered. She had a fair idea of what the answer would be, but with hope dwindling fast, she felt she had to ask.

He lifted the pint to his lips and while he drank his eyes scanned the room and scrutinized the faces of the people he'd known all his life. Several caught his eye and gave him a half wink or a barely perceptible nod of the head -- or both at once. He wiped his lips with the back of his hand. "Doesn't look like I can now, does it? Everybody knows".

* * * *

There were very few cars left in the Church car park by the time they left. Joggy unlocked the passenger side first for Alice and the children. As he walked around the front of the car, a black Anglia pulled up abruptly alongside him. Nancy's husband Ted, jumped out. He slammed the car door behind him and came marching over to Joggy.    "Jackson," he growled, as he approached, "you have a

fucking nerve coming around my place when I wasn't there, scavenging through John's things… browbeating my wife."
Joggy glanced over Ted's shoulder at Nancy; she was staring straight ahead; he knew then he was in trouble.

"What do you want?" Joggy already knew the answer.

"I want what you stole from me."

"I stole nothing from you. What I brought with me, Nancy gave willingly."

"I want them back and so does she."

Joggy took another look over Ted's shoulder; Nancy was still staring out through the front window. He knew what he had to do.

"Why the panic Ted, -- afraid Nancy might read what's in them?"

"What the fuck are you on about?"

"What John had to say about you… none of it too flattering. It seems the two of you didn't exactly see eye to eye. In fact, I think he was afraid of you and your quick temper."
He could see the rage building in Ted's face. He primed him and then prepared himself for what was coming. "Where exactly were you, on the Saturday that John was murdered?"

He saw the punch and rode it like an actor in a Wild West punch-up.  Ted's fist just glanced off his chin. He fell back against the car, and for effect, slid to the ground.

It worked. Nancy came running. "Ted," she screamed, "what the hell do you think you're doing?" She grabbed Ted by the arm. "Get back in the car."

"But he provoked me," Ted protested. "Get in the car," she demanded even louder. He got behind him a pushed.  With Ted ahead of her, Nancy turned around to Joggy as Alice helped him to his feet. "I'm really, really sorry, Joggy, you'll have no more trouble from Ted, I promise."

A smirk of satisfaction crossed Joggy's face as he watched the Anglia disappear around the bend.

"What was that about?" Danny asked, when his father climbed into the car. "Why didn't you hit him back?"

"Because I would have lost what I gained."

"I don't understand."

"I'll explain more when we get home."

* * * *

Joggy asked everyone to sit around the kitchen table. Then he told them, in outline, what he was doing. Afterwards, Katie was the first to speak. "Dad, will this make you famous? Will you be on T. V?"

"No pet, that won't happen."

"What makes you think you can catch this person," Danny asked.

"I don't know if I'll be able to catch him, but I owe it to Luke to try."

"And what is it exactly that you owe him," Helen asked.

"Years ago he did me a favour, and this is the only way I have of repaying him."

"What favour?" asked Danny.

"That is between me and Luke."

Danny jumped up from his seat on the sofa. "I'm sick of this," he said, his voice raised, but not quiet to the level of a shout. "Why do you treat me like a child, Dad? I'm eighteen; that's old enough to drink, drive and get married if I want to. But by your standards I'm not old enough to be told anything personal. Your family history is my history and I'm entitled to know it."

"You're only entitled to what I want to tell you." His response was sharp. "Eighteen is just a number, not the age of maturity." His response left no room for argument.

# CHAPTER 8

Ed McNeill turned up promptly the following Monday, same time, same place as the week before.

"Good afternoon Joggy." He squeezed the words out between his pipe and the corner of his mouth.

"What's good about it?" Joggy muttered. He drank a mouthful of tea.

"Well the sun is out and the birds are singing and we're alive to enjoy it," McNeill teased.

Joggy took a bite from his ham sandwich. He chewed in silence then washed it down with the tea. "This thing with Luke, I suppose you know it's all over the place. What am I saying? Of course you know. If everybody knows, you know."

McNeill sat back on the stone roller. "It was bound to happen sooner or later. In my book, better sooner than later. It's good to get it out there. You'd never know what might turn up."

"I could have done with a bit more time."

"For what?" McNeill pushed down the tobacco with his thumb. "So you could back out?"

Joggy stood up and walked to the open doorway, half a plastic cupful of warm tea still in his hand. A clear and disturbing thought was pushing its way forward through his up-to-now muddled thinking. He glanced sideways at McNeill, who was pulling on his pipe and looking at the ground.

"It was you that put the word out, wasn't it?" Joggy stepped back and stood in front of McNeill.

"I had to." He lifted his head and faced Joggy. "You were having second thoughts and I couldn't afford to have that happen."

For a split second he felt the urge to empty the cup of tea into McNeill's face, but it passed. "How did you know that?"

"In my experience there are only two reasons why anyone visits a church before eight in the morning; they're either praying for a miracle or they're very worried. I couldn't take a chance on you pulling out."

"You're a conniving bastard McNeill. What the fuck is in this for you anyhow? I know you're not doing it for Luke Baker."

"I'll do a deal with you. You tell me the favour you owe Luke and I'll tell you my reason for doing this."

"Fuck you."

"Right, at least now we know where we stand with each other, so can we get back to business?"

Joggy stared out across the gravel yard to the back lawn, where a pair of gaelic football posts were set up, and remembered when he was a kid kicking football with his cousins Luke and Tom and all his other childhood friends. A lot of them wandered away in different directions and got absorbed in their own lives, but Tom and Luke had stayed true.

He glanced at McNeill…Friend or Foe? At the moment the sergeant was one step ahead of him and he loathed the feeling. He tossed the remains of his tea onto the gravel yard, turned around and sat back in his old wooden chair. "I called to Nancy Canavan. I went through the contents of John's home."

"And…?"

"Nothing…. except for a small bundle of manuscripts which I brought home with me."

"Nothing else?"

"I did notice how he marked his books for identification. He scratched away a small portion of the bottom corner of the initials of the author. So if we ever find his copy of Robert Frost poems, at least we will know how to identify it."

"And the manuscripts. …anything of interest?"

"Not so far. I've only read a couple of them. They contain mostly quotes from other authors and bits of unfinished stories." He turned to McNeill. "And you, what did you find out?"

"I got a hold of a copy of the murder file. I was very surprised to see how thin it was. I was expecting it to be much heavier. To me it indicates a quick investigation; they found a prime suspect and then built their case around him. That said, it seems your friend Luke wasn't as saintly as you make him out to be. He had a previous conviction for arson and got two years."

"That happened when he was fifteen and it wasn't intentional; it was an accident. He was out rabbit hunting with his terrier when it started to rain. He took shelter in Waller's hay barn. Luke smoked. When the shower passed over; he put his cigarette out with his foot; obviously not successfully; the barn caught fire and burnt to the ground. Unfortunately, the judge was a family friend of the Waller's. He didn't believe his story and sent him down."

"I see. The file also has no eye-witness statements. They did however talk to Luke's immediate neighbours, but according to the report, no one saw or heard anything untoward. There were sightings of Canavan earlier in the day in Oldbridge, but after that nobody saw him. I can't believe that a man on a bicycle could just disappear and then turn up in a river six miles away. Somebody out there has information."

"Am I in the file?"

"Yes. You didn't tell me you found the body?"

"It's common knowledge. I just assumed someone who specializes in gathering news and gossip would have known that." Sarcasm oozed from every word.

McNeill grunted. "Right-- you're going to have to canvass houses and talk to people. Start at Walls and work your way home."

\* \* \* \*

The rattling sound of Pete Wall's old flat-bedded truck coming up the avenue distracted Joggy's attention from the flower-bed he was preparing for planting. Pete pulled up beside him and cut the engine. "God bless the work."

Joggy, leaned on the handle of his digging fork. "Isn't it well for some, sitting on their arse all day, driving around."

Pete laughed. "I hear you're playing detective these days."

"Who told you that?" Joggy asked defensibly.

"Ah, you know, word gets around."

"So, is that why you called in, to give me a hard time and to tell me I'm a fool?"

"Actually, Joggy, I called in to give you a piece of information; it might be of some help to you."

"Thanks Pete," he said. "I can do with all the help I can get. So, what have you got?"

"I reckon I was one of the last people to see John Canavan alive. The day before you found his body, he cycled past my place. I was just after getting out of the truck and was walking up the path to the front door when he cycled by."

"But," said Joggy, frowning, "what would he have been doing out your way? That's wasn't his normal route home."

"That's what I thought at the time."

"And you're sure it was him?"

"I'd recognise those long bandy legs on him a mile off."

"What time of the day was this?"

"It was just before twelve, I'm certain, because I heard the bells of St Marys Church just after that."

"Who would he have been calling to out there?" Joggy asked.

"The only person I can think of is Maggie May." Pete lifted his cloth cap and scratched his scalp through his thinning grey hair. "But he'd hardly call to her in the daylight."

"I suppose not. But if he didn't call to Maggie May, who did he call to?"

"Beats me."

"What had the guards to say, when you told them?"

"I never told the guards."

"Why not?"

"They never called."

"But surely they called to some of your neighbours?"

"No. We never saw hide-nor-hair of them."


Who did John Canavan call to on that day?
The question bothered Joggy; it would not leave him alone. For the rest of the day his mind roamed along that road and into the homes of everyone who lived there, but by the time he reached his own house – the last -- he was none the wiser. There was nothing for it, on the way home that evening, he would have to brave Maggie May's.

* * * *

Maggie May Brown was a widow in her mid-forties -- a buxom lady with a narrow waist and wide hips. Nowadays she wore her chestnut hair high in a bun. She lived at the top of a winding gravel lane in a narrow two-storey farmhouse. It was a small farm of thirty acres, dedicated mostly to livestock. She had been married six years when her husband, Tommy Brown, died. For the last two years of their marriage, they had slept apart; Tommy was not the most faithful of husbands.  Initially, the marriage was a happy one. They tried for several years for children but to no avail; finally they went to the doctor. The tests proved that Maggie was incapable of bearing a child, or "as barren as the Burren" as Tommy became fond of saying, after a few too many pints. He slowly returned to his old life and to some of his old girlfriends. Arguments ensued, which led to raised fists, flying crockery and, inevitably, separate beds. Thereafter they hardly spoke to each other.

One evening Tommy was attending to a cow with mastitis.  He squeezed the penicillin up inside the teat. The cow angered by his rough handling sideswiped him with her hips, toppling him to the ground. She then lashed out with her hoof, catching him flush on the temple.  It knocked him out cold. It was twenty minutes later when he woke up. Not feeling well, he took to his bed and there he was found the next morning, dead, the hoof mark of the cow clearly visible on his forehead. A brain haemorrhage they said. Several women grieved for Tommy, but Maggie May was not one of them.

The house had a peculiar stairway, with an acute turn at the top, which meant the funeral directors could not get the plain pine coffin around it. So they had to leave the coffin at the foot of the stairs and carry Tommy down to it.

"Would you like to take your final farewell of Tommy?" the priest asked of Maggie May.

"Thank you Father," she said calmly and, still calm, she leaned over her husband and spat on his face. "That's all I have to say Father."

One of the funeral directors extracted a handkerchief from his pocket.

"Don't," She snapped. "I want him to have something to remember me by."

"But you can't send him off like that," he argued.

"If you want to be paid for your services," she said sternly, "you'll leave him as he is."

Reluctantly, they closed the lid.

Maggie May did not attend her husband's funeral.

With Tommy gone, money became tight. The small farm barely made enough to pay the bills. Maggie May did not know in which direction to turn. She contemplated selling the farm. Then fate stepped in. Feeling a little lonely, she travelled to Coothill in County Cavan to spend a weekend with her elder sister, Noreen. During one of their many conversations, Noreen related the scandalous tale of a local woman whose husband had died and left her in dire financial straits. The lady, unable to get work, resorted to taking lovers for, she whispered, using the polite term -- monetary gain.

On the long bus journey back home, Noreen's story planted an idea that germinated and took root in the back of Maggie May's brain. By the time she arrived home, it had flowered. She now knew the way forward. She set about carefully and discreetly cultivating a small, but select clientele. The proceeds of which would eke out her meagre farm income. And so she had survived these past eleven years.

From her kitchen Maggie May heard the sound of a car coming up her laneway. She hurried up to her bedroom, releasing her hair from the constrictions of the bun as she went. She gave it a quick brush, touched up her lipstick and opened the top three buttons of her blouse before spraying herself liberally with perfume.

Joggy had barely finished knocking when she was back down to open the door.

"Joggy." She hid her surprise well. "How nice to see you. Come in."

Before he could politely refuse, Maggie May had disappeared into the house. He had no choice but to follow.

"Come through to the front room," she said.

It was a small cosy room, with an open fire, a two-seat settee and an armchair, on which her black-and-white collie was sleeping. It opened one inquisitive eye, gave a shallow guttural growl and then closed it again.

"Have a seat," said Maggie.

"I can't stay long."

"That's alright Joggy, it doesn't take long." She sat beside him and her hips pinned him against the armrest.

Joggy swallowed hard.

"I hear you're doing a bit of snooping," she said.

"I believe you and John had a relationship?" He spoke, despite his annoyance at fielding the now familiar question, in a pleasant manner.

"Who told you that?"

"He confided in Luke Baker."

"We didn't have a relationship; we had affection for one another. He was affectionate with me and I was affectionate with him. I miss him. He was gentle and kind." She smiled. "And he had loads of stamina." She leaned closer to him and her hand came to rest high on his inner thigh. Her hot breath was on his neck, her heady perfume assailed his nostrils and her ample cleavage filled his sight. "You know Joggy." Her chest heaved with her slow deep breaths. "I still haven't replaced him in my affections."

"I'm… I'm so sorry to hear that," he said hastily, "but I didn't come here to..er… be affectionate. I..I came to find out if John was here the day before his body was found. I'm sorry if you got the wrong idea."

"Oh!" She straightened herself up. "Well, you can't blame a woman for trying."

"I realise it's a delicate question, but I really need to know."

"No. He was not here; it was not his time of the week to call."

"I appreciate your candor Maggie, thank you. Now, I had better get home or Alice will have given my dinner to the dog."

He stood up to go.

"Are you sure, there's nothing I can do for you?" She smiled as she eyed the bulge in his trousers.

"No, no, I'm, I'm fine thanks," he said, his face hot with embarrassment, and left.

* * * *

Later that night with the children gone to bed, Joggy and Alice sat in the kitchen in two armchairs in front of the Stanley range. Alice was knitting a cardigan for Katie, while Joggy stared at the billowing flames through the open fire door.

"I had to call in and see Maggie May this evening," he said.

Alice stopped knitting and rested the needles on her lap.

Joggy described their meeting.

"That cheap tart," Alice spat, when he concluded. "Wait till I see that one, I'll give her a piece of my mind." She picked up her needles and began knitting again: This time a little faster than before. Half way across the new row she slowed and asked light-heartedly, "You weren't tempted, were you?"

"Well, if I'm to be truthful," he answered, becoming mesmerized by the tongues of red flames drawn by the flue up over the side of the firebrick and forgetting for a split second who he was talking to, "I suppose I was a little."

Silence. He looked at Alice then. Her face was changing colour rapidly as her good humour turned to shock and then into fury.

"You know I would never be unfaithful to you Alice." He quickly tried to reassure her. "No matter how tempting she was, I... I could never cheat."

"You were tempted?" she hissed through gritted teeth. She kept her voice low so the children would not hear. "You were tempted? How could you be tempted by that... that, trollop?"

"Look, it's like you're on a diet and you are offered a cream bun," said Joggy, scrabbling for a way out. "You're tempted; you know there's a price to be paid if you eat it, so you resist."

"What," Alice exploded. "You're comparing Maggie May Brown to a cream bun and what am I? Your diet? Just a slice of brown bread?" She stood up, threw her knitting at Joggy and stormed off to bed.

Joggy sank his face into his hands.

# CHAPTER 9

Danny had just parked his bicycle against the wall of the farmhouse when Fred Winter exited through the back doorway and came striding purposefully towards him, carrying a hold-all. "Danny!"

"Yes Mister Winter?"

"A couple of loads of turf were delivered during the week," he said, not stopping as he drew alongside Danny, who fell into step and walked with him down the yard. "The driver reversed as far as he could into the shed, but there is a good deal of it still outside." They stopped beside Fred's Woolseley. "There's rain forecast for the weekend, so I need you to throw it in before it comes." He opened the driver side door and flung the hold-all onto the passenger seat. "You think you can handle that?"

"Yes sir."

"Good." He slipped behind the steering wheel, banged the door closed and drove off.

Victoria watched from an upstairs bedroom window. She wasn't going to risk another confrontation – another refusal to go with him on this visit to the North. She had plans of her own for the weekend.

Shortly after Danny had undertaken his task, Victoria arrived with the empty wicker basket under her arm.

"I'll do that for you." He took the basket from her and placed it on the ground, then began to fill it.

Victoria eyed his broad upper back and wide shoulders. His coal black unruly hair covered the nape of his neck and blended with the colour of his Donkey jacket.

"Louise told me that Mister Winter wouldn't let you go last Saturday," said Danny.

"Yeah, said that only drunks go there and I'd only end up getting groped. He offered to take me to a fork supper instead. I had to bite my tongue otherwise I would have told him into which orifice he could stuff his fork supper."

Danny stood up and presented Victoria with the full basket.

She took it from him and studied his face, a face that was in transition, from the soft roundness of a boy to the chiselled handsomeness of a man. His eyes held hers.

"I suppose you're not going tonight either," he asked.

"No, sorry, I'm house-sitting."

"House-sitting, sounds really exciting. Where's he gone?"

"To the North... won't be back till late Monday."

"So what's stopping you from going out tonight? He's not going to know?"

"I can't. He said he'd ring around eleven o clock; His way of checking up on me."

"So what are you going to do with yourself for the weekend then?"

"I suppose the T.V will have to keep me company," Victoria said it with just enough inference.

Danny was not deaf, but still couldn't bring himself to ask.

She waited. His body-language told her everything she needed to know. *Louise was right*, she thought, Danny was never going to make the first move. *To hell with this.* She tossed the basket on the ground, grabbed Danny by the lapels of his Donkey jacket and pushed him back against the shed wall. "If you fancy me, kiss me, if you don't....." He covered her lips before she could finish the sentence.

After several seconds, she released him. "You're a good kisser for someone who gets little practice." she said, somewhat pleasantly surprised.

"Who says I don't get practice, I've had loads of practice." He looked a little miffed at the suggestion.

"With who?"

"My sister, Helen."

"What!" Victoria's mouth fell open in shock. "That's disgusting."

Danny burst out laughing.

"I'm only joking," he said, still laughing.

"Bastard." She punched him hard in the chest.

"I'm joking, I'm joking, I'm sorry," he wailed. He crossed his arms in front of his body to protect himself from further assault, "I couldn't resist." Then satisfied he wasn't going to be hit again, he asked, "Would you like me to keep you company this evening?"

"I don't know if I want you to now," she said teasingly.

Danny collected the scattered sods into the wicker basket and carried it to the kitchen door.

"I'll be here at eight."

"I mightn't let you in." She tried to keep a straight face.

With a parting smile and a bounce in his step, Danny returned to his work.

* * * *

Over the five and a bit miles that spanned the distance between Pete Wall's and Joggy's home, eleven families resided beside or close to the road. Six of them, including Maggie May, were farmers. One was a teacher of long-standing in Oldbridge Secondary School, two were newly married couples, one was a pair of old-age- pensioners and one was a hermit. On Wednesday he had decided to call to two houses each evening for the next three evenings and the remaining four he would call to on Saturday. Joggy's first port of call that Saturday morning was Fred Winter's. Victoria answered the knock on the front door.

"Yes? Can I help you?" she inquired politely.

He had heard that Fred had a new housekeeper, but it was her youth and beauty that surprised him. "Oh, hello, I'm looking for Fred? Is he about?"

"I'm sorry, you've just missed him."

"Will he be back later?"

"No, I'm afraid he won't be back "till Monday."

"I see. That's a pity; I'll have to wait till Monday so."

"Shall I say who called?"

"Ahm, tell him Joggy Jackson called."

Victoria's eyes lit up. "You must be Danny's father."

"I am for me sins. Well it was nice meeting you," He turned to walk away.

"I'll let Mister Winter know you called," said Victoria, and closed the door.

* * * *

The results were fruitless; not one in eight of the nine other houses had seen John Canavan. The grapevine however had been busy and by now they had all heard of Joggy's quest, which made it easier for him to ask the questions he needed to ask. If they had reservations, they managed to keep them to themselves. They were polite but inquisitive at the same time. Nearly all offered tea; the exception had been Delaney's. They were farmers and lived down a long gravelled lane. The house was large and over two hundred years old. It formed part of a square cobbled courtyard, butting as it did to grey stone sheds that encircled the yard. The doorways to the sheds had semi-circled archways and heavy slatted timber filled the windows. Joggy drove into the yard and pulled up outside the front door. He got out and knocked. Ann Delaney opened the door. She was the wife of Brendan, the oldest son, who now ran the farm. The parents had retired. They had bought a bungalow on the outskirts of Oldbridge and had moved there with the rest of the family. Ann was petite with plain looks and shoulder-length brown hair tied back into a ponytail. She did not speak. She looked warily at him. The fading yellowed remnant of a bruise was just visible on the cheekbone under her right eye.

"Hello," said Joggy. "Is Brendan about?" He would have liked to have asked her about her injury but since he had never met her before, he felt it was not his place. Just then, Brendan drove into the yard on a New Holland tractor. His wife, still without speaking a word, closed the door.

Brendan climbed down and came to meet Joggy. He was a tall man with a receding hairline and ruddy weather beaten face. "The very man," he said with a smile. "A fella told me something in the mart the other day. He said that you were looking into John Canavan's murder. He was pulling my leg, right?"

"No, he wasn't."

Brendan, burst out laughing. "What the fuck would you know about investigating a murder?" he said, still laughing.

"Nothing, I suppose. But I have to try."

"Why?" He asked incredulously.

"Because.... Luke asked me too."

"Because he asked you to! Joggy, I don't know if you are simple-minded or just naïve, but you haven't a hope in hell. The police investigated and found Baker to be the culprit and they are professionals. You're just a....a gardener. Stick to what you're good at."

The insult hurt, but he tried not to let it show. "I can understand your attitude, Brendan, but I still need to ask questions."

"Jesus, Joggy, did you not hear me? Leave it be. They're both dead. There's nothing to be gained." He turned back to his tractor.

"I met your wife. She seems nice. What are ye married now, about a year?"

He stopped and looked back. "Yeah, about that."

"Has she any family?"

"Four brothers and two sisters."

"The brothers, are they all older than her?"

"Three of them are. Why do you want to know?"

"Older brothers are usually very protective of their little sisters. I was just wondering what they might do if they found out that you were using one of them as a punch bag."

Delaney marched towards Joggy. The arteries on each side of his neck stood out; blood red and pulsing.

"You can take a swing at me if you want, Brendan," Joggy said unfazed, "but I can assure you, unlike that little girl in there, I return anything that comes my way with interest."

Delaney stopped and glared into Joggy's eyes. "What goes on between me and my wife is none of your fucking business, Jackson."

"You're right, it is none of my business, but, I don't think her brothers would see it that way."

"What will it take for you to leave this yard?"

"It's a simple question, yes or no. And then I'll leave you alone. On the day before John Canavan was found in the river, he cycled along that road out there coming from Oldbridge, all I came here to find out was, if you saw him? Maybe you were driving around in the tractor at the time."

Delaney said nothing for a few seconds. The veins in his neck seem to reduce in size and colour. "No," he muttered eventually. "I wasn't near the road that day. Anyway I never knew the man."

"Thanks Brendan." Joggy slipped behind the steering wheel and closed the car door. He rolled down the window.

"Just for your own information," said Brendan, looking thoughtful, "I didn't hit my wife. It was an accident. She tripped and hit her face."

"I'm sure that's all it was Brendan," said Joggy. He turned the key in the ignition and drove out of the yard; a smile of quiet satisfaction on his face.

One last house remained -- old Bill Weir; the hermit. Bill lived alone on a hill in a run-down cottage by the edge of the road. Joggy had called Thursday evening but received no reply. He tried again Saturday morning. Several times he knocked on the door, each time taking a step back out of the porch, so Bill could see who it was. Once, he thought he saw one of the grey—once white-- lace curtains move; a minute movement, but enough to satisfy Joggy, that Bill was home.

"Bill, Joggy Jackson here," he shouted. "I know you're in there. I just want to talk to you about John Canavan. I want to know if you saw him on the Saturday, the day before his body was found. Bill? Bill, please talk to me." He waited several minutes more for a reply, but none was forthcoming. Before he left, he imparted a final shot.

"Bill, I'm sorry if I disturbed you, but I thought because Luke was a good friend to you, delivering home your groceries and medication every week, you'd want to help!" He started to walk away.

"I didn't like John Canavan." Bill said from the outside corner of the house. He had left by the back door and come around.

Joggy turned. "I'm not doing this for John Canavan. I'm doing it for Luke. So if you know something, you'd be helping a friend."

Bill was a small man with a head of wavy-grey hair, which along with his clothes, did not look like they had been washed in a long while. A small blob of butter was adhering precariously to his stubbled chin. "I remember that Saturday. Some people think because you get old, your memory goes, but mine is still sharp. I can still remember my first communion. I made two shillings and six pence. Spent the whole damn lot in Murphy's shop on sweets. I was as sick as poisoned dog for two days."

"Ahmm," said Joggy, purposefully clearing his throat in the hope it would stop old Bill babbling on.

"Anyway." Bill took the hint. "I didn't see Canavan that day, but I did see something else. At least I think I did. It happened so fast. I just couldn't swear to it, on a Bible like."

Bill had a habit of speaking in short sentences; often pausing several times in the duration of a longer one.

"Bill, what exactly did you see that day?" Joggy was becoming perplexed by Bill's ramblings.

"I was out here digging up some weeds. It started to rain. I stood into the porch and waited. The road was quiet. I remember that. Then I heard a car coming from Oldbridge. It was Winter's Woolseley. It was pulling a covered trailer. You know the type; the ones you can carry a beast in. I thought someone else was in the car. But I couldn't be sure. Winter is not known for giving lifts. That's why I think I could be wrong. It happened so fast."

"Do you remember what time of the day that was?"

"I don't keep time. I have no clocks or watches." He pointed a shaky finger at the sky. "But it was close to mid-day, because the sun was directly overhead."

"Apart from Winter's reluctance to carry people, is there any other reason for you to doubt what you saw?"

"The memory is still sharp. But I'm afraid, Joggy, the old eyesight's fading. In those few seconds after the car passed…. I could have sworn there was someone else in the car. Joggy, has anything ever passed in front of you, quickly like, and you say what you saw, because it was the first thing that entered your head, but afterwards, you start to doubt what you thought you saw?"

"Yes, I know what you mean Bill. Did any other traffic go by?"

"I'm sure there did, but I didn't see them. I went for a bite to eat after Winter passed."

\* \* \* \*

The Jackson household's weekly shopping was done every Saturday morning in Dunnes Stores in Oldbridge and since Alice could not drive, Joggy had to bring her in. The atmosphere had not altered since Tuesday night… ice-cold silence.

"I'll be in the pub, give me a shout when you're finished," said Joggy. He winced as the passenger door slammed shut. "For fuck sake Alice," he muttered, "I didn't do anything."
Alice had a well-tried shopping system. She had a starting point and a finishing point and knew as well as the staff did where to find every item she needed. Usually she lolled along, taking her time, looking at products she was never going to buy, thinking

maybe there would come a day when she would. Today she did not loll, today she moved rapidly from one aisle to the next, filling her shopping trolley with essential items. Her last port of call was the freezer department. She examined a frozen chicken.

"Scrawny yokes, aren't they?" Alice instantly recognised the voice. She spun around.

"Call into me on the way home," said Maggie May, "and I'll give you a real one."

"My family don't need anything from you," Alice snapped.

Several women turned and stared in their direction.

"I don't blame you for being mad at me Alice." Maggie May, now realised that Joggy must have talked. "I jumped to the wrong conclusion the other evening. I shouldn't have compromised your husband. It was a genuine mistake."

"Is that what you call it?" she sneered. "A mistake! Someone calls to your door and you try and jump on their bones."

"I don't get too many visitors Alice, and the men who do call to see me, usually have something else on their minds. I don't get too many men with your husband's integrity."

"I see. Just how much integrity did my husband display the other evening?"

"He nearly jumped out of his skin. He reminded me of a rabbit caught in the headlights of a car; not knowing which way to turn. He's a rare one Alice, hold on to him tightly."

Maggie May was a person of ridicule in the area, a pariah, an outcast, someone you avoided and above all did not speak to.

The rage that Alice had nursed since Tuesday night gradually disintegrated and to her own amazement it was replaced by compassion. She suddenly felt sorry for Maggie May. Her words conjured up a lonely life.

Alice knew as did every other woman in the area that the only people who called to Maggie May were men and they only called under the cover of darkness. Up to now she had not thought about the human side of it, companionship, friendship, human warmth. "So why do you do it?" she asked.

"Ah, you know, it started out as a good idea. I thought I could keep it a secret and that the men would be discreet. How naïve was I. Men have big mouths when they drink."

"You could stop if you wanted to."

"I could, but it wouldn't make any difference. I'd still be known as a whore. No, better to let it die naturally."

Despite herself, Alice could not help being drawn to Maggie May. In her speech and manner she could hear resonances of her favourite grandmother. Her mother's mother was a straight-talking down-to-earth woman, who called it as she saw it. She had always said to accept what was different, understand and live with it.

Several women watched from a distance, Maggie May noted the condescending looks. "Look at them," she said. "They probably think that every time their husbands leave the house they're coming to see me. And they have a right to worry, because some of them do. And do you know Alice, their husbands wouldn't be coming to me if they spread their own legs a bit more often. I'd better go; you could lose friends talking to me."

"Don't worry about them," said Alice.

"Still, I'd better be going, thanks for the chat." She walked slowly away.

A little later Maggie May pulled in behind Alice at the cashier desk. Nothing more was said as Alice packed her shopping bags and placed them in the trolley. She paid the cashier. Alice looked for several reflective seconds at Maggie May. Eventually she said, "I'll call in some evening for that chicken."

"Call anytime, you'll be welcome." But there was scepticism in her voice.

They drove home in silence. Once the groceries were brought into the house, Joggy quickly changed into his working clothes and left by the back door. There was not a lot to do. But he felt more comfortable outside, pottering about, away from the glacial atmosphere.

Alice called everyone in for dinner. He looked up in surprise when his wife placed his dinner before him; lamb chops, new potatoes, onions, mushrooms and gravy; his favourite meal. She smiled benignly at him and then set about serving the rest of the family.

# CHAPTER 10

Terry Parker was watching the six o clock news on U.T.V when the soft, lyrical tones of the door chimes resounded in his hallway. "Will you get that, dear?" his wife said from the kitchen, raising her voice a little so she could be heard above the news announcer. Terry grumbled. He had settled in for the evening and hated being disturbed from his comfortable armchair by the open fire. He shuffled down the hallway in his red tartan slippers to the front door. He switched on the porch light. Through the opaque glass centre panel the shape of a large man could be seen. Terry peeped through the spy hole and smiled.

"Well, well, well, if it isn't Fred Winter. Come all this way for my big day, have you?"

"Wouldn't have missed it for the world, Terry."

"Come in, come in."

"All alone are you?"

"Afraid so."

"She'll be bitterly disappointed," Terry warned.

He stepped into the kitchen. "Liz, we have a guest for dinner."

Her face lit up when the tall, blonde figure of Fred Winter appeared and presented her with a bunch of red roses and a kiss on the cheek. Liz glanced expectantly at the kitchen doorway.

"Is Victoria not with you?"

"I'm afraid not Liz, couldn't persuade her to come. You know what teenagers are like, a bit selfish; parents don't always rank high in their priorities."

"Victoria is not selfish," she snapped," She's a kind and loving young woman."

"I'm sorry, Liz, it was a generalisation, I didn't mean it specifically."

Feeling a little guilty at her riposte, Liz quickly changed the subject. "Where are you staying tonight?"

"I've a room booked at the Shelton Arms."

"Have you checked in yet?"

"No, I came here first."

"Stay here then, there's plenty of room."

"I couldn't impose."

"Nonsense, I won't hear another word. That's settled. Now the two of you go into the sitting room and chat. I'm sure you have a lot to catch up on. I'll give you a call when dinner's ready."

"You must have started late to be only arriving now?" said Terry, as they settled into the two armchairs, one either side of the fireplace.

"Actually I started out early this morning. I had a couple of things to see to first." Fred did not elaborate.

At first Terry was stumped. Fred's answer had been curt, not encouraging further discussion. Then, he remembered the date.

"Did Victoria not ring to let you know she wasn't coming?" asked Fred.

"No, it must have slipped her mind. Liz believed because of the weekend that was in it, that she would be home for it. Personally," Terry lowered his voice and leaned forward so as not to be heard by his wife, "I would have been more surprised, if she did come. Politically, Vicky and I have never seen eye to eye and the one thing she's not is a hypocrite. I have to admire her for that."

After dinner was over, Fred offered to help tidy up, but Liz refused, said it was women's work and shooed him into the sitting room.

"Scotch?" Terry held up a three-quarter full bottle.

"That'd be lovely, thanks."

Terry handed over the drink, switched off the T.V and returned to his armchair. "Did you hear the news today?" he enquired.

"No, what happened?"

"Two more of our U.D.A boys were murdered."

"Fenian bastards!"

"Not to worry, I'm sure our boys will even up the score soon."

Fred took a large swig of whisky. "Your acceptance speech all ready?"

"Finished it last night."

"Any surprises in it?"

"Yes, as a matter of fact there is."

"Are you going to tell me?"

"If I told you, it wouldn't be a surprise, now would it?" Terry said mischievously. A half smile played on his face.

"Come off it Terry, I tell you everything."

"Everything but what goes on at your Royal Black Preceptory meetings."

"That's not fair, you know I'm bound by secrecy, I took an oath."

Liz came into the room. "The spare room is made up, I'm off to bed."

"So soon?" Fred stood up. "I hope it's not because of what I said?"

"Nonsense, I'm a little tired and anyway you'll only bore me with your talk of politics, so I'll say goodnight."

She kissed her husband on the forehead and left. Terry listened and waited until his wife had climbed the stairs and closed the bedroom door behind her before he spoke again. "Speaking of surprises," he said, "I received one recently while rummaging through my father's effects. I found a diary."

"Well that's hardly a surprise -- a lot of people keep diaries."

"This was a diary of murder, a chronicle of death no less." Fred rose up out of his armchair and made his way over to a teak cabinet with a sliding door. He slid the door back and extracted a dull brown leather briefcase. "Liz knows nothing of this." He tumbled the combination numbers and popped the latches, "I don't want to worry her. I want it kept between ourselves."

Terry pushed back some papers and lifted out a small red leather bound diary.

"She won't hear a word from me," promised Fred. He craned his neck for a look at the book.

Terry left the open briefcase on the carpeted floor and returned to his armchair. He topped up Fred's glass. "I'll leave that with you." He placed the bottle of Scotch beside Fred, "make free with it, I'll sip what I have."

"Thanks, that's very generous of you, I will."

"Do you remember me telling you about dad's paranoia and how he'd turned into a nervous wreck over the last year of his life?"

"Yeah, you said he was afraid to leave the house."

"Right, and every time the phone or the doorbell rang he would jump out of his chair hide in a corner and start muttering to himself, they're coming to get me... they're coming to get me. He would never say who was coming to get him or what he was terrified of. But that fear eventually led to the heart attack that killed him."

"Did you ever find out what his fear was?"

"Not until I read his diary."

Terry handed it to Fred, who thumbed quickly through the entries.

"I don't understand," he said, "even at first glance I can see that most of these murders happened abroad. What have they got to do with your father?"

"Everything." Terry took the diary back. "They were all at one time good friends of my father and I believe they all had a hand in the punishment beating and murder of Rory Donovan. According to the police reports at the time, the punishment beating got out of hand and they ended up killing him. Do you remember him?"

"Can't say I do, who was he?"

"He was a young catholic man. He was found tied to a tree in Blackfield Woods. His skull had been crushed with an iron bar. Remember it now?"

"No. But then there's been a lot of killing over the years. It's hard to remember them all. What makes you so sure it was Donovan's death they had a hand in?"

"Because, according to the diary entries the first of the reprisal killings happened the morning after Donovan was murdered."

Terry opened up the diary and searched for the entry. Aloud he read…"20 /04 /1955 Charlie Wright: the first to die. His brakes failed coming down Forkhill. Went through a red light at the bottom and was wiped out by an Ambulance."

He smiled grimly at Fred. "Ironically, it was speeding to pick up the body of Rory Donovan in Blackfield woods."

"I take it you think the I.R.A carried out the reprisals?"

"Yes, who else could it be?"

"I don't know, but what I do know is that Charlie Wright was not killed by those bastards. Charlie was a good neighbour and friend of my family. On the day that Donovan was killed Charlie was with my mother and father and we were all at the hospital."

"What makes you so sure it was that night? It was after all nearly twenty years ago?"

Fred topped up his whisky glass and leaned confidently back in his armchair. "Because that was the night my sister Susan died."

"Ok," Terry said thoughtfully, "we'll skip that for the moment and run through the other four killings. Perhaps they'll shed some light on the matter. "

Again he read aloud...26 / 04 / 1955 Bernard Magee: the second to die. Body found in a field. He was naked and found lying in the shape of a cross. Ash skewers had been driven through the palms of his hands. He was finished off with a bullet to the head. After Magee's and Wright's deaths, Seale, Manning and Ryder disappeared overnight."

He looked up, but this time Fred made no comment.

"'10 / 10/ 1956, Ian Ryder: the third to die. Killed in Australia. He was found in the outback in a burnt-out car with his hands, feet and neck bound by wire to the driver seat. He had been burnt alive.'

"'23 / 06 / 1959, Alex Manning: the fourth to die. Killed in the U.S.A.

Found on a building site in Arizona nailed to the gable end of a wooden house.'"

"'17 / 09 / 1964, William Seale: the fifth to die. Killed in Canada. Found in the Canadian Rockies hanging from a tree outside his cabin. He had been living a low-profile reclusive life.'

"And the last entry is just two words --I'm next.'"

Terry looked at Fred, searching his face for a response.

"Well." Fred answered the unasked question. "It's obvious they were all tortured; tortured for the names of the others involved. And, the big question that stands out from all of this is, why if he was involved didn't they come after your father?"

"I've no idea. Maybe they couldn't get to him. After all he had become rather reclusive."

"Maybe." Fred was not entirely satisfied.

"Let's go back to Charlie Wright," said Terry.

"What about him?" There was a hint of annoyance in Fred's voice.

Terry chose to ignore it.

"Where was Charlie between nine and ten that night?"

"I told you, he was with my family. I travelled home with Charlie that night and he stayed in our house till my parents came back."

"What time was that?"

"It was close to midnight. Can we drop this now, it's going nowhere and it's becoming tiresome?"

"Of course, I was just hoping we'd come up with some answers but it looks like all we came up with were more questions. So, for the time being it'll remain a mystery."

Reluctantly, Terry put the diary back in the briefcase, locked it and replaced it back in the sideboard.

The more they talked the more Fred drank. He eventually drained the last drop of Scotch from the bottle into his glass.

"It's getting late," said Terry. We had better be getting to bed. I've a big day ahead of me tomorrow." He stood up.

It took Fred several efforts to stand, and when he did he swayed like a ship on a storm-tossed sea. "With my last drop Terry," said Fred, his words heavily slurred. "Let's salute the Queen."

They pointed their glasses at the portrait hanging over the teak side unit.

"The Queen, God bless her!" they said.

Fred poured the last drop down his throat and then stumbled backwards. Terry caught him before he crashed into the furniture. He removed the tumbler from his hand and steered him to the door, up the stairs and into the spare bedroom. Fred collapsed face down onto the bed. Terry turned him over; then removed his shoes before lifting his legs onto the bed. He left the door ajar then went back downstairs to tidy up. He washed and dried the tumblers before going out the back and dropping the empty bottle in the dustbin. All tidied up he checked on Fred who was snoring his head off. He quietly closed the door and returned downstairs to the front hall, then searched Fred's overcoat and found what he wanted. He put on his own coat and left. An hour later he was back, returned the item and went to bed.

CHAPTER 11

Even though Victoria had reassured Danny that Fred was away for the weekend; a small doubt remained. What if he broke down? What if he had changed his mind? What excuse could he give for being in his house? These doubts niggled away at him as he cycled down Winter's stony, pot-holed laneway. To Danny's knowledge, no one local in Fred's or his parent's time had ever been invited into the Winter house. Even the farm labourers who worked the farm down through the years, none of them had been asked in for as much as a cup of tea in the kitchen.

One local woman, however, Maisie Brennan, who was selling raffle tickets at the time, did step inside the front door. While Fred was gone to fetch his money, she stepped out of the rain and into the front hall to use his hall table to write out the ticket.

"What are you doing there?" Fred had asked sharply when he returned.

"Well I couldn't very well write them in the rain, now could I?"

"I suppose not. Next time just wait till you're invited in." He had replied in the same sharp tone.

And so a shroud of secrecy surrounded the house.

Danny looked about warily as he parked his bicycle against the back wall and was relieved to see no sign of Fred's Woolseley.

Victoria was waiting in the back doorway. "Don't look so worried," she reassured him. "There's nobody here but us chickens."

Danny followed Victoria into a small scullery, where two pairs of black Wellingtons and a pair of tan hob-nail boots stood to attention against one wall. Turning right he entered a spacious kitchen and was instantly disappointed. He had expected something special, but it looked no different from many a farmer's kitchen he had been in before. It smelt of damp clothes and boiled cabbage. A Belfast sink sat low under the kitchen window and a large pine open-shelf dresser filled in the space between the window and the far corner. It displayed a wide variety of crockery of which no particular pattern or colour prevailed. The centre of the stone slab floor was taken up with a well-worn table surrounded by four equally well-worn chairs. The wood was marked and scratched and its origin indistinct. The Aga solid fuel range was the kitchen's only concession to the modern age.

Victoria opened a door in the left-hand wall. "We're in the living room," she said.

It was another large room and again he was disappointed. It had two windows through which the golden rays of fading evening sunlight fell upon a dull and jaded carpet. One of the two windows looked to the front, the second onto the orchard. Filling the two portions of wall between them stood a mahogany book case, loaded down with old books. Underneath the orchard window, overflowing with paperwork was a polished oval mahogany table. A lone mahogany chair sat in front of it, its seat threadbare.

"That's Freddie's office," remarked Victoria.

"He's messy," said Danny.

"I know. I said it to him but he just calls it organised chaos."

The white marble fireplace, in which Victoria had lit a cheery fire, was the only redeeming feature in the room. In front of it was a three-seat, well-worn brown leather settee. It was flanked on either side by equally well-worn matching armchairs.

Victoria closed the curtains and switched on the tall lamp stand that stood to the left of the fireplace. On the right sat a square double-door mahogany cupboard on top of which stood the T V. She sat into the corner of the settee and folded her long slender legs beneath her. She patted the settee with the palm of her hand. Danny did not miss the signal. But he was not finished snooping. His eyes continued to flick along the family photos that hung over faded cream heavily embossed wallpapered walls.
Sitting on top of the T V was a gleaming silver cup. Danny stooped to read the inscription engraved on the base.

*SPONSORED BY ETHEL WINTER IN 1958.*
*AND*
*DONATED TO KILPATRICK SPORTS COMMITTEE.*

"That's Freddie's pride and joy," said Victoria. "He first won it three years ago for bale tossing and has retained every year since."

At last, Danny removed his duffel coat and flung it onto the armchair to the right of the fireplace. He then joined Victoria on the settee. He planted himself in the opposite corner and stretched his long legs towards the fire. Above the fireplace, Queen Elizabeth looked down on them: her smile seemed to carry a hint of disapproval.

"Do you not feel uncomfortable with her nibs looking down on ya?" he asked.

"She doesn't bother me. But then again I'm use to seeing her in the same way you're probably used to seeing portraits of the Sacred Heart or the Pope."

"Of course," he said mischievously, "I forgot you're one of them."

Victoria bristled at the remark. Even though she realised that Danny was jesting with her, she couldn't help feel a wave of tension swell within her. It was like an automatic warning sign.

"One of them! What do you mean… one of them?"

"You know; a protestant."

"What makes you think I'm a protestant?"

"Well, because no Catholic would name their daughter after an old English Queen, plus the Winter's are renowned for hiring their housekeepers from the protestant ranks."

"Actually, he didn't hire me… I volunteered," she mocked haughtily.

"Volunteered?"

"Yes, volunteered. Freddie and my father have been friends for a long time. I finished my A levels last year and with a little persuasion from dad, decided to take a year out. He thought I was too young to start college. So I went to work in his office. Then early in the New Year, Freddie came up North on one of his frequent visits and mentioned to my father that he was looking for a housekeeper. Dad suggested to me that I fill in till the end of the summer and hey presto, here I am."

"So what's it like being Fred's housekeeper?"

"Pretty easy really. I do a little cooking, a little cleaning, a little dusting and as long as the rooms, with the exception of his bedroom, look tidy," Victoria shrugged her shoulders, "he's happy."

"What? He likes an untidy bedroom?"

"I don't know whether his room is tidy or not, I'm not allowed into it."

"But surely you've taken a sneak look?"

"Of course I tried, but he keeps it locked."

"Why would he lock his bedroom? Is he afraid someone will make off with his jocks?"

"I don't know and I don't really care. At least it's one less room for me to clean."

An easy silence fell between them, as they both stared into the flames. Victoria was first out of the blocks. "I met your Father this morning. He called looking for Freddie, but he had just missed him."

"Oh, Fred must be part of his enquires into the John Canavan murder."

"Your Father's a policeman?" she asked, surprised.

"No, he's a gardener."

"I'm lost."

"He's doing it as a favour for a dead friend."

"I still don't understand. Tell me more about this murder and what part your father has to play in it?" She pulled her knees up to her chin and wrapped her arms around them.

Danny talked at length about what he knew, which wasn't a lot, but he did his best. "My father's involvement is something I don't fully understand. He says it's a debt of honour, and won't tell me what it is. But I intend to find out, with or without his help." He took a deep breath. "Anyway, that's enough about my family, tell me about yours?"

"I'm an only child. My father's an estate agent and my mother stays at home. There, all done."

"Not so fast, you don't get away that easy."

"What else is there?"

"You must have some interesting skeletons in your closet, like is your father involved in politics?"

"In a way." The wave of tension that had receded was back. "Why the sudden interest in my father's political views?" She folded her arms.

"From what I see on T V, everyone up there seems to be involved in one organisation or another and they all seem to have affiliations with some political party. I was just wondering which side of the political barricade he was on."

"In other words you want to put a label on him. You're just like all the rest of them Danny Jackson; pigeon-holing," she snapped.

"Everyone has to be labelled or you don't feel comfortable around them." She quickly unfolded her long slender legs and stood in front of the fire, from where she glowered down at him. "Let me tell you something, I don't believe in my father's politics nor do I believe in labels, because from where I come from, labels get you fucking killed. Whether you're a Protestant, Catholic, Unionist, Republican, English or Irish, it doesn't fucking matter, because up there you'll always find some disillusioned bastard who wants to harm you and you don't even have to be a target to die." She paused and took a shuddering breath. She placed a finger to her lips.

"I'm sorry," said Danny, taken aback by the outburst.

"Sorry! You're not sorry. You know why? Because you don't know why you're sorry and like everyone else down here, you're ignorant. I had a friend once, a very good friend" There was a slight quiver in her voice. "Josie was fifteen and mad in love with Mark Bolan. One Saturday morning, just over two years ago, she walked down to the newsagents, like she did every Saturday, to pick up a copy of 'Jackie' The centrefold was her idol. As she walked back home, totally engrossed, she passed between a car and a bookies; the blast tore her to shreds. What was left of her could have been buried in a Sainsbury shopping bag. So stop trying to fucking label people."

"I'm so sorry. I didn't mean to be insensitive and upset you. I was just trying to get to know you better by finding out what your family was like."

"Yes well, from where I come from, those kinds of questions can get you killed."

"This is not the North, Victoria. Down here we ask questions of people we want to get to know. It's a way of getting a handle on them. So, please, can we start again?"

No answer. Her angry eyes bored into Danny's. He feared opening his mouth in case he again said the wrong thing. The anger passed as quickly as it came. Her eyes softened. She lifted her head and looked to the curtains that hid her view of the orchard. Her eyes were more reflective now, as if she was reviewing a treasured memory. "I need a drink," she said suddenly. "Do you want one?"

"Yeah, why not?"

She opened the double doors of the mahogany cupboard and turned the bottles around to read the labels.

"We got Vodka, Scotch Whisky, Sandeman's Port and bingo, we've got a whole bottle of Brandy and not any old Brandy, but Remy's." She handed it to Danny, "You open that. I'll fetch the glasses and the red lemonade."

"Will Fred not miss it?" Danny felt a little apprehensive at drinking someone else's property.

"Don't worry about Freddie, I'll deal with him."

Danny swallowed hard when he read the label: it contained 40% alcohol. When Victoria had asked him to have a drink, he was thinking more on the lines of a mineral. The nearest he had previously come to alcohol was taking a sip from his father's pint. Now he was going to be drinking for real and he couldn't back out.

Victoria returned with the red lemonade and two brandy glasses. "Stop admiring it and open it," she said. She sat now in the centre of the settee.

Danny caught her hand. "I'm sorry about before. I didn't mean to re-open fresh wounds. Your friend's death must have been horrible for you."

"It's alright, I forgive you; you weren't to know."

Victoria poured.

"Let's toast," said Danny. "To your good friend Josie, may she never be forgotten."

* * * *

Vinny and Louise had two reasons for standing at three o clock on Sunday morning under the Elm tree to the side of Louise's house. The first was so they could kiss out of sight of Louise's parents, should they by chance, get out of bed and peep through the closed curtains for any sign of their daughter and the second was to avoid the shower of rain that was falling. The brief shower suddenly stopped and the moon re-appeared. Vinny gave Louise a last lingering kiss, whispered goodnight and started for home -- home was a fifteen minute walk.

He lived half way between Danny's house and the stone railway bridge. There was lightness in his step as he sauntered along. Things were going well with Louise.

He had just passed under an arch created by the convergence of two trees, when he heard the sound. He stopped and listened. It sounded like snoring, light snoring. "A cow? But he could see no cows in the moonlit field and anyhow he'd never heard of cows snoring. He came closer to the sound which seemed to be coming from the grass margin at the foot of the whitethorn hedge. He was now close enough to make out the shape of a person lying prone on the grass verge. Vinny rolled him over and was shocked to find it was Danny. "Danny, Danny." He shook him by the shoulder. "Wake up, wake up."

Danny, half opened one bleary eye. "Ah, for fuck sake, it's still dark. Go away," he slurred.

Vinny waved his hand in front of his face in a vain attempt to dispel the fumes of alcohol rising out of Danny's mouth. He grabbed Danny's arm and tried to lift him. "Come on Danny, up, you can't stay here, let's get you home."

"I am home."

"No you're not; you're on the side of the road, so come on, up."

Slowly, very slowly, Danny rose to his unsteady feet. He leaned heavily on Vinny, who was four inches shorter. They eventually arrived at Danny's house. He steadied him against the pebble dashed wall and searched his pockets for a door key. Within seconds they were inside.

"You're a good friend," slurred Danny, a little too loud for Vinny's comfort, as they made their way across the kitchen floor. He dropped Danny on his bed and began to remove his shoes.

"I'll do the rest," said Alice.

Vinny spun around. "I'm not responsible for his condition Missus Jackson," he protested.

"I never said you were Vinny." Alice knelt down and slipped off Danny's socks.

"I'll give you a hand Missus Jackson; he's dead weight."

Between them they stripped Danny naked of all his wet clothes and tucked him in.

"Do you know where he was tonight?" Alice enquired as they left the room.

"I'm afraid not Missus Jackson. Finding him on the side of the road was the first time I'd seen him all night."

"Thanks for seeing him home safely Vinny, I'm much obliged."

"Tell him I'll call later today ... to see what sort of head is on him."

"I'll do that and hopefully it'll be a whopper."

\* \* \* \* \*

Vinny stuck his head around the door-jamb of Danny's bedroom. "It's two o' clock; are you well enough to get up?"

The room was chilly. Earlier, his mother after she came home from mass checked in on him. She had found the overpowering odour of alcohol, sweat and farts so repugnant, that she held her nose, ran across the room, opened the top window and ran out again before she felt able to take another breath.

Vinny closed the bedroom door behind him and shuddered. "It's fecking freezing in here."

"I know. Shut the window will you."

Vinny obeyed and then sat on the edge of the bed. "How's the head?"

"I'm dying. There's a cunt inside kicking a football against the gable-end of me skull." He gingerly lifted himself up in the bed. "Do me a favour will you, get me a shirt out of the wardrobe?"

Vinny picked a white one and resumed his spot on the bed, "So, are you going to tell me where you were last night?"

"If I tell you, you have to keep it to yourself."

"Yeah, of course."

"No I mean you can't tell anyone, and that includes Louise. This is to remain between you and me, ok?"

"Fair enough, if that's the way you want it. My lips are sealed."

Danny glanced at the closed bedroom door and then back to Vinny.

"I was with Victoria, in Winter's," he whispered. "We were drinking brandy; Winter's brandy."

"You and Victoria... alone?" Vinny spoke a little too loudly for Danny's liking.

"Ssh, keep your voice down."

"Sorry."

"I've no memory of how much we drank. But I remember toasting some dead friend of hers; after that, nothing."

"You don't remember cycling home and falling into the ditch?"

"No, nothing."

"I reckon ye must have drunk the whole feckin bottle and if the state you were in is anything to go by, I'd hate to think what condition you left her in. Wouldn't it be terrible," a wide grin stretched across Vinny's face, "if ye did the deed and now have no memory of it?"

"Fuck off Vinny, that's not even close to funny."

"For you maybe, but I think it's hilarious."

"You would."

Suddenly there was a knock on the door and Danny's mother walked in. "Dinner's ready. You'd better get up for it because I'm not bringing it in to you." She reached into her apron pocket and extracted a small piece of white paper.

"I found this in your coat pocket when I was cleaning it out for the wash." She handed it to Danny. "It probably makes more sense to you than to me."

Danny waited for his mother to leave before he looked at it.

"Same time, same place," it read. He smiled with relief. "I've another date. I must have done something right."

# Chapter 12

It had become Joggy's Sunday ritual. Each time he crossed the river bridge on his way to visit Tom Baker, he would stop, lean his legs against the parapet and look down upon the spot where he found Canavan's body. His image would stare back at him from beneath the wavering water. He would then recite a silent prayer, bless himself and move on.

As he walked on further he became aware of a familiar sound. But because a thicket of young trees blocked his view, he could only guess at who was making it. He stood for several seconds at the gate of the second house of the four, and watched a young red-haired boy taking pot shots at a row of tin cans lined up at the base of the front wall of the house. A tin can took flight.

"You're getting pretty handy with that hurley and sliother, Stephen."

"I'm practicing."

"For the Kilpatrick under tens?"

"Yeah, and for the county."

"That's a mighty ambition," said Joggy, as another can became airborne. "What exactly are you practising?"

"My accuracy. Goalkeepers find it hard to stop low hard shots." Yet another can pinged into the air,

"Are you interrogating my son, Joggy Jackson?" Jenny Roache, said in jest as she stood in the open front doorway. She made her way to the gate.

"He wields a mean hurley. He'd make a good suspect."

Jenny was a small, pretty, dark-haired woman in her early thirties. She had three children, all boys. Stephen was eight and the twins were five. Her husband, Alfie, was a lorry driver who spent most of his spare time and money in O Meara's. Joggy's hand rested on the wooden gate. Jenny tapped it gently. "How's your investigation coming along?"

"Slowly, I'm afraid."

"There's not many I know would take on such job, even for a friend. I think it's very brave of you."

"Oh, I don't know about being brave, Jenny. More foolish I think"

"Foolishness or bravery, people will still appreciate what you're trying to do. 'Though, and I won't beat about the bush, Joggy, there are the be-grudgers hereabouts. They're all sweetness to your face but sneer at your efforts when your back is turned. But I'm not one of them. I liked Luke."

"Most people did."

"He would baby-sit the boys for me went I went to the shop. He was a good neighbour. I for one would like to see his name cleared."

He looked back towards the bridge and found his view blocked by the thicket. He turned back to Jenny. "Do you remember that weekend," he asked hopefully.

She nodded. "It's not one we're likely to forget, is it? After all, it happened right on our doorstep. That was the weekend Fred Winter brought his boar up to Bakers. I remember hearing those iron wheels rolling like thunder from a long way off. The kids were really excited, wondering what was coming. We waited at the gate for ages. They started clapping when that big Clydesdale of his passed, pulling the iron wheel cart, with the boar sitting there, proud as punch, high, like a king on his throne of straw."

A thought crossed Joggy's mind. "Can you remember, did the noise of the wheels stop or pause at any point?"

"No, it was continuous. I would have remembered if it had. Why do you ask?"

"Oh, just ruling out possibilities."

"Mommy," a small, brown-curly-haired boy came running out the door, "Jack hit me."

Jack came running close behind his twin brother, "I did not, he's telling fibs."

"I am not."

"You are too." With that Jack kicked his brother Frank on the leg and ran off with his brother in hot pursuit.

"Their getting big," said Joggy.

"Big and bold," retorted Jenny. "I have to love you and leave you. Alfie will be back shortly, looking for his dinner."

He was close to Tom Baker's when he heard an American voice calling after him.

"Hey Joggy!"

He turned to face the tall broad shouldered figure of Rick Worrell; Jenny's next-door neighbour and the sole occupant of the third of the four cottages. Rick was Irish/American. His uncle Peter, in his will, left the cottage to his only sister, who, in turn passed it on to her son. She did not want to see her family home sold or fall into decay. Rick was a writer; mostly articles and short stories for magazines. "Can I have a word?"

"Sure. What about?"

"If you wouldn't mind stepping into my parlour, as you Irish like to say. We'll have a bit more privacy there."

The interior of the house caught Joggy by surprise; it had been completely renovated. The kitchen and living-room were all one. Under the front window was a very untidy writing desk with a typewriter sitting in the middle of a sea of paper. The rest of the room, by contrast, was neat and tidy. There was no T.V. Every available space was filled with books. Joggy had never seen so many in one room. "Wow, you've done some job here."

"You like the open-plan effect?"

"It's great. I didn't think you could have this much space in a small cottage."

"When I took over the place seven years ago, Joggy, I couldn't believe how small the rooms were. They were claustrophobic, they had to go. I had to redesign it all."

"I see you kept the open fire."

"Yeah, I loved that. It adds cosiness to the room. Have a seat. Will you have tea… or coffee?"

"No thanks, it's too close to my dinner." Joggy sat on the sofa.

Rick stood in front of the open fire. "Let's cut to the chase, Joggy. I'm fascinated by this detective work you've taken on. As you probably know I'm a writer and I think what you're doing would make a great story. Would you talk to me about it?"

Joggy didn't answer. Instead he rose to his feet and crossed to the fireplace where he stood in silence studying a large photo of an American football team. A banner behind them spelt out NOTRE DAME.

"That's my final-year collage team. See if you can pick me out?"

"Number twenty-two."

"No, that's my….my brother. Try again."

"Seventeen."

"Good spot."

"It wasn't too hard, you're very alike."

"He was the quarterback and I was a linebacker."

"Linebacker, what's that?"

"A bit like your game of rugby. I was in the scrum and he was like a scrum half. So getting back to this story, Joggy, would you be willing to talk to me?"

"Not right now. I have to get it clear in my own head first. But, when I do, you'll be the first to know."

When Joggy reached the road again he looked at his watch and found it was too late to continue to Tom's so he turned for home. He couldn't get his mind off that photograph. Something about it niggled at him.

# CHAPTER 13

Three loud evenly spaced knocks fell upon the hall door and resonated in the silence of the room. A man with a purple, red and blue sash worn diagonally across his chest arose from his seat on the front row and made his way slowly down the centre aisle. When he reached the door he called out in a loud authoritarian voice, "What do you want?"

"I seek entry."

"Whence came you?"

"From the land of Moab".

"Whither do you go?"

"To the plains of Jericho".

"How do you hope to get there?"

"By a password."

"Have you the password?"

"I have."

"Will you give it to me?"

"I will divide it with you: the Ark of God."

"What is your colour?"

"Purple."

"Why do you make purple your colour?"

"Because the ornaments of the curtains of the Ark of God were purple, blue and red; and I chose purple for mine."

With that the man with the sash opened the door. "Enter and lead us to Jericho."

Two Lambeg drummers started up and led Terry Parker into the local orange hall and  the crowd, who up to now, had kept a dignified silence, suddenly let loose. Clapping, whistling and shouting, the noise very nearly drowned out the drumming. When Terry eventually reached the podium, he threw his arms in the air and gratefully accepted their acclaim. One of the loudest was Fred Winter, his whistles echoed from the back of the hall.

"Enough, enough." Terry gestured with his hands for everyone to sit down. "You're embarrassing me, please." Slowly and in piecemeal fashion, everyone resumed their seats.

Terry took his time. He scrutinized the eager faces that sat patiently waiting and watching. He did not want to be hurried.

What he had to say was too important to be rushed. He raised his right hand and pointed to the portraits that adorned the walls of the hall. "Like all my illustrious predecessors," his voice was loud and clear, "my role as head of this order is to promote and protect our customs, our heritage and above all the evangelical principles of our faith. As you are all well aware, our order extends back to the Battle of the Diamond and the Peep O' Day boys. And from that time we have manfully resisted all challenges and seen off all threats to our way of life. Along the way, for protection, we have had to arm some of our brethren. They have not alone protected us but they have also bravely protected our nation in two world wars. In the past, the threats have come from without, but today, I fear, the threat is coming from within. It is my belief, that we have a traitor in our ranks. He may be sitting beside you, behind you, or in front of you. But make no mistake he is there. You may ask, what proof I have to make this vile accusation, and I will tell you. Over the last four years seventeen of our protectors, our brethren, have been murdered. All of them have been members of our local order. They have been ambushed as they travelled to work. They have been blown up in their cars and they have been singled out in public houses for execution.

"His voice rose to a shout. "It is my belief that someone among us has sold his soul to the papist devils. It is not common knowledge which of our members is armed and which are not. It is not common knowledge where they work, where they live, what they drive, and where they drink. That kind of information is known only to the members. So I say again, we have a traitor among us. It is your duty as members to address this problem. It is your duty to report suspicious behaviour to the proper authorities and I don't mean the R.U.C. Into your hands I deliver this problem." He threw his arms out to his silent and stunned audience.

They looked at one another in abject shock. It was as if he had read their inner-most fears, given it a name and now it made absolute sense. Fred Winter stood up and started clapping. Within seconds the hall vibrated with thunderous applause. The man in the sash stepped up onto the stage. He waited patiently for the noise to subside, then stepped to the microphone and announced, "Tea and sandwiches are now being served in the committee room."

Danny started out for his second date with Victoria. Nervous excitement buzzed through him at the prospect of seeing her again. He still could not remember how the previous night finished. This time he left his bicycle at home. He had no choice. Earlier, his father had recovered it from the whitethorn hedge; both wheels flat. His parents had questioned him about the night before but got nowhere. When pressed by his father on the matter, Danny became belligerent and chided him. "Why should I tell you my secrets, when you won't tell me yours?"

With his parent's words ringing in his ears, "not to come home drunk," he shoved his hands deep into the pockets of his trousers and marched towards Winter's.

Victoria met him at the back door. She threw her arms around his neck and kissed him. "I've got a great night planned."

Danny swallowed hard. "I hope it doesn't entail brandy?"

"No, no brandy. There's none left anyway, we drank it all last night."

Victoria took Danny's hand and led him through the kitchen to the sitting room, where she had a blazing fire. They sat on the settee.

"What happened last night?" he asked in a faltering voice. "Toasting the memory of your friend is the last memory I have. Did... anything ... happen?"

"You can't remember a thing?"

"No."

"We talked and kissed and then talked and kissed a bit more. Actually, you talk a lot when you drink."

"That's all, nothing... else?"

"No, you passed the test with flying colours."

"Test... what test?"

"My test. Last night was about me finding out about the real you. My father once told me that if you want to find someone's real personality; get them drunk. And he was right. When you're drunk, your barriers come down and the real you, comes out to play. Some people turn nasty; some become argumentative, but you, you... apart from being talkative, your personality hardly changed at all."

"How could you see that if you were as drunk as I was?"

"I wasn't as drunk as you, I drank the same amount but I wasn't drunk. I have a little secret Danny; I have the constitution of a goat; I can drink any man under the table."

"So what was I last night, some sort of guinea pig?"

Victoria placed a warm hand on his cheek. "Don't be angry with me Danny. When I like a guy I need to be sure of them; that way I feel safe in moving to the next level."

She stood up, grasped his hand, pulled him to her and kissed him tenderly. Without releasing his hand she led him out of the room and up the stairs. Victoria's bedroom was moonlight and music. Moonlight poured in through the window, cutting a swath of rectangular light, stretching diagonally across the wooden floor, illuminating the single iron-framed bed and wooden locker. A small Phillips pocket-size transistor radio stood on the white locker, tuned to Radio Luxemburg. Nilsson's, 'Without you,' filled the air. Victoria kissed Danny again and then glided to the locker side of her bed. She smiled mischievously back at him, gripped the bottom edge of her tie-dyed navy t-shirt and yanked it over her head, revealing perfect breasts. He could not take his eyes off them. She then slipped off her skirt and panties and slid in between the sheets.

She was the most beautiful creature he had ever seen. In the adult magazine's that had been passed furtively among his friends, and in the fantasies they created, he, was the experienced seducer that women found irresistible, undressing them, laying them down, kissing, stroking, nipples between lips, penetration, ecstasy… and although it felt so real, his still moist jocks the following morning always reminded him it was only a dream.

But this was not a dream. This was for real. For the second night running, she had surprised him. Always one step ahead, challenging him, scaring him.

"What are you waiting for?" she said. "Strip."

Danny quickly undressed. Modesty made him keep his jocks on as he joined her between the sheets.

"All of it," she demanded.

He reached under the covers, removed the last item and dropped them on the floor. He turned and faced Victoria, unsure of what to do next. On the outside he was calm and composed but on the inside he was shivering, his rapid heartbeat echoing loudly in his ears.

"Have you ever made love before, and don't say your sister or I'll hit you where it really hurts?"

"No, no I haven't. Have you?"

"Several times. Do you know what foreplay is?"

"I've a fair idea."

"I'm going to show you. You follow my lead. What I do to you, you do to me."

She took him in her arms and kissed him. She was soft and warm, her mouth tasted sweet and her breasts felt surprisingly solid against his chest. Her free hand moved slowly down his belly, her long nails scraped teasingly along his abdomen. His body quivered involuntarily. She continued to his manhood and began to fondle. Danny's hand followed the contours of her body and rested on the silky smooth roundness of her bottom. Suddenly, he knew he was in trouble. He tried valiantly to hold back but the more she fondled him the harder it became not to succumb to the unbelievable build up of pressure, till he couldn't hold on any longer. A series of pleasurable grunts arose out of his throat and a tide of erotic bubbles exploded in his brain.

Victoria felt the wetness on her stomach. "You haven't, have you?"

"I'm sorry," he said, mortified, "I'm so sorry, I'm so sorry."

"It's alright, it's alright, it happens a lot with first timers," she said, placing a consoling hand on his cheek. "Do you think you could be ready again when I come back from the bathroom?" She pulled back the covers and slipped from the bed.

"Easy," he assured her.

She walked out of the room and down the hall. Within minutes she was back. She opened a drawer in the locker and removed a small box. "Are we ready to go again," she asked climbing back into bed.

"Yeah." He watched her extract an item from the box.

"Put this on," she said.

Danny studied it

"You look like you'd never seen a condom before?"

"Don't be silly, of course I have" he lied, "It's just that you can't buy condoms in this country."

"That's stupid."

"I know. Now how do you put this on?"

Victoria slowed Danny's eagerness by turning him on his back and straddling him. She reached out and gripped the top bar of the bed-head. With hands now free he squeezed her breasts.

"Not so hard," she said, feeling the pressure of his fingers, "they're not for building muscles, you know."

Victoria closed her eyes and began to build up a slow rhythm. Her body gyrated like a belly dancer and the iron bed fell into step. The sounds of the bed banging against the wall and her rising groans of pleasure grew louder and louder into a deafening crescendo as Victoria let rip, holding back nothing, until eventually reaching orgasm, her groans turned into a loud shuddering hiss.

Danny was a fast learner. After Victoria got what she wanted, they fell back, exhausted. She sat up and lit a cigarette. He slipped out of bed.

"What will I do with this?" he said, peeling off the used condom.

"Flush it down the toilet."

When he came back, she was standing by the window looking out over the apple trees into the moonlit open countryside, her beautiful naked body bathed in the pale cool light. Danny sat on the windowsill. "When was your first time?"

"I was fifteen."

"Were you in love?"

"No, I was in mourning."

"For your friend?"

"I wanted to know what it was like before I died too. Josie had experienced nothing of life. I was determined it wouldn't happen to me."

"Good for you."

She sat into the other side of the window. "I told you a lie yesterday."

"Really?"

"It wasn't because of the drunks that Fred stopped me from going to the Park for that dance. It was because I would be hanging out with the wrong crowd."

"What -- me, Vinny and Louise?"

"Yes, because you're Catholics. He said I should hang out with only my own people."

"Good luck with that, there's not many of ye around here."

"He also said that we had moral standards to uphold and a bloodline to keep pure." She sniffed. "Fucking hypocrite."

"What do you say that?"

"I sleep naked. I like to fall asleep looking at the moon, so the curtains are never drawn. Every night before I go to bed I have my last fag, usually, standing at this window, looking out over the orchard into the open countryside… and down there among the Apple trees, he's watching. He thinks I can't see him…. but I do."

"Mister Winter?" Danny exclaimed.

"Yes, the hypocrite."

"How do you know it's him… it could be anybody?"

"Because the night I first spotted him, I left the window and opened my bedroom door and listened. I heard the backdoor latch click as he closed it."

"So if you know he's down there, why stand at the window. Why expose yourself to him?"

"Because I like to torment him. It must drive him wild to see me and know he can never have me."

"Are you not afraid that he might attack you?"

"He wouldn't dare. My father's a powerful man with powerful connections. Freddie would be too terrified to do anything."

# CHAPTER 14

A chorus of birds chirped and cooed in the high branches of the trees surrounding the garden. They provided a soundtrack to an otherwise silent and peaceful setting as Joggy sat on a low wall having his mid-Monday-morning cup of tea. Cedric and Ethel Mercer lived three miles from Oldbridge. Of all the gardens he serviced, theirs was his favourite. It was set in woodlands surrounded by oaks, elms, ash and hazel. He felt if he ever had any real money, this was where he would like to live. Close by, high on a branch, a wood pigeon cooed. It brought a smile of remembrance as Mrs Wren story automatically came to mind.

He could still visualize the little white haired old lady who cycled out from her home in Oldcastle once a month to instill in the pupils of Kilpatrick the love and enthusiasm for nature that she so obviously felt. Her enthusiasm was infectious. Her eyes lit up and her voice sang as she explained how to recognize the various trees, flowers and animals. Birds she made clear, are not always visible, but you can always recognize them by their tell-tale songs. She was a fantastic mimic. But of all the wildlife stories she told, the one of how the wood pigeon came to have its distinctive sound, was the only one that Joggy could still recall.

Many years ago she said, a young boy was herding his family's cattle. The Wood Pigeon, who was sitting high on a branch, spotted a gang of marauding cattle thieves, stealthily making their way through the high grass. The Wood Pigeon called out a warning to the boy. Take the cooes Tadie, take the cooes Tadie, quick. The Wood Pigeon repeated the warning until Tadie escaped with the cows.

"Mister Jackson," the voice inquired, putting the brakes on Joggy's trip down memory lane. He spun around. A tall man sporting a brown neatly trimmed moustache, slicked-back hair and a navy-blue anorak came walking smartly towards him. Under the half-zipped anorak was a dark blue patterned silk tie over a light-blue shirt. Joggy frowned as he swung his legs back into the yard and stood up.

"Yes," he replied, cautiously.

"I'm Detective Sergeant Owen Reilly."

"What can I do for you, Owen?"

"Detective Sergeant, if you don't mind."

"Is that what your mother calls you?"

"Detective Sergeant is my official title, Mister Jackson. I have earned that right."

"Well good for you, Owen, now as I said before, what can I do for you?"

"I can see you like to make trouble for yourself, Mister Jackson."

"And what trouble would that be, Owen, because I can assure you I can handle any trouble I make for myself?"

"These enquires you've been making into John Canavan's death… on whose behalf have you been making them?"

"My own behalf; not that it's any of your business."

"It becomes my concern, when you interfere in police business. Your enquires, Mister Jackson, are illegal and must stop immediately. Otherwise you could end up in prison."

Joggy burst out laughing.

"This is no laughing matter Mister Jackson; think of your family."

"It is," said Joggy, still laughing, "when a gobshite like you thinks he can come in here and frighten me into submission." He stopped laughing. "Let me tell you something, Owen. I thank God every day that this is not a fucking police state. You must think that just because I'm a gardener, I must be thick and ignorant. But I know the law and I know my rights and if you think you can frighten me, then, like John Canavan's murder, you've not done your homework very well."

"You're making a big mistake, Jackson, crossing me." Reilly wagged a warning finger at him.

"The Mister didn't take long to disappear, now did it?"

"You go on being a smart arse, but you just remember one thing, Jackson, this cosy lifestyle of yours can disappear overnight."

Joggy took a step closer to Reilly; the look that had unnerved Danny was on his face.  "You interfere with my family or my livelihood, Reilly," Joggy said coldly, "I'll come after you, no matter how high or how safe you think you are."

"Are you threatening me?"

"You interfere in my life and you'll soon find out."

Reilly gave Joggy one last stony look before turning and walking away.

Later that day at lunch time, Ed Mc Neill turned up. Joggy was surprised to see him as earlier that morning he had had to change clients.

"How did you find me?"

"It wasn't too hard. You'd be surprised how much common knowledge is out there. Everyone thinks that no one is watching, but we're all being watched by someone."

"I had a visitor this morning, one of your guys, a nasty piece of work by the name of Reilly; kept insisting I call him Detective Sergeant."

McNeill turned pale grey. "I hope you didn't say anything."

"No, I didn't give the game away. But I made sure he left here with his tail between his legs."

"Shit," McNeill exclaimed, "that's all I need."

"I take it he investigated the original murder?"

"Yes, and he won't be happy at us digging up the past. Speaking of which, did you find out anything?"

Joggy filled him in.

"Right." McNeill clapped his hands together. "You make sure you talk to Winter. Find out if that was Canavan in his car. I'll have another word with my source... see if I can speed up those scene photos."

"Someone dragging their feet, are they?" Joggy teased.

"They won't be after I've finished with them. Now listen, we can't meet like this again. We'll have to be more subtle about it. You've made yourself a dangerous enemy in Reilly and from now on he's going to be watching your every move. We can't be seen together again."

"But, how are we going to make contact?"

"Don't worry, when I want too, I'll find you. From now on," McNeill warned, "watch your back."

\* \* \* \*

Fred Winter arrived home late on the Monday afternoon. "Make me a mug of tea and a sandwich like a good girl," he said to Victoria, as he tossed his hold-all onto the kitchen table.

"Will ham do?" she enquired.

"Yeah, anything at all, I'm starving."

He moved to the sitting room and collapsed into an armchair. After a short while he stirred himself, opened the drinks cabinet and pulled out the Scotch Whisky.

"Bring us in a glass when you're coming, Victoria." he shouted. "Oh and that lot on the table have to be washed."

He was beginning to doze when Victoria arrived in with a mug of tea, a ham sandwich and an empty glass.

"Your tea," she said, in a louder than normal voice.

"Thanks." Fred blinked himself awake. "Anything I should know about happen while I was away?"

"No, all was quiet on the western front. So quiet, I became bored, so bored I got drunk on the two nights you were away. I'm afraid I drank all your brandy."

"There was a full bottle of Remys in there." His eyebrows rose in alarm, He opened the cupboard. "You couldn't have drunk it all?"

"I'm afraid I did. Brandy and I get on very well together."

Fred's eyes narrowed in suspicion, "Are you sure you didn't have help?"

"And who would I know that would help me drink a full bottle of Brandy?"

Winter stared impassively at Victoria, scrutinizing her face for tell-tale signs.

"Well you didn't take it from your father," he said, coldly conceding the point. "He wouldn't drink water,"

\* \* \* \*

On the way home that evening, Joggy detoured via Kilpatrick. He slowed down as he approached Canavan's house. He was in two minds whether to stop or not. He had searched it in the dark, now he wondered if he would have any better luck in broad daylight. He parked the car and waved at old Mrs Quinn across the road as he entered the front gate and made his way around to the back.

It had not changed since his last visit. The holes were still there and loose debris was everywhere. With the daylight streaming into the rooms he got a better look at everything, but still found no hiding spaces. He eventually gave up and made his way back through the kitchen. Annoyed at finding nothing and not watching where he placed his feet as he tramped across the room on broken pieces of ceiling plaster, his left foot stood on the edge of a large piece, it lifted the other end up like a see-saw. His right foot stubbed the risen end and he went face first towards the floor, hands flew instinctively out. His right hand caught the edge of the brick fire surround, spinning him and landing him flat on his back, winding him.

He lay there for several seconds stunned and staring at the pot-holed ceiling before gingerly checking his limbs, slowly raising each leg and twisting the joints. Apart from his right hand which was grazed and now stinging, everything else seemed fine. He climbed stiffly to his feet and glanced with annoyance at the offending piece of ceiling plaster before heading for the door. He stopped in the light of the open doorway and examined his grazed palm. He licked his thumb and rubbed some debris from the graze. Just then, a memory; a sensation of movement when his hand struck the brickwork came back to him. He turned back to investigate, and there it was, two of the facia bricks had moved. He slid them out and the pain in his hand disappeared – forgotten, when he saw the black notebook. He sat down on the backless chair and for several seconds excitedly turned the notebook around and around in his hands, dusting it, wiping it, as if waiting for an instruction from someone to tell him it would be alright to open it. He could not be happier. Carefully, he opened the first page; then frowned as he quickly leafed through the rest. By the time he reached the last entry, he was crestfallen; all the entries in the notebook were written in lettered code.
G VIQZ Q ZQFUSTR VTW VT VTQCT VITF YOKLZ VT HKQEZOLT ZG RTETOCT.

Later that evening Joggy walked to Fred Winter's; he needed to think. A set of three steps kerbed by a two foot wall on either side led to the front door. Victoria answered the knock.

"Mister Jackson," she smiled, "I presume you want Fred?"

Joggy gave a tight-lipped smile and nodded.

"I'll go and get him for you."

Fred was asleep in the armchair. Victoria tapped him on the shoulder.

He arrived in the front doorway sleepy eyed and in slippers. "You've woken me from a good snooze, Joggy. What can I do for you?"

"Sorry Fred, I didn't know. I can come back another time if you want?"

"You're here now, let's get it over with."

Joggy cleared his throat. Even though he had been doing this for about a week, the initial approach always made him apprehensive.

"You probably heard that I've been making enquires into the murder of John Canavan?"

"So it is true." He snorted, "I thought someone was pulling my leg."

"Would you mind if I asked you a few questions?" He ignored Fred's derisory tone.

"Are you serious, Joggy?" Laughter rose steadily in his voice.

"I'm glad you find it funny."

"Not funny, amusing, and ... quite frankly, absurd. You're like me, Joggy, a man of the land. This is not a job for you, please, leave it to the professionals."

"Fat lot of good that did. The last time it was left to them, they sent an innocent man to prison."

"That's wishful speculation, Joggy. Twelve loyal and true citizens of this county found him guilty."

"They had no choice on the evidence that was put before them."

"Anyway, the man is dead… nothing is to be gained by digging up the past."

"So I take it, you're not interested in answering my questions?" He lifted a twenty packet of Sweet Afton from his jacket pocket and withdrew one.

"That's not what I said Joggy. And please don't take this the wrong way, but I just don't think you're equipped to do this job. You're a gardener for God's sake."

"That's fair enough." Joggy took a couple of quick pulls. "You think I'm wasting my time?"

"Quite frankly, yes. I think you're pissing against the wind here."

"Thank you for your honesty Fred. And you're right, I do run the risk of getting wet but it's a chance I'm willing to take."

"So be it, but don't say I didn't warn you."

"Thank you, I consider myself duly warned. Now will you answer my questions?"

Fred gave a large almost theatrical sigh. "If I can."

"I've an eyewitness who says he saw John Canavan in your car the Saturday he
died. You were pulling a trailer. My guess is that his bike was in it."

"I see. Who might that be then?" Fred sat on one of the low walls.

"That's confidential... sorry." Joggy took a slow drag as he climbed the steps and sat on the wall opposite.

"Your eyewitness is spot on," he said cautiously. "I picked Canavan up just outside of town; it was raining. He had a puncture and was leading his bike. I felt sorry for him, threw his bike in the trailer and gave him a lift as far as the head of the lane."

"Did he say where he was going?"

"Yes. He said he was going up to Baker's."

"Did he say why?"

"No... I didn't really know the man that well to ask. Does that satisfy you?"

"That's all I wanted to know. Thanks for your time."

Joggy started back down the steps when a notion he had entertained earlier came back to him. He turned around to face Winter. "I was just wondering...why do you bring the boar up to Baker's in the horse and cart? Would it not be faster with the tractor?"

"It would, but I can't get him to travel by tractor: He refuses every time." Fred stood up, a thin smile on his lips. "He has ideas above his station, Joggy. He thinks he's someone."

Joggy turned and walked away, a large smile lit up his face. The remark had not fallen on deaf ears, but Joggy did not care. His ruse had worked. He now had a confirmed sighting of Canavan.

# CHAPTER 15

"Cedric Mercer was here." Alice told Joggy as he entered the kitchen. A doleful expression hung about her face.

He felt something move in the pit of his stomach, "What did he want?"

"He said he wouldn't be needing you anymore. He was babbling a bit. I think he was looking for excuses. He eventually said a nephew of his was taking on the work."

"That's bullshit."

"Do you think it's got anything to do with the run in you had with Reilly, this morning?"

"I don't know, but we can't afford to lose anyone else."

"What are you going to do about Mister Mercer?"

"I'll call and see him tomorrow evening, see if I can change his mind."

\* \* \* \*

After the children were in bed, Alice and Joggy sat at the kitchen table, paper and pen in hand and tried to decipher Canavan's lettered code. For the next two hours they tried every permutation and combination they could think off, but to no avail: It remained locked. But the exercise was not a total waste; they did discover that the code used all the letters in the alphabet.

\* \* \* \*

The next morning Joggy went to work as usual. Today it was Doctor Kelly's garden he was attending. Doctor Kelly's wife, Doreen, was waiting for him when he arrived. Normally she smiled when she met him, but not this morning. Again, his stomach turned.

"Joggy," she said, "I have bad news for you." Her voiced was shivery…uncertain. "We have to let you go. We won't be in need of your services again." The corners of her eyes were filling up with tears. "I'm sorry," she said finally.

"I don't understand," said Joggy, "is it something I said… or did?"

"No, no, Joggy, it's not you…it's, it's us. It's a personal decision we have to make. I'm sorry. I'm really, really sorry."

Joggy climbed back into his car and watched as Doreen retreated into her house.

He sat there for over fifteen minutes analyzing the situation. He knew what he had to do but to get results he had to go about it the right way. He knocked on Doctor Kelly's front door.

"I'm sorry to annoy you, Doreen," said Joggy, "but do you by any chance know who's in charge of Oldbridge Garda station?"

"Inspector Bob Murray." She tried hard to restrain the curiosity in her voice.

Joggy turned and drove directly to Oldbridge. The Garda station was new with a counter that fronted a large open room. Several desks were occupied on the floor while doors on both sides lead to offices. The duty officer was on the phone. He wrote a message onto an A4 pad and then hung up. He glanced up when Joggy approached the desk.

"Yes sir, how can I help you?" he asked, in a businesslike manner.

"I'd like to see Inspector Murray please."

"Is he expecting you?"

"No."

"Then may I ask what it concerns?"

Joggy raised his voice just enough so everyone could hear. "Police interference in my livelihood."

"That's all right, Pat." Detective Sergeant Reilly emerged from a door on the right, "I'll deal with this."

Pat moved away leaving Joggy and Reilly facing one another across the counter.

"Inspector Murray is a busy man," said Reilly. "He won't be able to see you today or any other day for that matter."

"One way or another, Reilly, I will see Inspector Murray. If you don't get him for me, I'm going to have to start shouting out his name."

"Do that and I'll have you thrown out of here quicker than you can say Jack Flash."

"Inspector Murray," Joggy shouted. All heads turned to look. "Will someone tell Inspector Murray that Joggy Jackson would like to see him?"

Everyone looked but no-one moved.

"Inspector Murray! Inspector Murray!" Joggy shouted even louder.

"Pat, Ian," said Reilly, to two on-looking guards, "throw him out."

The two came around the end of the counter, grabbed an arm each and twisted them behind his back.

"Inspector Murray, Inspector Murray," shouted Joggy again, as they frog marched him to the door, "my business concerns John Canavan."

A small man with a pair of oval-shaped spectacles perched precariously on the end of his nose, who had been watching proceedings from the doorway of one of the side offices, suddenly spoke up. "Garda Doyle, Garda Slevin" he bellowed, his voice belying his small stature. "Bring that gentleman to me."

The two Gardai turned and escorted Joggy to the Inspector's office.

"Have a seat, Mister Jackson," he commanded, as he moved around and sat behind his desk. "Now." He removed his glasses, leaned back and folded his arms. His face was taut and his eyes hard. "What's this all about?"

Joggy explained how he came to be making enquires into Canavan's death, discreetly sidelining McNeill's involvement. While he talked, Murray stared intently at him, sizing him up, working out what kind of man he was dealing with.

"Yesterday, your man, Detective Sergeant Reilly, called to see me. He tried to get me to drop the case and when I didn't back down he threatened my livelihood, said it could disappear overnight. Since last night I have lost two customers -- two of my longest -- standing customers. You might say it was a coincidence, Inspector, but I don't believe in coincidences."

"Have these people named Detective Reilly."

"No sir, they're too afraid."

Murray leaned forward and picked up his pen.

"Give me the names of the two clients you've lost, Mister Jackson."

"Cedric and Ethel Mercer and Doctor Tom Kelly."

He placed his pen slowly and thoughtfully down on the writing pad, musing over the two names he had written. He leaned back in his chair again and placed his hands on the armrest. This time his features were less severe and his manner became more cordial. "Mister Jackson, you've made a serious allegation against one of my men, an allegation that is founded on suspicion only." Slowly, he lifted his arms, leaned forward, planted his elbows on the desk to form a bridge with his hands and spoke to them as if it was a microphone, " Nevertheless, I take all complaints against my men personally. If true, it reflects badly on me and this station and I will not tolerate that. Mister Jackson, do you wish to make an official complaint?"

Joggy paused before answering. Having experienced the change in the Inspector's attitude, he wondered. "Do I need to?" His tone was leading, gambling on the answer he wanted to hear.

"No, that might not be necessary. If you could leave it with me, I'll make some enquires."

The Inspector escorted him to the front door. He pulled the door towards him and held it open. "Mister Jackson, while I believe you're on an honourable quest, I feel it's incumbent upon me to warn you. What you are doing is not illegal, but, should you use illegal methods to achieve your goal, I will have no choice but to arrest you. Do we understand one another, Mister Jackson?"

"Yes, Inspector, we understand on another very well."

Murray walked smartly back to his office. He sat behind his desk leaned back in his chair and began clicking his pen to a certain rhythm, two clicks slow, three clicks fast, two clicks slow, three clicks fast… He stopped, dropped the pen on the desk and picked up the telephone and dialled an internal number.

"Detective, my office, now," he said evenly.

Reilly found his superior standing with his back to him staring through a window to the right of his desk. The window looked out to a bare block wall. Together with the brightly lit office it turned the window into kind of mirror. Murray's left hand held his right wrist behind his back. In the fingers of his right hand he held one leg of his wire rimmed glasses. He swished it back and forth like a cow's tail. The Inspector observed Reilly in the window as he closed the door behind him

"You wanted to see me, sir?" He had a defiant expression.

"This window, Detective… a futile exercise, don't you think?"

"Yes sir. All it looks out on is a bare wall."

"An exercise in vanity."

"Vanity, sir?"

"Yes vanity. Defined as too much pride in our own abilities and achievements. The man who placed this window here will always deny he made a mistake. And vanity, Detective, eventually leads to a fall."

Murray watched Reilly's reflection intently. Whether the man picked up the insinuation or not, Murray could not tell. Reilly's face gave nothing away. He turned, moved behind his desk and sat down. He laid his glasses down and picked up his pen. The rhythmic clicking began again. "Explain to me, Detective, the totally unnecessary and unseemly drama that just took place at the front desk." The clicking stopped.

"Jackson is a trouble maker, sir, and was making a nuisance of himself. He had no appointment and wouldn't leave when asked."

"He wanted to see me, Detective. Since when did you become my secretary, vetting who sees me and who doesn't?"

"Sorry sir, you're a busy man. I didn't think you'd want to be bothered with trivialities."

"So you think police interference in a man's livelihood is trivial, do you?"

"Of course not, sir."

Murray leaned back in his chair and observed, Reilly who still wore an expression of defiance. The only sign he gave of the pressure getting to him was an almost imperceptible movement from one foot to the other and Murray did not miss it.

"Mister Jackson has made a complaint against you, Detective. He says that you threatened to interfere with his livelihood and it seems that after your little chat with him the other day, two long-standing customers of his have since left him."

"That's purely coincidental, sir."

"Like Mister Jackson, Detective, I'm not a big believer in coincidences."

"It must be a coincidence, sir."

The rhythmic clicking started again and continued for several long seconds. Then it stopped.

"Do you play golf, Detective?"

"No sir." Reilly was baffled at the sudden change of topic.

"My wife does. Strange game; could never get the hang of it myself. But she loves it. Plays it twice a week, Monday and Friday, and loves nothing better than to fill me in on who her partners were and how she played every boring bloody shot. She seems to play with the same people a lot. One name she mentions regularly is Ethel Mercer, who happens to be coincidentally, the wife of one of Mister Jackson's lost clients."

Reilly changed feet.

"My wife, Detective, has the happy knack of wheedling information out of people, even when they don't want to talk. I suppose it has something to do with her trusting face. So what I propose is for her to talk to Missus Mercer and see if she can locate the source of the problem. What do you think, Detective?"

"I don't think that will be necessary, sir," he said quickly, "I'll have a chat with them myself and see if I can find a solution. Will that be all, sir?"

"For the moment."

The Inspector waited until Reilly was turning the handle on the office door.

"Mister Jackson lost two clients, Detective," he said, "Would you like the other name... or maybe, you already know it."

That evening two very relieved gentlemen, Mr Mercer and Dr Kelly, apologising profusely, called to re-instate Joggy as their gardener.

# CHAPTER 16

Ed McNeill was in rare good form on Wednesday morning. He crossed the floor of his bedroom and pulled back the curtains. A red sky the previous evening had foretold a good day today. He smiled as he watched the sun climb steadily from behind the Church opposite. Charlie had come through with Baker's file and although he was being tardy with the scene photos, he knew he would come through with them also. He had Joggy where he wanted him; doing the legwork and making steady progress; and now an added bonus; Reilly's cage had been rattled. Yes, things were shaping up very nicely. He whistled as he descended the stairs to the kitchen in his stocking feet and made straight for the saucepan of porridge on the solid-fuel range. "Morning dear," he said, over his shoulder to his wife, Mary, who he knew from a life-time of habit, would be sitting at one end of the small kitchen table under the front street window, fondling a cup of tea. "That porridge smells wonderful," he continued.

"Ed," said Mary. There was a hint of urgency in her voice but he ignored it – time enough to listen to her fussing when he'd be eating.

"Mmm?" He just about acknowledged her as he searched the cupboard for a bowl and saw none.

"Ed," said Mary, a little louder and with a little more urgency.

"Yeah, yeah, just a second." He decided to eat from the saucepan. He shook salt on the porridge, then poured in the milk. "I was thinking, Mary, now that Dermot's not coming up from Templemore this weekend, maybe we'll go and visit your brother in Carrick-on-Shannon. We could do with a night away."

"I think that's a great idea," said the deep voice that Ed instantly recognised. "Mary could do with a couple of days, relaxation."

"Inspector!" Ed nearly dropped the saucepan. "I didn't see you there." Nervous tension instantly replaced his good humour. "Mary, why didn't you tell me the Inspector was here?"

"My fault, Ed, I asked Mary not to disturb you. But you'll be happy to know that she has been looking after me very well." The

Independent stood up. "Mary, thank you for your hospitality. That was a wonderful cup of tea."

"You're welcome Bob, call anytime, the kettle's always on the boil."

"I have the office key, Ed, I'll let myself in. You sit and have your porridge." He gestured to the now vacated chair. "There's no hurry, I'll wait for you inside."

The Inspector made his way down the hall and opened the office door.

"Jesus, Mary," exclaimed Ed, after hearing the office door close, "why didn't you warn me?"

"He asked me specifically not to wake you," she protested," What else was I to do?"

Ed grabbed his boots from beside the range. "And what's all this, you calling him by his first name?" He planted each boot in turn on the chair and with his fingers moving at high speed, tightened and knotted the laces. "He's the Inspector, Mary; you don't address him by his first name?"

"He insisted I call him Bob, what are you rushing for, sit and have your porridge, he said he'd wait."

"Jesus, Mary, are you naïve?" He slipped the noose of his ready-made tie over his head. "That was for your ears only."

Ed grabbed his jacket from the back of Mary's chair, "You don't think that he came out here at this hour of the morning just to have tea with you and to hang around the office while I have my porridge. Cop yourself on." He buttoned up his jacket and walked warily down the hall.

The file cabinet drawer with the initials I,J,K, was open when he entered and the Inspector was sitting on the corner of Ed's desk, reading.

"I see you haven't forgotten your special branch training, Sergeant." Murray, closed the file in his hand.

"I like to keep tabs on everyone, male and female, over the age of sixteen, sir. It tends to make my job easier when I know who I'm dealing with."

Murray dropped the file on the desk and nonchalantly walked to the window. His left hand held his right wrist behind his back and he swished his spectacles back and forth.

With the inspector's back turned, Ed glanced at the name on the file, closed his eyes tightly, clenched his teeth and swore under his breath. "Shit."

"Nice view of the church you have here, Sergeant," said Murray, "I hope it keeps you honest?"

"Yes sir, indeed it does."

"Interesting character this Joggy Jackson." Murray kept his back turned to Ed. "Family man, wife and three children, self-employed gardener. Nice clientele he's got, some well respected people. What's this about him breaking into Canavan's?"

"He didn't exactly break in, sir; he knew where the spare key was kept and let himself in."

"What was he looking for?"

"I don't know sir. He wouldn't say."

"I see he was a good friend of Luke Baker's and was the last visitor Baker had before he died."

"Yes, sir, been friends since childhood."

"The break-in at Canavan's wouldn't have anything to do with Luke Baker, would it?"

"I don't know, sir."

Murray turned around.

Ed's collar and tie was now like a heated element around his neck.

"For a man who keeps such meticulous records, there seems to be a lot you don't know, Sergeant."

"Yes sir."

"So, let me tell you what I do know. I know you and Mister Jackson have hooked up together to re-investigate John Canavan's murder, with you backstage and Jackson out front under the naked spotlight of public opinion. I also know your motives. You figure if you can come up with some new evidence that will dispute the original findings and find a new leading man for the murder, then you will have slayed two dragons at once. Am I correct, Sergeant -- and remember you are facing God's holy temple?"

Ed could see no way out. The Inspector obviously knew the story and Ed feared the worst. "Yes sir, it's true."

"You'd hoped that by somehow finding John Canavan's real killer and thereby proving that Detective Reilly had imprisoned the wrong man, you would embarrass him, stunt his promotional prospects and perhaps, get yourself promoted back to Detective. Is that true?"

Ed lost his temper. "I wouldn't have been in this position if that bastard had kept his mouth shut."

"Detective Reilly did the right thing," the inspector snapped back. "For God's sake, you put a man in a coma."

"He was a queer. He came onto me and grabbed me by the balls."

"He was drunk, Sergeant. There are ways to handle those situations and beating a man to a pulp was not one of them. You were lucky the man came out of the coma and couldn't remember what had happened. You were also lucky to be only demoted to Sergeant. If I was in charge, you would have done time, and now, you have involved a citizen in a Garda investigation."

"He had started his own investigation...."

"Don't play the innocent with me," snapped Murray. "You and I would not be having this conversation if you had allowed Mister Jackson go his own merry way, but ooh no, you just had to drag him into your own little clandestine plot. Your methods, Sergeant, are totally unorthodox, they are sharp, provocative and foolhardy; and against Garda regulations. You risk bringing the force into disrepute, Sergeant."

"Yes sir, I'm sorry sir." McNeill's shoulders slumped in anticipation of the sack. He was dreading the thought of having to tell Mary that they would soon have no home, no job and no pension.

"I have little time for people like you, Sergeant." The Inspector, glared at McNeill, his blue-grey eyes as cold as Arctic ice. "People who don't walk the straight and narrow."
Murray turned back to the window. He clasped his hands behind his back and took another look at the Church -- this time longer. "Fortunately for you, Sergeant," he said eventually, "I live in the real world and in that world people like you get results, so getting rid of you would be like expecting an engine to run smoothly without ever having to get your hands dirty."

McNeill could not believe what he was hearing as relief and confusion washed over him together.

"When I took charge of Oldbridge two years ago," continued the Inspector, still looking up at the Church, "one of the first files I pulled was that of John Canavan's. What I found disturbed me. It seemed my predecessor liked an orderly and tidy desk; he did not want an open murder left on his watch before he retired. Unfortunately for Luke Baker, a quick case and a quick result is what transpired." He turned back to McNeill. "I'm not cut from the same cloth, Sergeant. The possibility, no matter how slight, of an innocent man spending time behind bars does not sit well with me. So, going against everything I hold true, I'm going to allow you to continue this covert investigation."

"Thank you, sir." McNeill's throat was now as dry as tinder.

"There's nothing here to be thankful for, Sergeant," snapped the Inspector. "I should by rights be throwing you out on your ear. From now on, you keep me fully informed of what's happening."

"Yes sir, I will sir."

"No face-to-face contact. You ring me each Monday night at my home, eight o' clock sharp."

"Yes sir, I will."

"You try and keep me in the dark about any detail of this investigation, Sergeant, and your arse will hit the pavement so fast you won't get time to say, yes sir."

"No sir, I will keep you fully up to date."

"Good. Now, two things to keep in mind, one… you're on your own. Anything goes wrong, the sky will fall on your head, understand?"

"Yes sir, you know nothing."

"Two -- if you ever hope to be promoted again, you make, absolutely sure, that nothing happens to Mister Jackson."

"Yes sir, I'll be his shadow."

"You'd better be." Murray made his way to the hall door. Suddenly he stopped, reached into his inside coat pocket and extracted a large brown envelope. He tossed it to McNeill. "They're the scene photos you were looking for."

McNeill caught them.

Murray opened the front door.

All of McNeill's instincts were telling him not to ask, let sleeping dogs lie, but he ignored them; he simply had to know.

"If you don't mind me asking, sir, how did you find out?" The Inspector gave a wry smile. "You should have chosen your accomplice with a bit more care, Ed," said Murray, returning to the informal, "The nervous ones tend to panic when they see me approach and leave incriminating evidence behind them in photocopying machines. It was then only a matter of following that individual."

Murray climbed into his navy blue Cortina. "You see Ed, I haven't forgotten my special branch training either." He then drove away.

* * * *

He moved silently in the shadow of the high wall, slipped into the angle of a supporting pillar and waited. The dull illumination from a single street lamp did not reach all the way back to where he hid. The high wall on O Meara's side of the church car park gave him the perfect cover. Dressed all in black, he felt safe in the knowledge that he could not be seen. It was also the perfect spot to observe McNeill's upstairs bedroom window. At eleven, McNeill appeared in the window. He took his time surveying the street before closing the curtains and quenching the bedroom light.

He waited patiently; gripping and re-gripping the heavy wooden baton; years of waiting about, had taught him to be still. His intended victim's car was only yards away, parked facing the church.

Now that the summer was imminent, games of twenty-five were becoming fewer and farther apart. A good crowd had turned up tonight and having won the pot, Joggy was the happiest. He left O Meara's with his well-oiled neighbour, Alfie Roache. "Joggy, I'm in bad need of a slash, you go ahead, I'll catch up," Roache slurred. He made a quick detour into a gateway.

Reilly moved swiftly and stealthily as Joggy fiddled with the car key in the gloom. He brought the heavy baton down hard on the back of Joggy's skull, crumbling him to the tarmac. "That's for fucking with me," he snarled.

With Joggy out cold on the ground, Reilly drove a boot hard into his ribs. "That's for humiliating me, you bastard, and this is for sticking your nose in where it's not fucking wanted." He drove his boot in for a second time. The beating would have continued only for the voices. Spit Sweeny had joined Alfie as he stumbled his way to the car park. Spit was first to react and was relieved to find Joggy still breathing. He looked about him and listened, but saw or heard nothing.

"You stay with Joggy," said Spit," I'll Get McNeill."

While they were on their way to Doctor Kelly's Joggy slowly came too on the back seat of McNeill's car. His body ached and his head was swimming.

"You wait here Spit," said McNeill," as they helped Joggy out of the car, "there's no need for the two of us to be cluttering up the doctor's surgery."

"But he might fall or something," said Spit.

"He's fine," assured McNeill, erring on the side of caution in case Joggy should inadvertently say something and Spit overhear. "He won't fall; I have a good hold of him." McNeill paced up and down the waiting room while Joggy was being attended to. His brain was working overtime. He was going to have to tell Murray before he found out from someone else. "Fuck it," he swore under his breath as the Inspector's warning came to mind. Make absolutely sure that nothing happens to Mister Jackson.

"Nasty bump, Joggy," said Dr Kelly, feeling around the affected area. Joggy winced. "I'm pretty sure nothing's broken. The same applies to those ribs of yours, but I'm going to send you for an X ray just in case. As he turned on the hot water, he added: "Did you get a look at your assailant?"

"I'm afraid not. I heard nothing and saw nothing except stars, and they weren't in the bloody sky."

"Have you any idea who would have done this?" He soaped his hands.

"I could think of one or two. It's probably something to do with John Canavan's death."

"That's right I'd heard something about that." Dr Kelly dried his hands and turned back to Joggy. "It's ironic really, if the killer had waited for a couple of months, cancer would have done the job for him, and no crime would have been committed."

"What? John was dying?" Joggy grimaced as the effort of taking a breath hurt his ribs,

"Yes, he had less than two months to live."

"Did John know he was dying?"

"He did. I told him about a week before he was killed."

"How'd he take it?

"He surprised me actually. Most people when told would naturally become upset, but John took it very calmly. In fact he was philosophical about it. His last words to me were…all good things must come to an end, I suppose.

Doctor Kelly's diagnosis was correct; no bones were broken, only bruising. The nurses reassured him and sent him on his way.

It was two in the morning when he arrived home. Alice was sitting up in bed, frantic with worry. All sorts of thoughts had run through her mind, including Maggie May.    "Where have you been," she demanded.

Joggy described his evening.  Alice's anger turned to sympathy, but by the time he finished his story, she was angry again.  "That's it," she said, "you're not doing this anymore; the next time it could be a knife."

Joggy agreed.

* * * *

Alice's happy voice travelled back to where Joggy lay in bed. She was humming along to the radio. The children were gone to school when she brought in breakfast; two bowls of steaming hot porridge.

"I shouldn't be here, I should be at work," he complained.

"Not after the beating you took last night, you need at least a day's rest."  She handed over one bowl then sat on the bed next to her husband and tucked into her own breakfast.

"What did you say to the children?"

"I just said that you were coming down with something and that you weren't feeling well. No need to worry them now that you're finished." Alice, not unlike a lot of wives married for twenty years, had developed a kind of telepathy; to read what is said by how it is said and more importantly by how it is not said. In the silence, her antenna picked up the warning signals. She stopped the spoon half-way to her mouth and glanced sideways at her husband. "You are finished, aren't you?"

Joggy stopped eating. He tried to come up with a soft answer but none was forthcoming. "It's too late Alice."

Alice dropped the spoon into her bowl, porridge droplets splashed onto the bed-cover. "Damn it, Joggy, last night, you agreed to end it."

"Last night I was in pain and in no mood for an argument," he said, irritably.

"Luke would not want you putting your life in danger. If he was alive, he would understand."

"I know that."

"Well, do it for me then. Do you think it's fair that I should sit at home anxious, worrying, wondering will this be the night you don't come home? If you won't do it for me, do it for your children." She was pulling all the emotional strings she could think of.

"It's not that simple," he said gruffly.

"It is that simple. People will understand. It's just too dangerous to go on."

"I can't Alice, I just… can't."

"Give me a good reason, one I can understand."

"It's gone too far, it's become personal. Besides," He dreaded the thought of having to tell her, "there's someone else involved, I've… I've got a silent partner."

"Who?"

"Ed McNeill."

"McNeill," she shrieked. "That," she was about to swear but changed her mind and her words piled up on one another in her mouth, bursting out with "…calculating snake in the grass. What the hell are you doing with him?"

"He found out about my chat with Luke from a snitch in Portmand prison. I don't know his reasons. All I know is he gives me the inside track. It was too good an offer to turn down."

"Does he know your reasons?"

"No. All he knows is I'm repaying a debt."

"Why didn't you tell me this before now?"

"I was afraid you'd be disappointed in me; taking help from someone you detest."

"I am disappointed, but not in you." Her smile was fleeting, "I could never be disappointed in you."

She slipped off the bed. "I should have listened to my inner voice," she added as she picked up the morsels of spilt porridge and dropped them in her bowl, "it was telling me this was too good to be true, but I didn't listen. Instead I got my hopes up."

"I'm really sorry, Alice."

"You were never one to back away from a fight." She walked to the door, "I don't know what made me think this time would be any different."

# CHAPTER 17

It was raining Friday evening. Everyone was inside. Country hour was playing on the old Bush Radio. Alice sat in the light of the front window and read the local paper. Katie lay prone on the floor drawing a picture on white cardboard in imaginative colours of a house with matchstick people. Helen sat in the armchair beside the Stanley range reading the latest copy of "Jackie" while Joggy and Danny sat around the angle of the kitchen table trying again to decipher Canavan's notebook. They were endeavouring to weed out the letters representing vowels from the consonants.

"This will take forever," said Joggy. He banged the pencil on the table, leaned back in his chair and removing his reading glasses. He massaged the top of his nose.

"What's wrong?" Alice asked, lowering the paper.

"He's running out of patience," said Danny, trying another combination of letters.

"Canavan wasn't that clever," said Joggy. "Going by what he typed in his manuscripts, he was no John B Keane. The code has to be something simple, something we're overlooking."

"It's a twenty-six letter code, using every letter in the alphabet," said Alice. "So it's hardly one word. Maybe it's a sentence made up of words that don't repeat any letter twice."

"Or maybe it's the typewriter alphabet," ventured Helen, from behind the pages of her teenage magazine.

Joggy sat bolt upright. He suddenly remembering the Olivetti typewriter he found in Canavan's belongings. "What did you say, Helen?"

Helen closed the magazine, marking the page with her finger "I said… it could be the keys of a typewriter."

"A typewriter has twenty-six keys?"

"Yes," she said, in mild exasperation.

"But do the keys not follow the alphabet from A to Zed?"

"No, it starts with a Q and finishes with an M. I don't know the sequence of the letters in-between. We've only just started using them in school."

Joggy jumped up, grabbed the notebook and ran out the door.

"Where're you off to?" called Alice

"To see a man about a typewriter. I won't be long."

"Where's the fire?" said Rick, when he answered the frantic knocking on his front door

"Can I see your typewriter?" said Joggy.

"Certainly, come in. What's this about?"

"It's about solving a mystery." Joggy marvelled at the keyboard. "Could you do me a favour?"

"Yeah, sure, if you can explain to me what's going on?"

"I will, later, I promise, but right now I need you to type me out a copy of the keyboard alphabet."

Once back home he quickly got down to work. Under Rick's typewriter alphabet he wrote out the original one. And under that he began to write out Canavan's entries.

Q W E R T Y U I O P A S D F G H J K L Z X C V B N M
A B C D E F G H I J K L M N O P Q R S T U V W Y X Z

The first one translated as,

G VIQZ Q ZQFUSTR VTW VT VTQCT VITF YOKLZ VT
HKQEZOLT ZG

O WHAT A TANGLED WEB WE WEAVE WHEN FIRST WE
PRACTICE TO

RTETOCT.

DECEIVE.

PTFFB KGQEIT... KOEA VGKKTSS

JENNY ROACHE...RICK WORRELL

YOCT HGXFRL

FIVE POUNDS

Quiet and all as he tried to be, sneaking into the bedroom, he nevertheless awoke Alice from her fitful slumber. She could never sleep properly when her husband was not beside her. She squinted at the bedside alarm clock. Its luminous hands pointed out the time. "It's nearly half-one."

"Yeah sorry, I tried not to wake you."

"Did you get it done?"

"Yeah, yeah, I did."

Alice sat up. She could tell by the tone of his answers, that something was amiss.

"What'd you find out?"

Joggy hesitated.

"Are you going to tell me or not?" she asked impatiently.

"I think the "Horse" was blackmailing people."

"Blackmail? Are you sure?"

"Yeah, I'm pretty sure."

She turned on the bedside lamp. "Who was he blackmailing?"

"I'll tell you in the morning," he said, as he undressed.

"Are you joking, I won't be able to sleep wondering."

"You won't be able to sleep if I tell you."

"I'd prefer not been able to sleep knowing, than not knowing. So come on, is it anyone we know?"

Joggy slipped in between the sheets. "I'll give you two entries that I can recall of the top of my head. Canavan first used a well known quote to outline the act he was blackmailing them for, and then wrote their names under it and the amount of money he was extracting from them. The first one was,

*O what a tangled Web we weave when first we practise to deceive.*

The two names under it were, Rick Worrell and Jenny Roache."

"Jenny and Rick," said Alice, in amazement. "What were they up to?"

"Well whatever it was, they were paying him five pounds a month to keep his mouth shut."

"Who's the other one?"

"The other one is strange."

"Strange? How?"

"Because the quote, *The love that dares not speak its name,* doesn't match the two people named under it.

"And the two people are?" asked Alice, losing her patience again, as Joggy paused teasingly dragging out the suspense.

"Ann Dwyer and Kevin Barrett."

"You're joking?"

"Nope, the priest's housekeeper and the headmaster are having a homosexual affair and they were paying Canavan ten pounds a month to keep it quiet," he said whimsically.

"That's not possible."

"Well it is possible really. He could be telling her to turn over and take it like a man."

"Stop, that's disgusting."

"Sorry, I just don't know how else to make sense of it. So now you know." He slid down onto his pillow. "Turn off the light, will you, and sweet dreams."

\* \* \* \*

Saturday afternoon came wet. The rain ran in rivulets down the glass. Joggy sat in the armchair by the Stanley range looking past it, trancelike, at the watery brightness on the horizon.

"Penny for your thoughts," Alice enquired, when she came in from the back kitchen drying her hands on her apron.

"I think you know what they are."

"You just have to go about it the right way, that's all"

"Is there a right way? I didn't know there was a right way to ask a married woman if she's having an affair with her neighbour. But you obviously think there is. So let's hear it, I'm all ears."

"There's no need to be sarcastic. I'm only trying to help."

"Sorry. I didn't mean it to say it like that. I just didn't think this would be so hard."

"I'm sure you'll think of something."

A little later he rose from his seat and walked across the kitchen floor to the dresser and collected his car keys from a yellow ceramic bowl with hand-painted red roses on the side. It was a gift from Helen who bought it on a recent school tour.

"Are you going up now?" Alice asked.

Joggy nodded. "Alfie will be in O Meara's by now."

"What are you going to say?"

"I've no idea. I think this is one of those situations where you just can't make up the questions in advance. So I'm going to play it by ear."

\* \* \* \*

Joggy," said Jenny, surprised to see him standing in the rain.

"I need a quiet word with you Jenny." He moved into the doorway out of the wet.

"You'd better come in so." She turned back into the house.

Her three children sat around the kitchen table. Stephen the oldest was building some kind of machine with his Lego set, while the twins shared a colouring book, each painting a page.

"How do you tell them apart?" Joggy asked. He studied one and then the other.

"A mother knows. Besides, they've very different personalities. She moved into the back kitchen, pulled out a packet of cigarettes and offered Joggy one. He accepted. Nothing was said while they lit up. Nervous restlessness kept him on the move, eventually he stopped in front of a window that looked out into the back garden. Though, garden was probably too nice a word for what he saw -- long unkempt grass strewn with discarded bric-a- brac and broken children's toys. A trodden path had been worn in the grass.

"Good neighbours are ye?" Joggy asked.

Jenny followed his gaze. "The path you mean? I do some housekeeping for Rick; a bit of hovering, a bit of ironing, wash his clothes, that sort of thing. It's a little extra money. Makes up for what some of what Alfie spends," she said ruefully. "But I'm sure, Joggy, that's not what you wanted to talk to me about."

Joggy stared intently through the window: His mind working overtime on the best way to start the conversation. He did not want to startle her. Keeping her calm was the key. Then, as if by magic, the words popped into his mouth. "What did you think of John Canavan?"

"I wasn't a fan. He was too much of a slieveen for my liking. Why do you ask?"

"Because I think he was blackmailing people."

"Really?"

"I recently found a notebook belonging to him. In it he kept details of the people he was blackmailing." He turned around and faced Jenny. "Your name's there, attached to Rick Worrell."

Jenny leaned back against the stainless steel sink -- took a drag from her cigarette and folded her arms. "Does it say why our names are there?" She seemed unfazed.

"He's a bit cryptic on that point. He made a habit of writing out well known phrase's to describe the acts. Yours went something like... O what a tangled web we weave, when first we practise to deceive. Any idea what he meant by that?"

Jenny shrugged her shoulders. "None. I've no idea why he has us in there and we certainly would never have paid him any money."

"Yeah, it's certainly strange all right. I think I'll go and have a chat with Rick. Maybe he knows something."

"Maybe, but I doubt it."

"Thanks for your time and the fag," he said.

"You're welcome."

As he made his way to the front door, he paused again and took a final look at the twins. "I still don't see how you know one from the other."

"Sorry, I wasn't much help to you," she said.


Rick answered the door on the second knock.

"Joggy." He rubbed his eyes with his fingers. "Sorry for the delay. I was half-asleep on the couch. I thought I was dreaming when you knocked first. Come in, come in, you're getting drenched standing there.  Did my keyboard solve your mystery?"

"It did, thank you, but it created another one."

"Oh?"

"It seems Canavan was blackmailing people."  Joggy, ambled into the centre of the room. He stopped and faced Rick. "I believe he was blackmailing you and Jenny Roache."

"Don't be ridiculous. What could he have possible blackmail us for?"

"Infidelity, I suppose."

"That's a scurrilous accusation."

"It's only scurrilous if it's a lie, Rick. Personally, I believe it's true. He somehow found out that you and Jenny were lovers. Not that I blame either of you for getting involved, after-all, you're single and she's lonely: Can't be easy for her being married to an alcoholic."

"Now you're really grasping at straws. If we were having an affair and I'm only been hypothetical here, why would we pay him? What proof would he have?"

Joggy walked to the fire place and studied the Notre Dame football team photo again.    "You know, that very same argument has been going on in my head for the last few days." He looked back over his left shoulder at Rick, "He had to have more on ye?" He reached up and placed two fingers on the glass, obscuring the players between the Worrell brothers. It was all he needed to confirm his suspicions. He turned around. "You're the father of Jenny's twin boys. That's what Canavan had on ye."

Rick who hadn't moved away from the front door, opened it. "I've had enough of this. You've outstayed your welcome, I want you to leave."

"I thought all writers were naturally inquisitive. Are you not even a little bit curious as to how I know?"

"No I'm not. The scribblings of a deranged dead man are of no interest to me. Now please leave."

Joggys eyes lit up and the beginnings of a smile creased the corner of his mouth. He suddenly veered towards the back kitchen, his eyes darting right and left.

"Where are you going?" said Rick, alarmed, "I said I wanted you out; now."

"It was the eyes that gave the game away," Joggy said without turning around. "Everyone has talents and one of mine is faces. I never forget a face. The first time I saw you and your twin brother in that football photo, I knew I'd seen those eyes before. It was only in the last hour I realised they were next door."

The door of the bedroom to the right of the kitchen was open. On the floor leading from the backdoor and in the framed picture of W.B Yeats hanging on the opposite wall close to the bedroom door, Joggy saw what he was looking for. "Come out Jenny. I can see your reflection in the picture glass."

Jenny left the bedroom with tears streaming down her face.

Rick closed the front door. "Now look what you've done."

"Let me ease your minds here," said Joggy, "I'm not interested in your personal lives. That's none of my business. All I'm interested in is clearing Luke's name. Anything else I find out will remain private. You have my word on that. So, that said, are the two of you now going to tell me the truth?"

Jenny sat down in an armchair and dried her eyes with a tea-towel. She looked at Rick. "You tell him."

Rick came and sat on the arm of Jenny's armchair. He gently rubbed her back. "We don't know how he found out. He must have added one and one and came up with twins. He threatened to have a conversation with Alfie, said that blood tests would prove him right. We weren't willing to call his bluff, so we paid him off; five pounds a month."

"Tell me, Rick, when you were renovating the kitchen, what did you do with the old gun-barrel plumbing?"

"I tossed it into the back shed."

"Is it still there?"

"No, the tinkers have it. I gave it to them when they came looking for scrap."

"How convenient. Did you see Canavan on the day that he died?"

"No."

"Are you sure? He didn't call in looking for an increase in wages?"

"What are you saying? Are you trying to pin Canavan's murder on me now? Is that what you're at?"

"Well you did have motive. He was blackmailing you. You also had opportunity. Probably called into to see you and when he left, you followed him up to Luke's yard. You also had access to the murder weapon and you're strong enough to have pulled it off."

"That's ridiculous," protested Jenny. "Rick wouldn't hurt a fly."

"You seriously think I murdered John Cananan?"

"I don't know if you did or not but all the facts fit."

"All but one."

"Which one is that?"

"The fact that I didn't kill him. I'm not the violent type. Look at it this way. It was only five pounds a month. I could comfortably afford it and it certainly was not enough to kill someone over."

"I'm not the violent type," said Joggy parroting, Rick. "That's a crock of shit. You know as well as I do that if someone pushes your buttons often enough and hard enough, you'll snap. You could live with paying out the money, galling and all as it was, but I bet it pissed you off no-end, that he had the power to change your world. One word in the wrong ear and the course of your life was changed forever. I'd say you smiled when you heard he was dead."

"His death lost me no sleep, if that's what you mean." Rick stood up and moved closer to, Joggy. "Let me make this clear." He stared directly into Joggy's eyes. "I detested the man for what he was doing to us and I'm not unhappy that he's dead, but, I didn't have anything to do with it"

Joggy stared long and hard back at Rick before slowly lowering his gaze. "I'd better be going," he said. "I'm sorry if I upset you,

Jenny. It was not my intention. And you needn't worry about your secret, it's safe with me."

"What about me?" said Rick, "You upset me as well, you know?"

"If I've accused you in the wrong, I will, but I don't know if I have." He made his way to the front door.

"Joggy," called Jenny, "How did you know I was here?"

"You were the only one I mentioned the notebook to."

Jenny's back suddenly straightened and her slumped shoulders squared.

"You set me up, didn't you?" Realising for the first time she had been played. "You knew I'd warn Rick?"

"I had an idea you might."

"You're too clever by half," said Rick.

Joggy, with a glint of satisfaction in his eye, closed the door behind him.

When he entered the kitchen, Alice's face was alight with expectation. "Well, what happened?"

Joggy slumped into the armchair by the solid fuel range. "I was right, Canavan was blackmailing them," he said grimly. "And what's more, I think I've found Luke's killer."

"What, Rick?" Alice said, alarmed.

Joggy nodded.

She pulled out a chair and sat facing her husband. "Alright, start at the beginning."

Joggy filled in the blanks.

"And are you sure it was, Rick?"

"Yes… no… I don't know." He placed his hands on his hair and pulled his head down until his elbows touched his knees. "I was hoping to finger someone nasty, like… you know, Ted, Nancy's husband, I didn't expect it would be, Rick. Problem is." He raised his head again to look at Alice. "If I've found him, what do I do now? How do I clear Luke's name? There's no evidence, only doubt. And that's not enough."

"Are you sure you're not missing something?"

"Like what?"

"Like, if it was Rick, why was it necessary to frame Luke for it? They liked Luke."

"Maybe it was accidental. Maybe Luke came back before he had time to clean up."

"Maybe, you should stay shopping."

"What're talking about?" Joggy had a look of incomprehension. "What… what's shopping got to do with this?"

"Everything. It's the difference between men and women when they go shopping. Men drop into the first shop they come to. If they find something they like and it's in their size -- they buy it. A woman, on the other hand, may do the same but, instead of buying she reserves her judgement until she sees what all the other shops have got to offer, because, you never know what you will find. Maybe, she'll find something even better, or maybe she won't, but either way, she has satisfied herself that she has picked the best."

"You know you're right." A ray of hope returned to his eyes. "I might be jumping the gun here. Canavan's blackmailing ways would have made him a lot of enemies. It could have been anyone in his squalid little notebook."

While Joggy spoke, Alice kept nodding; a self-satisfied grin plastered on her face.

"You're not as dumb as you look," he said jokingly.

Alice picked up a tea-towel from the kitchen table. "Cheeky bastard." And chucked it at him.

# CHAPTER 18

Her Hazel eyes turned lilac. They mirrored what they saw and the delight she felt as she walked hand in hand with Danny on Sunday afternoon. Dappled sunlight spotlighted their path as they weaved their way around the numerous beds of bluebells that carpeted the Hazel-wood floor.

"It's so beautiful," she said. "It's like something out of a famous painting. It's the prettiest birthday present I've ever had."

"Today's your birthday?"

"Yes, I'm eighteen today."

"Why didn't you tell me, I could have gotten you something?"

"Because I didn't want you to, besides, I've something else in mind."

"What?" Victoria had him on the back foot again.

"I want you to make love to me."

"Here, you mean…. here?"

"Yes, why not? She swept her arm out in an arc. ."We've beautiful beds and beautiful places deserve beautiful things done to them. You're not afraid are you?"

"No, no, it's just… what if someone sees us?"

"Who's going to see us? Fred's gone to the agricultural show and won't be back for ages. Besides, nobody knows were here – so -- relax."

* * * *

Indifferent eyes watched from the edge of the wood. Thomas Matthew Flynn was the only full-time employee of Fred Winter's. He was known locally as "Tomato", but not to his face. The name was derived from two sources: his two first names and his high red colouring. He was a bachelor in his early fifties and lived alone in a small cottage near the entrance to Winter's lane and next door to Victoria's friend, Louise.

Fred trusted him, because he was religiously indifferent. He was born into Catholicism but cut all ties when he left school at fifteen. He had worked on Winter's farm since then. Whenever Fred was away on a Sunday, Tomato did the herding. He was making his way from there when he spotted two people in the distance entering the wood. Satisfied now that he knew who they were, he turned and left them to their love making.

* * * *

Danny and Helen came through the open front door on Monday afternoon. They traipsed across the kitchen floor and dumped their schoolbags outside their respective bedroom doors. Without a word, they turned around and sat at the kitchen table.

"Have you two lost the power of speech?" Alice asked. She had been standing by the solid fuel cooker in the kitchen stirring the oxtail soup. "Hello mum or what's to eat mum wouldn't hurt ye. I don't think I'm looking for too much by asking for a simple greeting, am I?"

"No mum, sorry mum," they answered.

Alice poured the soup into three bowls then took a seat at the table. "When you've finished, Helen, I want you to bring Nellie up a loaf of brown bread and a Currant cake."

"Why do I always have to do it, you know she gives me the creeps?"

"She's an old lady. Let's see what you're like when you're seventy-six."

"If living till seventy six means being half-blind, living on my own and having to depend on my neighbours for hand outs, then I don't want to live that long. She also smells and she's always trying to grab my hands."

"Don't exaggerate; it's only the smoke from the open fire. Anyway all seers touch people; it's how they read their future."

"Yeah well, if she's so in touch with the future, how come she didn't warn granny J, about her future?"

"Are you talking about dad's mother?" asked Danny, suddenly taking an interest in the conversation.

"Yes," said Alice.

"Did she know her well?"

"She was your grandmother's best friend."

"Oh, I didn't know that."

"How did they meet?" asked Helen.

"Your grandmother and Nellie?"

"No, granny J and granddad."

"What is it with you and love-stories?" she answered dismissively.

"I'm just interested in how the old fogies got it together in their day."

"Less of the old fogies, miss. At least in our day people knew how to dance. We actually had steps, which is more than can be said for your lot."

"We have our own rhythm and our own steps."

"Shaking like epileptic in the middle of a seizure is not a dance step."

"Very funny, mum. I just love romantic stories, that's all. Their story is romantic, isn't it?"

"Yes…and tragic."

"So, please, please, tell us." Helen playfully begged, her hands joined as if in prayer.

"Do you want to hear it as well?" She looked at Danny.

"I'm all ears," he said.

"I can only tell you what Nellie told me. According to her, they met something like your father and I -- at a dance. Nellie said for Kate it was love at first sight. Unlike your father and me who knew one another from childhood -- she didn't know him at all. He was sitting at the far side of the dancehall his hat on his knee, tapping time to the music. He waved and smiled benignly at the people he knew dancing by him. Some of his friends tried to get him to join in but he stubbornly refused to budge from where he sat. Kate could not take her eyes of him. He was handsome with a fine head of wavy jet-black hair."

"Was there not a ladies choice?" Helen asked, recalling the story her mother had told her a few weeks earlier.

"There mustn't have been. He was twenty-four at the time. He worked as a farm labourer for a man called …ahm, wait now, his name will come to me in a minute." She closed her eyes and tried to visualise the name.

"Waller, his name was Waller," said Danny.

"That's right, Waller. How did you know that?"

"Dad told me."

"So you two do talk sometimes, then?"

"Yeah, but only when it suits him and even then he fobs me off with excuses."

"You have to be patient, Danny."

"You said that to me before, mum, well I'm all out of patience."

"Well I can't help you. It's between you and your father and I'm not getting involved. Now, can I return to the story?"

"Yeah, sorry."

"Your grandmother made some discreet inquires about him and then set herself a plan of action. Dan didn't know it at the time, but he was about to be hunted. Your grandmother worked at that time as a file clerk in a solicitor's office in Oldbridge. A couple of times a week, particularly if it was a fine evening, she'd cycle two miles out of her way from work in the hope of meeting Dan on the road driving the herd of cattle from the pasture to the milking shed.

When she was successful, she stopped and to Dan's delight chatted. He fell for her. But, he was too bashful to ask her out. He felt intimidated by her and stupid in her company. She was eighteen and well educated, Whilst, Dan, beyond the ability to read and write, had no real education.

Life was tough in your grandfather's day. For the common man, work and education were hard come by. Labouring was the only work open to him and from the age of twelve that's what he worked at. He was in his late teens when he came to work for Waller.

But he needn't have worried because Katie thought him intelligent in an understated way. She loved the wide felt hat he wore -- it gave him an aura of mystery. Like you Helen, she was a romantic. Dan was like the heroes in her romance novels. He was tall and handsome, masculine and gentle, sensitive and understanding and in some ways, was a man out of era. Eventually Katie became inpatient with Dan's ways. The next time she met him she complained of not having a date for the next local dance. Somehow he gathered up the courage and said he would take her if she could not find anyone else. They married two years later."

Alice paused when Danny placed a hand over his mouth to stifle a yawn. "I'm not boring you, am I? Lads your age are generally not interested in romance."

"I'm not bored, I'm just tired. Go on. I'm actually more interested than you think."

"Your grandfather it seems was not good at expressing how he felt in words, so he did it with flowers. Every Saturday evening on

138

his way home from work, he'd pick whatever flowers were in season, snowdrops, daffodils, bluebells, daisies, forget-me-knots, honeysuckle and Katie loved him for it. It wasn't the flowers but the gesture that endeared him to her. She loved that he was thinking about her as he crossed the wet fields in the winter and the meadows in the summer back to their two- bed- roomed cottage.

Your grandmother was very independent and stubborn. Not the kind of woman that would stand idle and allow her man to be the only one earning a living. So she started her own business by growing vegetables and selling them in the local town market. The extra money was a godsend for the family. You do know that it was from your grandmother that your father inherited his green fingers?"

"Yes, we do know that, you told us before, mum," said Helen

Alice returned to the story. "Then Tragedy struck. One warm late summer's evening, your grandmother was standing up on the back of the cart, sweeping it out after a day at the market. The Ass was still harnessed to it. A neighbour passing the road shouted in a greeting. It startled the Ass. He made a sudden lurch forward. Kate lost her balance and fell backwards striking her head on the baked hard ground -- snapping her neck. Dan panicked. Not knowing what to do, he did the most obvious thing -- he picked her up and carried her into the house and laid her gently on their bed. She died before the doctor arrived. She left behind a husband and three small children. At five years of age your father was the oldest."

"Poor granddad," said Helen. "He must have been heartbroken."

"Nellie said -- he became a shadow of the man he was. Now Helen, you've got your ration of romance and tragedy -- are you bringing the bread up or not?"

Danny rose up from the table. "I'll bring them up."

His reply surprised Alice -- he had never volunteered before. "Are you sure?"

"Mum," Helen said, indignantly. "He just said so."

"Ok, that's settled then."

\* \* \* \*

Nellie Roe lived alone in the first of the four cottages. It had been her home from the first day of her marriage. She married

Charlie Roe on her twenty-second birthday and he made her a widow on her sixty-sixth. No children graced their home. For a while after Charlie's death, Nellie tried to keep the cottage, known locally as Rose cottage, as tidy as possible. But with the advancement of old age and poor health, the place slowly deteriorated.

Above the little sagging wooden gate, branches of an out-of-control privy hedge reached out to touch one another. Danny ducked and pushed, scraping the gate across the crumbling concrete path. The gate came to a halt by the edge of the tall meadow grass. Dandelions now forced their way up through the fissures in the concrete, and the roses that Charlie had once been so proud off, were now wildly out of control -- threatening on windy days to whip and lacerate everything within reach. The curtains were closed on the one window that looked to the front. He knocked on the door.

"Who is it?"

"It's Danny Jackson, Missus Roe -- my mother sent me up with some bread."

"Come in, come in and close the door behind ya like a good lad."

Danny stood in the closed doorway and allowed his eyes and nose to adjust to the dim and smoke-pungent room. "Where will I put these?"

"Put them on the table like a good lad" -- Nellie was out of sight. She sat in a high-backed armchair facing the turf fire —"then come before me till I get a good look at ya."

"It's a bit dark in here. Do you want me to open the curtains?"

"No thanks child, they're fine. The light only hurts me eyes."

Danny came and sat on a wooden chair to her left.

She studied his face in the warm light of the open fire. "My God -- I'm looking at a ghost. You're the spitting image of your poor grandfather: Same eyes, same handsome features. If I didn't know better I'd say he was back among the living."

She was a small woman, dressed all in black. Her white hair was wispy and unkempt. She had a kindly face. She slowly leaned forward -- her eyes like distant clouds, staring directly into Danny's. She gently grasped his hands, closed her eyes and began to sway, back and forth, back and forth. Her hands at first cold began to heat up, generating a tingling sensation in Danny's fingers that began travelling through his wrists and up his arms. Spooked, he tried to pull free but found he was powerless. Suddenly she stopped rocking, her eyes shot open, her grip released and she settled back into her armchair -- her body settling down like a deflating balloon into blackness.

"I hope I didn't frighten you. I know Helen was never comfortable with me. She didn't understand. But you – you're different."

"In what way?"

"Helen turns from what she doesn't understand. You don't. You're a seeker. What do you want from me, Danny?"

"You probably already know that."

"I do, but I want to hear it from your lips."

"I want to know about dad's parents. I know his mother died in an accident when he was very young. He won't talk to me about them, particularly his father."

"Your father just can't bring himself to talk about what happened to them. He's still angry."

"About what?"

"His father's death. What do you know about your grandmother?" Nellie asked, changing the subject.

"I know how she died and how they met."

"Anything else?"

"Only that she was strong willed, single minded and a romantic."

"Yes, your father inherited the first two and so have you. Helen inherited her romantic side. Tell me, does Helen, help out in the garden in any way?"

Danny laughed at the notion. "No, she avoids it like the plague."

"Pity -- the green fingers are hers now."

"Will you tell me about granddad?"

"Your father still reluctant to talk, is he?"

"He's fairly tight lipped on the subject. It's like he's keeping some big secret."

"There's no secret, Danny." Her face became dark and sad. Her eyes rested on the fire and the flames danced in them. She stayed that way for several seconds before responding. "Go to the dresser like a good lad and open the bottom right-hand door."

Danny did as he was asked.

"There should be a red biscuit tin in there. Bring it to me."

Danny brought the faded red biscuit tin back to Nellie.

Nellie's frail arthritic fingers pressed hard against the lids edge, but found she had not the power to prise it open. She handed it to, Danny. "Will you do the honours like a good lad?"
He prised it off and handed it back.

"It's important, Danny…." she said, rummaging through yellowed envelopes, birthday cards and faded photographs. She stopped when she recognised one, pulled it out and looked adoringly at it. "That's Kate and Dan's wedding photo." She handed it to, Danny, and then continued her rummaging.

Danny leaned forward and studied the old black and white photo in the light of the turf fire. In the posed photo, Kate sat in a chair and Dan stood beside her with his hand on her shoulder.

"They're very sombre -- they don't look like they're having a good time".

"I can assure you me lad," she said, not raising her head up from her search. "They were very happy that day."

"We'll they don't look it."

"That's because in those days you had to pose for something like five minutes for a photo. You try holding a smile for that length of time… agh, found it." She lifted up a copy book from close to the bottom of the tin, then placed it underneath the tin, replaced the lid and handed it to, Danny. "Put that on the floor beside you."

Danny once again did as he was asked.

"It's important to remember the period of time in which your Grandfather lived." She leaned back in her armchair, her hands rested on the copy in her lap. "The new century was but an infant and times were hard. Jobs, particularly in the countryside, were difficult to come by. Having a job-any job-was a godsend. Dan worked on a large farm, milking cows, cleaning out byres and numerous other jobs that needed to be done. He laboured with three other men, 6 days a week, from sun up to six each evening for small money. It was hard back-breaking work, but at that time they were glad of it. The farm was owned by a man named Waller."

Nellie suddenly sat up and spat into the fire. "I cannot abide the taste of that devil's name in my mouth and it'll be the last time I'll mention it." She settled back into the armchair.

"Dad said that Mister Winter was an uncle of Waller's. Is that true?"

"It is and I can assure you that in his case, the apple did not fall far from the tree."

When Danny did not respond, Nellie took a shallow wheezy breath and continued. "Kate and Dan's story is a tragic one. It still upsets me to talk about them. A long time ago I wrote their story in this copy book. They were two wonderful people and I didn't want them to be forgotten -- because if they were forgotten then what was done to them would be forgotten -- and I wasn't about to let that happen. So if you want to know about your grandfather, you'll have to read it for yourself." She handed the copy to, Danny.
He opened it, leaned forward into the fire light and began to read.

*This is the story of two beautiful people. Their names were Katie and Dan Jackson.*
*The details I've enclosed here were told to me by friends, relatives and witnesses to the events. The finer details were told to me by Dan.*

*Katie died young. She fell from the back of an ass and cart and broke her neck. She left three young children. The oldest was five years old.*

*With Kate only freshly in her grave, Dan, still numbed by her death went hat in hand to his employer, a farmer by the name of Waller. He knocked on the back door of the big house. The farmer seemed unsurprised to find him standing there -- it was like he was expecting him. He held the door open, allowing Dan to enter the flagstone kitchen.*

*"This has to be a very difficult time for you and your young family," he said. He pulled out a chair from beneath the pine kitchen table and indicated that Dan should sit.*

*Dan sat down and rested his hat on his knee. The farmer took up a position in front of the old pine dresser -- his hands firmly clasped behind his back. "It's also a very difficult time on* money." He looked down on Dan. "It's in that department I want to help you."

Of course Dan was hugely relieved. After been warned by his fellow workers about the farmer's manipulative ways -- he had dreaded the thought of asking for a raise -- those fears now seemed groundless.

"Thank you sir, you don't know how much this means to me."

"It's times like this that we need to be there for one another and to ensure your young family has a future by continually putting food on the table and keeping a roof over their heads. Isn't that so Dan?"

"Yes sir, it is."

The farmer paused, as if mulling something over in his mind. Dan, now relaxed, waited patiently, for the next piece of good news.

"Dan," said the farmer eventually, "there is an aspect of your wife's tragic death that I've been meaning to ask you about, and I hope, I'm not being too insensitive by speaking of it so soon," he said, apologetically.

"Of course not sir, ask away."

"Why did you move your wife from where she fell?"

"Well I couldn't very well leave her there for everyone to gawk at. Now could I sir?"

"But did you not realize, Dan, she may have broken her neck and by moving her, you were placing her life in danger?"

Dan's face drained of all colour. "What are you saying sir, that by moving her, I killed my Katie?"

"I'm not saying that, Dan, but, it's well known within the medical profession, that if you move someone who has a broken neck, that you hasten their death."

"And, if I didn't move her, my Katie could still be alive?"

"Yes, that's a possibility."

The possibility that he could somehow be responsible for the death of his beloved Katie, now ran blind in his mind. He vaguely heard what the devil said next.

"Anyway, as I was saying earlier, I'd like to help your family. So this is what I propose. I'll allow you to work two extra hours each evening and three out of every four Sundays. The extra hours will keep you and your young family afloat."

Dan's mind was in turmoil. The thought that he may have contributed to his wife's death frightened and bewildered him. The proposal went unheard, muffled by the confusion.

"Well, Dan, what do you say, have we a deal?"

"Yes," said Dan, not understanding what he was agreeing to.

They shook hands on it and Dan left. He climbed on his bicycle and rode into Oldbridge. He propped it against the white pebble dash wall of Doctor Myles surgery. The surgery was full. "I'd like to see Doctor Myles," he said to the receptionist.

"Doctor Myles is with a patient at the moment," she said." If you'll take a seat he'll see you in turn."

There were no seats available, so he remained standing. Several of the people waiting knew him -- they came to him and offered their condolences. The inner surgery door opened and an elderly woman came out, followed closely by the Doctor. Dan walked briskly up to him. "Did I kill my Katie?" he asked. A look of sheer terror was in his eyes.

Doctor Myles stared at him stunned by the question and wondered how he could truthfully answer him. "You had better come through, Dan." He placed a sympathetic hand on his shoulder. "I can't talk to you out here."

Dan jumped back as if hit by a dart of electricity. "O sweet Jesus, O sweet Jesus, it's true," he said. He backed away from the doctor and crunched his hat into a ball. "I killed my Katie."

He ran out and was seen that evening pedalling furiously out of town. They said it was like the devil was after him. Shortly after that the nightmares began. He'd wake up with a start and could not go back to sleep again. So he dressed, walked the half-mile to his wife's grave and sat beside her till dawn. And life went on like that for the next fifteen years until tragedy struck for a second time. Dan suffered a massive heart attack. On the day he died, he, along with two of his fellow workers were tossing bales of straw high above their heads into a loft. All of a sudden he stopped and clutched at his chest. His face was contorted into a grimace as the pain hit him crumbling him to his knees. And then a strange thing happened-- as if in silent slow motion and just before he keeled over the expression on his face changed -- to sheer joy. The men who witnessed it didn't understand why that happened, but I know.

*In those last few seconds of life he saw his Katie. She had come for him.*

*One of the workers ran and fetched the farmer. He knelt and checked for a pulse -- found none and declared him dead. The farmer then astounded all present. He ordered Dan's fellow workers to move his body into the ground floor of the barn, where he picked up a large dusty jute sack and covered him with it. It was like he was covering an old dog that had been put down after outgrowing his usefulness. He then ordered everyone back to work. The men asked him was he going for a doctor or an ambulance. He said he would, once the working day was over. That evening long after the men finished, an ambulance called to the barn and collected Dan.*

*The farmer did not call and sympathize with the family or attend the funeral. Dan's last pay packet arrived and he was duly paid for only the hours he worked -- nothing more, nothing less. The farmer was never made pay. His actions prevented the slim possibility of Dan's survival, yet, he wasn't even questioned by the police. No charges were ever brought against him: The perks of privilege I guess.*

*On the evening of Dan's funeral, the farmer's hay-barn was burnt to the ground.*

Danny looked at Nellie. "Dad burnt the barn down," he said, in triumphal satisfaction.

"No. Luke Baker did." She momentarily held Danny's gaze before turning back to the fire. "It was an accident. The story goes that Luke was out hunting rabbits with his Terrier when it started to rain. He took shelter in Waller's barn. But when he was leaving he was careless with his cigarette and the place went up.

"Pity," Danny said, deflated. "It would have made for sweet revenge."

Nellie was silent.

Danny leaned back from the fire-light and sat upright in his chair. For several seconds he contemplated what he had just read. "I don't understand why he stuck to the deal, I mean, it was only a handshake, it wasn't legal -- nothing was in writing."

"Today child that might be the case, but back then, a man's hand was his bond. Honour was hugely important. And even though he shook hands on a bad deal, Dan would not dishonour himself or his family by reneging on it."

He rose from his chair. "I'd better be going, Missus Roe. Thanks for filling me in."

Nellie's eyes were now closed "My gift," she said, "Doesn't always allow me to see the future clearly. Sometimes the vision is hazy, hard to interpret."

Danny sat down again.

"I saw danger in your future... smoke, lots of smoke, coughing and terrible heat. Someone else is with you, I can't see who it is -- they're lying down."

A cold shiver ran down Danny's back. "Do we survive?"

Nellie opened her eyes. "I could say yes, but the honest answer is, I don't know. Sometimes that's all my gift will allow me to see." She grasped Danny's hand as he rose to leave. "You be careful now," she said, patting the back of it. "You come back and see me again and next time," she said with a knowing smile. "Bring that nice young lady of yours."

Danny gave Nellie a quizzical look, then reddened a little with embarrassment and wondered had she seen his past as well as his future. "I will," he said, "I will."

"Oh, and ask that father of yours to call in and see me soon. He's overdue a visit and don't worry, Danny, I'm sure everything will work out fine."

# CHAPTER 19

For McNeill, the silence coming from the other end of the telephone line was sheer torture. It reminded him of his days in national school. The headmaster had him by the wrist, tapping the tips of his fingers with the cane, little stinging tips that seemed to go on forever -- his eyes closed tightly as he waited and waited for the big one -- the one that really hurt.

Inspector Murray sighed deeply. He was uncomfortable with the whole situation -- it went against all his instincts. He had to make a decision. If he called off McNeill, he thought, Jackson would be alone. Eventually his leads would come to nought, his investigation would fizzle out and he would give up. Murray leaned his head back, looked up at the ceiling in his hallway and gave another large sigh. He realised the impression Jackson had left on him was not of a man who gives up easily. He also realised he was smart enough to solve it and by doing so put himself in harm's way. As a member of the force who put his pal behind bars -- he felt somehow responsible. "Only bruises you say?"

"Yes sir, he was lucky."

"Providing he exists, could it have been Canavan's mystery killer?"

"No sir. If he does exist, it's too early for him to show his face."

"So who do you think did this?"

"Someone who doesn't take kindly to being humiliated."

"You think it was Reilly?"

"It has his trademark."

"You know this from experience?"

"Yes sir. I covered for him on numerous occasions when we were partners. He doesn't look kindly on people who make him look foolish."

"Must have hurt when he didn't cover for you then?"

McNeill bit his lip.

"Right" said Murray. "From now on, you'll have no more trouble from Reilly. I'll tie him up in so much work -- he'll think he's in a straitjacket. In the meantime, try like a good man, and keep Jackson out of trouble."

* * * *

Danny walked out of Columb's shop in Kilpatrick on Tuesday evening, swigging from a bottle of Orange. He was thirsty after a minor hurling training session. He wiped his lips with the back of his hand.

"How's it going Danny?" Spit asked. He was sitting on the window sill of the shop, picking his nose. What he excavated from his right nostril, he briefly examined, rolled it vigorously along his trouser leg to dry before flicking it into the street.

"Not too bad, Spit, and yourself?"

"Ahh, you know, dragging the devil by the tail. Fancy your chances in the championship this year do ye?"

"We've as good a chance as any."

"Aye, I suppose it's all on the day."

Danny turned his bicycle for home. Spit stood up.

"You don't mind walking with me as far as my place, do you Danny?"

"No, of course not."

"I remember your dad when he played. He was the goalie." Spit, started laughing. "We use to call him kamikaze."

"I never heard him called that before. Why was he called Kamikaze?"

"Because he threw himself at everything. Unfortunately a bad knee injury brought an early halt to his hurling career. It was a pity -- he could have made the county; he was that good."

Spit spat onto the road.

"Did you play yourself?" asked Danny.

"I did, very briefly. Soon found out I hadn't an athletic bone in me body. We had some good players back then, particularly the Baker brothers. Luke was a monster. Jaysus there were times when I was glad I was on the sideline -- he took no prisoners. But the craic was always good after a match, especially if we won."

"So you were all friends then?"

"Of course. We were all off the same age."

"Must have been a bit of a bummer when Luke went to jail for burning down Waller's barn?" Danny, was quick to spot the opening.

"Yeah, tore the heart out of the team. Pity, with Luke playing we could have been county champions that year."

"Did he really do it?" Danny asked, with an air of nonchalance that did not fool Spit for a second. He was an old hand at the information gathering game and could spot someone on a fishing trip a mile off.

Spit stopped walking. "You're about as subtle as a sledge hammer," he said. His eyes narrowed.

"What do you mean?" Danny asked innocently.

"You get nothing for nothing, young Jackson."

"You mean a trade?" He realised the game was up and any further protestations of innocence would only make him look foolish.

"Precisely."

"What do you want?"

"What have you got?"

"Nothing at the moment, but maybe later I'll have something."

"I don't deal in maybes. You'll have to come up with something more concrete than that, young Jackson."

"If you want me to betray my dad, forget it. I can't do that."

"I wouldn't expect you to. What I want is the inside track on what went down when it's all over."

Danny thought for a moment then agreed.

Spit spat on his hand and extended it to Danny. "Shake on it. A man's word is cemented with his hand -- it's unbreakable." He stared sternly into Danny's eyes.

Danny did so reluctantly. Not because he did not want to give his word but because he was repulsed at the thought of having Spit's saliva on his hand.

With the deal sealed Spit started walking again.

Danny wiped his hand on the arse of his jeans "Now, what about Luke, did he do it?"

"At that time, Danny, Waller, was a hated figure in this area and people were delighted when they heard his barn had burnt down and Luke became a hero. Luke never talked about it after he was released from prison, which was strange because he always loved talking about his exploits. Particularly when he was hurling -- he'd have you in stitches. He was never boastful, just had a humorous turn of phrase."

"Why do you think that was?"

"Well, when you do something popular, you tend to milk it for what it's worth: Luke never did. Rumour has it he didn't burn down the barn -- that he took a fall for someone else. Now, Danny, as you know, I don't deal in rumour, only in the truth."

"So who do you think he took a fall for?"

"You're a smart lad Danny, you work it out. I have."

* * * *

Maxwell's of Heatherville Lodge was Joggy's oldest client and at seventeen miles distance, it was also the farthest away. It was a stately pile. Twelve uninterrupted generations of Maxwell's had resided there. The three story building was at the end of a long gravelled avenue, surrounded by lush green fields and a dairy farm.

Joggy's job every Wednesday was the rectangular shaped walled vegetable garden: the pride and joy of Mrs Maxwell. In the bottom right hand corner was a stone tool shed stocked with everything he required for the work. A line of garden tools hung in an orderly fashion upon a row of wire nails driven into a wooden lath three-quarters way up a side wall. An unlocked wooden door in the back wall of the shed linked the farmyard to the house. In the garden was a large heap of farm manure had been brought in and left composting in the corner opposite the stone shed. Waiting in the shed to be sown was a large bag of shallots and a smaller bag of scallions.

Showers persisted throughout the morning, forcing Joggy on several occasions to retreat to the shelter of the shed. With the exception of Mrs Maxwell nobody else was about. Her husband and only son were attending the cattle mart.

It was close to mid-day as Joggy walked back from the main house, having delivered Mrs Maxwell her day's requirement of vegetables and potatoes. He had not reached half-way when the heavens opened up again, forcing him to sprint for cover. He reached the doorway, brushed the loose drops from his bibbed overalls and swore silently at the weather: Straight lines of water were coming down.

It took him several seconds before his nose told him he was no longer alone. Drifting on the still air was the unmistakable aroma of tobacco smoke that he knew so well. "I was wondering when you'd turn up," he said.

"I figured this place was a safe bet, husband and son at the mart, wife in the house, not much chance of been spotted." McNeill, came from the shadows and leaned against the wall beside the front doorway. "No after effects from your injuries I hope?"

"No, thank God. Any ideas on who done it?"

"Afraid not, he didn't leave a trail. I've got something for you though." McNeill, reached for his inside coat pocket and extracted a thick brown envelope "Scene photos." He handed them to Joggy.

Joggy feared the horror of that day would return when he looked at Canavan's lifeless body photographed from different angles and was surprised when it did not. The discovery of Canavan's nasty secret life had somewhat diluted the initial horror. In his mind a justification of sorts had set in. He examined the photos of the body and surrounding area, the murder weapon and where it was found plus the farmyard and the blood-spattered straw. "What's that?"

"What's what?"

"That." He pointed out something high in the white thorn bushes above where the body was found.

McNeill examined the photo, tilting it back and forth in the light. "Hold on," he said, and reached into his inside pocket again and withdrew a small magnifying glass.

"What else have you got in there, rabbits?" Joggy said in mock curiosity.

"I always carry a few necessities with me when I travel. You'd be surprised how often they come in handy." McNeill examined the photo again. "As far as I can make out it's a piece of straw."

"Are you sure?"

"Here." McNeill handed over the photo and magnifying glass. "Have a look for yourself."

"You're right, it is straw and it looks fresh. But what's it doing there?"

"It probable blew of a load going by."

"In April? Who moves straw in April?"

"Well I don't know. I'm not a farmer, am I? Maybe it was blown by the wind off the body when it was thrown from the bridge."

"As far as I can remember, there was little or no wind on the Saturday his body was dumped."

"Yes, but there was plenty of wind late Saturday night and Sunday morning!"

"Can I hold on to these?"

"Yeah, sure. Just don't show them to anyone else."

"What do you take me for, a moron?"

McNeill ignored the comment. "Have you got anything for me?"

"Did you know that Canavan was dying from cancer and had only a short time to live?"

"Really, who told you that?"

"Doctor Kelly. He said that Canavan had known for about a week before he died."

"Interesting. But I don't think it bears any relevance to his murder."

"What makes you think that?"

"Because he obviously told nobody or we would have heard about it by now. Have you anything else?"

"I found Canavan's notebook."

"Great. Now we're getting somewhere. Have you got it with you?"

"No, it's at home. It wouldn't do you any good to read it. It's written in a lettered code."

"Shit."

"Fortunately for us, I cracked it."

"Well done, and….?"

"And…. he was blackmailing people, and… for a number of years,"

"Fantastic, can you get it to me." McNeill rubbed his hands together in eager anticipation. He loved having the power, being in control, twisting and turning people to his advantage -- it was his aphrodisiac and the salacious details encased between the covers of Canavan's notebook practically gave him an erection.

"I don't think so."

"What do you mean, you don't think so?"

"Because it holds a lot of sensitive information."

"That's precisely why you should get it to me. You don't want it falling into the wrong hands."

Joggy burst out laughing. "You're some blaggard McNeill. I've no intention of giving you that notebook. As bad as Canavan was -- you'd be ten times worse.

"Don't start messing me around, Jackson, that's not the deal we had."

"Maybe not, but I have a responsibility to protect those people from the likes of you."

"Who the fuck do you think you are? I am the law around here and I want that fucking notebook. It's material evidence."

"In an official investigation, maybe, but not in this case; unless, that is, the rules have changed?"

"Fuck you, Jackson." Minute drops of foamed spittle flew from his mouth. "I've kept my side of the bargain, now you keep yours."

"Sorry, Ed. I'd lose my credibility if I did that."

Powerlessness tasted alien in McNeill's mouth. He had put up with Inspector Murray having the upper hand because he was his superior but not from an upstart like Joggy Jackson. Seeing he was getting nowhere, McNeill turned back into the shadows. In the dark he fumed. Sharp intakes of breath could be heard, like a bull about to charge.

Joggy was determined to keep his cool. He didn't want to be drawn into a heated argument and end up saying something he hadn't meant to. He had to admit to himself, he quite liked having the upper hand, being in control.

McNeill suddenly emerged from the shadows. "What have you got against me? What did I ever do to you?"

"You, personally?" Joggy shook his head. "Nothing. It's that rag of a uniform. I lost respect for what that stood for -- a long time ago."

"Really? And what cataclysmic event made that happen?"

"Let's just say that justice proved itself to be two-faced and biased."

McNeill clenched his jaw and ground his teeth. He peeled his gaze away from Joggy and onto the heap of steaming farmyard manure. The downpour had stopped and the Sun had once again made an appearance. He took a long slow deep breath, turned and stared hard at Joggy. "Okay. Let's play it your way then. What information are you and your superior moral conscience willing to let me have?"

"No names. There are only a couple of active leads worth following up. The rest are null and void. The people involved have either died or moved away. Or maybe they just called his bluff and refused to pay anymore. One way or another, those accounts are now closed."

"How do you know that?"

"Because he had a line drawn diagonally across their names. And by the way when I'm finished -- I'm burning it."

"You said there were a couple of leads worth chasing. Have you?"

"I've chased one of them." He paused to gather his thoughts and pondered on how much he would reveal. He didn't want to give McNeill any clues. He spoke slowly choosing his words carefully. "Canavan was blackmailing this particular couple for adultery. They were paying him five pounds a month to keep his mouth shut. I've spoken to them and the man had motive, opportunity and access to the murder weapon. The only piece that didn't fit was their motive for framing Luke. They both liked him."

"You're tying my hands here, Joggy. If you get into trouble -- I won't know where to go."

"That's a chance I'll have to take."

"You said you had another lead?"

"I have and I'll tell you how it pans out the next time we meet."

# CHAPTER 20

Later that night, Spit Sweeney stepped out of O Meara's and into the still night air. Before starting for home he surveyed the street and found it empty and quiet. He pulled up the collar of his jacket as he crossed the street. Even-though it was now mid-may a late spring chill still existed. A large puff of pipe smoke floated out from an open doorway.

"A word." McNeill said, as Spit drew level.

"Evening sarge. A bit late for you to be up?"

"In here," McNeill, stood aside.

Spit paused. Beyond McNeill the hall that divides the station from the dwelling was in pitch darkness. Spit entered slowly and cautiously.

McNeill closed the door most of the way, leaving just a shaft of street light, a light Spit was glad to stand in.

"Well Sarge what can I do for you?" Spit, for once swallowed his own saliva.

"It's late, so I won't beat about the bush. You and Joggy Jackson know one another a long time, don't ye?"

"Aye, we go back a bit alright."

"Good. I want you to tell me everything you know about him, including what happened to his parents."

"Sorry Sarge, I don't do charity."

"Of course, of course, how naïve of me to think you'd work for free. Would a little incentive help?"

"Now you're talking my language." Spit smirked, believing he had the sergeant by the short and curlies.

"Ok Spit. How about me not turning a blind eye the next time you work and draw the dole at the same time -- how about the next time it happens, me having a quiet word into the ears of the social welfare boys. How often do you think you'd be able to visit O Meara's after that?"

"Good incentive, Sarge," The smirk wiped clean from his face.

"Thought you'd see it my way. Start talking and don't leave anything out."

Spit stuck only to the basics. This time, unlike his earlier conversation with Danny -- he did not embellish anything nor did he give opinions. In Spit's world, freebies just did not come with privileges.

Joggy sat at the end of the kitchen table on Friday evening and waited while Alice assembled his dinner of potatoes, bacon and cabbage onto a plate. The children had been fed earlier and were playing outside.

"I suppose you heard the news?" She placed the hot food in front of him.

"No, I didn't hear anything." He picked up the salt shaker and gave his food a liberal sprinkling. "Why what happened?"

"I can't believe you heard nothing, the place has been buzzing since it happened."

"I haven't spoken to a soul all day. So what is it?"

"Ah, it'll keep till you're finished your dinner." She sat down to her own food.

"Can't you tell me now?" He cut off a chunk of butter and placed it on the side of his plate.

"No, I'll wait till you're finished. It might only spoil your dinner." Alice was enjoying herself. It was not often she got a chance to play Joggy at his own game.

"Stop messing, woman, and tell me what happened?" He was not enjoying the tables been turned on him.

"Eat your dinner," she said, with a large teasing smile.

Alice cleared away the plates and made the tea. She poured out two cups. Into her own she placed two heaped spoonfuls of sugar and a small drop of milk and then slowly stirred it for several teasing seconds.

"Well, are you going to tell me or not?" Joggy's patience had finally snapped.

"God, now, aren't you the inpatient one."

Joggy glared at her.

She took a sip from her cup and then placed it back on the table. "Rick and Jenny are gone -- eloped and taken the kids with them."

"Gone!" Joggy leaned forward onto the table. "What do you mean gone?"

"They're gone to America."

"Are you sure? How do you know it's America their gone to?"

"It was in the note they left for Alfie."

"Poor auld Alfie."

"He can only blame himself. If he stayed out of the pub more often, he'd still have a wife and child."

"Ah bollocks." Joggy exclaimed, as the facts hit home. "What am I going to do now? There goes my main suspect. I must have frightened him away."

"Oh I doubt that." Alice had more time than her husband to digest the news and had come to her own conclusion. "Their getaway has to have been planned for awhile."

"What makes you think that?"

"Because he would have had to organise visas for Jenny and the kids and that doesn't happen overnight. She worked with your sister, Chris, in St Mels. Nurses would be in big demand over there."

"Well bollocks again. What if it turns out to be him? What am I going to do then?"

"Pray it's not him and stay shopping, that's all you can do. I thought you were to call and see, Ann Dwyer and Kevin Barrett."

"I've been busy. I'll call to them next week."

"And what's wrong with this evening?"

"Nothing, I guess. I suppose I need a new suspect now that Rick has flown the coop."

* * * *

Kevin Barrett lived with his artist brother Edwin in a three bed-room bungalow, up a short twisted avenue a mile, Joggy's side of Kilpatrick. Between the high whitethorn hedge on the roadside and a row of Evergreen trees along one side of the avenue, which over the years had knitted together, the house was completely obscured from public view. The wooden gate was open. There was no car outside the house when Joggy called. He knocked on the door but no one answered. He walked around the house looking in the windows in the hope of catching Edwin snoozing in a chair. One room was full of artist materials, canvases, brushes and slashes of paint everywhere. In another was a double bed, followed by a private study or office, followed by the kitchen/living room. Outside the back door were two cardboard boxes full of empty Vodka bottles. The bathroom was the one with the frosted glass and to the left of the front door was a sitting room. Joggy was about to leave when he heard the sound of the car: it was the Barrett brothers.

"You looking for one of us, Joggy?" Kevin climbed out of the driver's side.

"I need a quick word with yourself, if you don't mind."

Edwin got out and closed the door. His eyes appraised Joggy from head to toe. "Join us for tea, won't you Joggy? It's not often we have such delectable company."

"Thank you, Edwin, but maybe another time."

"Pity, another time it will have to be then." Edwin opened the front door and disappeared into the house.

"So, Joggy, what can I do for you." Kevin Barrett smiled and sat back against his car.

"It's a bit of a sensitive matter."

"You're among friends, Joggy, go on."

"As you probably know I've been trying to clear Luke's name by looking into the John Canavan murder."

"It has come to my notice."

"Well I found a notebook belonging to Canavan. It seems that he was blackmailing people. The little black notebook holds some very delicate information."

Barrett slipped his hands into his trousers pockets, looked down at the ground and began nudging gravel out of the way with his right foot.

"Your name is there, tied in with Ann Dwyer. The love that dare's not speak its name was the quote he used to describe the act he was blackmailing ye for. Do you know what that was about?"

Barrett raised his eyes and focused them intently on Joggy. The bright beaming smile was gone. His face was grey and serious. He took his time before answering. "Who have you spoken to about this?"

"My wife.... no one else knows."

"And the notebook?"

"I have it at home."

"What are you going to do with it?"

"At the moment I'm using it as part of my enquires. But as soon as I've cleared Luke's name, I'm destroying it. Like you, I don't want it to fall into the wrong hands. In the meantime, any information I gather will be kept in the strictest confidence. What I need to know, Kevin, is what he meant by that quote so that I can decide whether it has any bearing on his murder."

"Trust me, Joggy, it was a personal matter and it had absolutely nothing to do with Canavan's death."

"That may be so, Kevin, but I'm the one who makes that decision. I still need to know why he was blackmailing you?"

"Is my word not good enough?"

"In this case I'm afraid not. He was blackmailing you, Kevin, for God's sake. Your car was seen the Saturday his body was dumped in the river, travelling that same stretch of road."

"I travel that road several times a week. The fact that I travelled it on that particular day means nothing. And since my word is not good enough for you," he said becoming annoyed, "I want you to leave and stay the hell out of my personal business. Get out of my yard." He turned and walked into his house, slamming the door behind him.

Joggy was left with no choice but to climb into his car and head into the village of Kilpatrick. He drove in by the side of the church and around the back, to the parochial house. He gave a sigh of relief when he saw, Ann Dwyer's red Mini Minor still in the yard. He rang the bell. She opened the door, stepped out into the porch and then pulled the door closed behind her.

"I don't mean to be rude, Joggy," she said, getting the first word in. "Kevin rang me and told me what you were up to. And I'm telling you what he told you, this is none of your business. Now go about your own business and leave us alone." Ann moved briskly towards her car.

"But that's just it, Ann." He fell into step with her. "I have to know your business before I can move on with mine."

She climbed into her car. "I've said all I'm going to say. Please respect my wishes." She slammed the door and drove away.

\* \* \* \*

Instead of going home, Joggy parked his Morris Traveller in the car park in front of the Church and made his way to O Meara's. Rejection had left a salty taste in his mouth and given him a thirst. Spit Sweeny and Squeek Malone were sitting in their usual spot in front of the fire, nursing the remnants of their pints. No one else was present.

"Spit, Squeek," said Joggy.

"Joggy," they answered in harmony.

He took a stool at one end of the bar and lit a Sweet Afton. "The usual, Joe."

He traded small talk with the barman while he waited for his pint to settle.

"Howya Joggy," said Spit. He hopped onto a stool next to him.

"Howya Joggy," said Squeek, in his high pitched voice, taking the stool next to Spit.

Spit turned and glared at him, sending a silent message that even Squeek, could not misunderstand.

"I'm thirsty too," he mumbled, and sulked his way back to the fire.

"Well how are you Spit?" Joggy asked, as he sorted through the loose change in his hand.

"Fine, couldn't be better."

The pint arrived and he paid the barman.

Spit lifted his near empty pint glass, drained the dregs and planted the empty glass on the bar counter beside Joggie's full pint

Joggy ignored the gesture. He extracted the Sweet Afton from his lips, lifted his pint and took a mouthful.

"I had a chat the other day with a man," said Spit, picking up the empty glass and turning it around and around in his hand, watching the cream foamy residue sliding across the surface. "He wanted me to tell him all I knew about you and your family."

"Another pint there, Joe." Joggy knew it would be futile to ask questions while Spit, was thirsty. "Now, you were saying?"

"The Sarge accosted me the other night while I was on my way home. He was very keen on knowing all about your family, your parents, grandparents etc, etc; in fact, anything at all to do with you."

"What'd you tell him?"

Spit's, pint arrived. He took a decent swig and related his encounter with the Sergeant. "That's all I told him -- the basic facts. I left the rest to his imagination."

"There's nothing for him to imagine." Joggy, lifted his glass and took another mouthful.

"Yeah, yeah, he'd want to have a powerful imagination all right. So, anyway, how's the detective work going? Any closer to proving them wrong?"

"Ah it's slow. Clues are few and far between."

The small talk continued until Joggy had finished his pint. He slipped off his stool. "Thanks for that. There's the price of a pint for Squeek, he's looking a bit dehydrated over there. He placed the money on the bar counter, patted Spit on the shoulder and left. He visited the toilet before heading for home.

The piece of white paper jammed under the wiper of his car immediately caught his attention when he turned the corner into the car park. He glanced warily around him before lifting it from under the rubber wiper. He sat into the safety of his car and read it: ASK JOSIE TYRELL WHY SHE PLACES FLOWERS ON JOHN CANAVANS GRAVE.

Joggy stared straight ahead at a row of low roofed detached cottages. Josie Tyrell's was the white one with the bottle green door and flowering window boxes. A double gate separated her house from the Garda station. She was not a lady he was overly familiar with. She did not venture into the public domain to often - - keeping her daughter and herself very much to themselves.

Even though this piece of curious information intrigued him, it did nothing for his despondency. It just meant it was another door to knock on and possibly another door slammed in his face. Feeling he had all the rejection he could handle for one day, he turned the key and drove slowly out of the car park and across the street. "Fuck it." He brought the car to a sudden halt. He realised he was going to have to talk to her sometime and this was as good a time as any. He knocked on the door. Josie opened it. She was a short round woman with straight brown hair, tied into a ponytail.

"Hello, Missus Tyrell, my name's Joggy Jackson. I wonder if I could have a quick word?"

"I know who you are," she replied, flatly.

"Do you mind if I come in?"

"I'm sure whatever you have to say can be said on the doorstep," she answered, in the same unemotional tone.

"As you might have heard, I'm looking into John Canavans death and it has come to my notice that you have been leaving flowers on his grave, which under normal circumstances would be none of my business or anybody else's. but..."

"You're right -- it is none of your business." She closed the door in his face.

Joggy bent down and pushed open the letterbox. "Look I'm sorry if I've offended you, Missus Tyrell. I'm only trying to clear Luke Baker's name and all I'm trying to find out is if your relationship with John Canavan has any bearing on my inquires. Again, I'm sorry if I've offended you." When she did not answer he released the brass flap of the letterbox, straightened and waited -- but the door did not open again. He made his way back to the car.

"Talking into letterboxes now are ya?" McNeill sneered, from the doorway of the Garda Station. "That's your new interrogation technique is it?"

"Yeah, it's right up there with dragging people in of the street in the dead of night," Joggy retorted sarcastically,

The sneer rapidly disappeared off McNeill's face.

# CHAPTER 21

Joggy could not sleep. His mind was in turmoil as he tried to make sense of everything. The investigation was turning and twisting him in all kinds of weird directions and just when he had settled for one, it suddenly shunted him in another. He decided to put all the confusing bits aside and concentrate on one thing at a time. His concentration fell on Kevin and Ann Dwyer.

He had seen another side of the normally affable and easy-going Kevin Barrrett a side he had not seen before and it disturbed him. Was it possible, that on that day, while travelling along that road, he came upon Canavan pushing his bike and saw an opportunity? Joggy was certain of one thing, he was not going to learn anything more from Kevin Barrett. Edwin Barrett was the weak link, he was sure of it, but how was he going to get him to talk? He fell into a deep sleep, no nearer to an answer.

Alice woke him the next morning by pulling back the curtains, revealing the onset of a bright day. She reached up and opened the top window. A light breeze rushed in and ruffled the net under-curtain. In the half light of the room Alice slipped her pink cotton night dress up over her head. Joggy quietly watched -- her hands high in the air and her breasts exposed -- an erotic moment that never failed to stir his loins -- the highlight of his mornings. Alice finished dressing, brushed her hair and left the room to start her working day.

Along with the morning light and gentle breeze that filtered through the net under-curtain came the sounds of the day -- birds chirping and chattering away in the thorny branches of the whitethorn bushes at the back of the house, and across the field's the constant barking of farmer Kelly's black and white collie dog, who seemed to think because he was awake everyone else should be.

From the kitchen came the grating sounds of the Stanley solid fuel range been raked, the ash box been dragged out of its place, the front door being opened as Alice went to dump the ashes into the compost heap at the bottom of the vegetable garden.

He thought again of the problem he had gone to bed with, and the answer slowly dawned on him. His sub-conscious had obviously been hard at work while he slept. The plan that slowly emerged was audacious. It appealed to his sense of adventure and at the same time made him very uneasy. It would mean he would have to call when Kevin was at school and it would also mean taking time off from work. It also meant not telling Alice because she would surely stop him.

* * * *

Because they sat up front in the pews close to the Altar, Joggy, Alice, Helen and Katie were among the last to leave the Church. Josie Tyrell watched from the front door of her home. When she saw them emerge she closed her door and marched across the car park, coming to an abrupt stop in front of Joggy.

"I want a word with you," she said curtly,

"Certainly, what's the problem?"

"Not here, over there." She nodded to a vacant section of car park.

Joggy followed her.

She stopped and turned on Joggy. "I want to make this clear, Joggy Jackson. I had no relationship with John Canavan and I don't want you going around telling people that I had."

"I can assure you Missus Tyrell, I have not been going around, saying any such thing"

"You men are all the same -- two faced." Her face screwed up in contempt. She marched back to her house.

"What was that all about?" asked Alice.

"She doesn't trust me."

"Don't take it personally. It's not just you. Since her husband left her she doesn't trust any man."

They walked towards O Meara's. Then Alice stopped. "You go ahead I'll be there in a minute."

"You're wasting your time, Alice," said Joggy, when he saw the direction she was heading. "She's not going to talk."

Fifteen minutes later Alice rejoined her family.

"Well?" asked Joggy.

"You have to call in before we go home." She wore a grin of quite satisfaction.

"How'd you manage that?"

"Ah, you know, a little one to one girl talk never fails."

This time Joggy was invited in. He sat at the kitchen table.

"Will you have some tea?" Josie cradled a slightly battered aluminium teapot in her hands.

"Thanks, but no thanks. It'll only spoil me dinner."

Josie placed the teapot on the draining board, turned around and folded her arms.

A young girl stood shyly in the kitchen doorway. "Joggy, have you met my daughter, Hannah?"

"No I haven't. Hello Hannah." Hannah held her hands and smiled shyly at the floor.

"This is Mister Jackson. He's a friend. Say hello."

Hannah moved quickly and threw her arms around Joggy's neck and hugged him. "Thank you, Hannah, that's very kind of you," said Joggy, surprised by the sudden burst of love. She released him and moved back to the doorway.

"We have to talk now, Hannah. Can you go and play in your room," said her mother.

"By, by, Mister Jackson." Hannah waved a hand at Joggy.

"By, Hannah, nice to have met you."

"She's lovely, Missus Tyrell," said Joggy."

"Yes she is and please, call me Josie," She unfolded her arms and took a seat at the table opposite Joggy. She stared hard at him, still a little mistrustful. Finally she took the plunge. "I'm only talking to you because of Alice. She's a lovely woman and one of only a few around here that I have any time for. She says you can be trusted and are a man of your word. So I'm going to tell you of my connection with John Canavan."

She took a deep breath. "One morning I woke up and found that during the night an envelope had been pushed under my front door. It contained twenty pounds. There was no name, no address, nothing to indicate who it was from. It continued for several months. The amount of money in the envelope always varied between ten and twenty pounds and it always arrived late at night and always within the last few days of the month. I decided I had to find out who my generous benefactor was. So in the last few days of the following month, I stayed up. And on the second night of my vigil it happened. John got an awful fright when I opened the door."

"I'd say he did," said Joggy.

"I asked him what he wanted and why he was doing this. He said he felt sorry for us. Said it can't be easy raising a mentally handicapped child on my own. I told him if he was holding out hope of some form of repayment from me, he wasn't getting it. He said he wanted nothing, just to help and the fact that I had caught him wasn't going to change things. And so it continued for near on five years -- until his death. I never knew his reasons and maybe I never wanted to know. The money dug me and Hannah out of a hole."

"It can't have been easy raising Hannah on your own?"

"No it wasn't. Hannah needed special education and until the money turned up, I couldn't afford it. Now the only way I can say thanks, is to mark his anniversary by placing flowers on his grave."

Joggy now had the answer to one question -- what Canavan was doing with the money. But it now raised a bigger question. Why did he pick, Josie and Hannah? If he was simply being charitable to the poor of the village, why did he not split the money and give a little to each.

"Only one thing bothered me in all that time and that was where the money was coming from. I mean the man was on the dole. He couldn't afford to pay fifteen pounds a month off that. So where was he getting it?"

"I believe he was working on the side for a farmer -- a few days a week -- must have saved it from that."

Josie was not a fool. She knew as well as everyone else in the village that John Canavan had never worked a day since he returned from England. Josie read Joggy's face and suspected he was not telling the whole truth. She got the feeling he was protecting her and that the truth was darker than Joggy let on. She did not push it. Her mind was curious but in her heart she really did not want to know.

# CHAPTER 22

Danny did not go with his family to mass in Kilpatrick, instead he decided to go to twelve o' clock mass in Oldbridge. At eleven o' clock he stood on the road outside his house and waited for Tom Baker. Tom was the slowest driver he knew, never travelling above twenty miles per hour. He had one piece of the puzzle to clear up and Tom would provide that missing piece. It was quarter past eleven when he spotted Tom's off-white Renault 4 coming slowly down the hill on the opposite side of the grey stone railway bridge. He did not have to thumb, a smile and a wave was enough.

"Gawnee, gawnee, young Jackson, would ya ever stop growing or you'll shortly won't be able to fit in me car."

Danny laughed and adjusted the passenger seat for more leg room.

By the time they travelled the six miles to Oldbridge, manoeuvred their way around the town to the Church and found a parking spot -- it was ten to eleven. The conversation on the way in was of a general nature. Danny decided to keep his powder dry until the drive home. After mass he waited by the car while Tom bought a Sunday paper from Gorry's newsagents -- waiting also until they had made their way around the streets and out of town. Then he began. "When you and Luke were teenagers, Tom, what did ye do for fun?"

"Gawnee, Danny, that's a long time ago."

"It's not that long. I know there was no T.V. then."

"No, but we had other things. We had the football and of course the hurling. The occasional dance and… the pubs were a big thing … though I didn't drink myself."

"Hunting, did ya do much of that, like for Fox's and Badgers?"

"Gawnee no, that was never me. I left that to Luke. God rest his soul. Me, I preferred cars and messing around with engines."

"That's right I'd heard Luke was a demon for the rabbits: Travelling miles to hunt them."

"Sure why would he do that? Weren't there loads of warrens in our own fields: more rabbits than you could shake a stick at?"

"I must have heard it wrong so." Toms answer drew a smile of quiet satisfaction.

* * * *

Joggy was basically a loner, always uncomfortable in crowded settings. So whenever family life became claustrophobic and impinged too closely upon his universe -- he went walking. Short walks, long walks, road walks, field walks, forest walks, always to a designated seat. The duration of the walk depended on his mood. This evening it was a short field walk to a patch of green that nestled between the railway tracks on one side and the river on the other. His seat was an old trailer that sat in the corner, its rubber wheels flat and perished, its metal frame rusted and its wooden floor rotten and full of holes.

It was there that Danny found him. His mind was a torment since putting the pieces of the puzzle together. He had earlier been excited with the results of his own maiden investigative efforts but when the initial wave of euphoria had receded -- it left behind emptiness. A mourning process had begun. He felt a part of him was becoming void, as if a constant in his life was been removed. He found himself in the dark of his bedroom at night, close to tears. Disillusionment had turned to sorrow and finally to anger. Now more than ever, as he walked across the field to his father, he wanted the torment to end -- he wanted answers

* * * *

Joggy sat on the trailer resting on what was left of the backboard and holding a Sweet Afton cigarette in the base of his fingers. A hovering Hawk had his undivided attention. It had been hovering patiently for several minutes a good twenty feet above the grass. Below was possibly a Field Mouse or a baby rabbit: its life about to expire. A sudden movement at the end of the field broke his attention. It was Danny climbing the round barred Iron Gate. It was diagonally across from where he sat. The same Iron Gate he climbed to find Canavan's body. He looked back to the Hawk, but it was gone.

Danny's head was down. His long, lithe frame glided with an effortless grace through the lush green grass. It was for, Joggy, like watching his father as he made his way home in the evenings through the fields. His hand covered the bottom half of his face as he took a long slow thoughtful drag from his cigarette. He exhaled it slowly and evenly into the evening air.

"Something wrong?" Joggy asked, when Danny came within talking distance.

"No nothing's wrong. You don't mind if I sit with you, do you?"

"It's a free country." Joggy was amused at his son's formal politeness.

Danny stood on the perished wheel and with a hop and a twist sat up on the edge of the trailer. Rocking himself from side to side he inserted his hands, palms down, underneath his thighs. They sat in silence.

Joggy took another thoughtful drag on his cigarette and wondered what was on his sons mind. He recognised the signs. Danny only came looking for him when he wanted something -- usually it was something he did not want the others to hear.

Danny looked momentarily at his father and then slowly back to the grass below his feet. "Missus Roe told me to tell you to call."

"That's right I heard you brought the cakes up to her. You certainly caught your mother by surprise. Why'd you do that?"

"Curiosity." He glanced at his father and back to the grass again. "Mum said something about Missus Roe being Gran's best friend and since I wanted to know more about her and granddad -- she seemed the best person to ask."

"And did you?"

"Yes. She told me about Waller and what he did to granddad and how his barn burnt down the evening of granddad's funeral. She told me Luke Baker accidentally burnt it down. But I had a problem with that -- it made no sense. It felt all wrong." He looked steadily at his father. "Because I think you burnt it down. I know if I had been in that situation, I would have."

"I only wish that was true, Danny."

There's no point in denying it, dad. I know your secret," he said sharply. The anger he had tried to suppress and contain began to leak.

"And what would that be?"

"That you allowed another man go to prison for something you did. You burnt down the barn, dad, and you let Luke take the rap for it."

"You're wrong, Danny, it's....

"I'm not wrong," shouted Danny, his composure shattering. "All my life I've looked up to you, wanting to be just like you. And then I find out that all along you were a fraud, a fake. What sort of man lets his friend to go to jail for something he did. You disgust me." He jumped down of the trailer.

Danny's words stung like a slap in the face. "You've got it all wrong, Danny."

"No I haven't. All our lives you've taught us to be honest and truthful. What a hypocrite you are." Danny turned and walked hurriedly away.

"You think you've got all the answers, don't you?" Joggy shouted. His own anger rising. He stood up on the frame of the trailer.

"Yes I have, and none of them came from you." Danny shouted back over his shoulder.

"Then answer me this. If I let Luke take the rap for me, why then did we remain friends?"

Danny's gallop came to a halt. He suddenly realised he had not thought of that and for the first time in days a doubt descended upon his conclusions. He turned around. "So why did he remain friends with you?"

"You're so fucking smart, you figure it out."

Danny was shocked. His dad had never sworn at him before. And for the first time he felt guilty. He heard the hurt in his dad's voice. He had gone about it the wrong way. Now he cursed himself and wished he had waited and discussed it with Victoria. But impatience had got the better of him. He could not wait until she came back from her weekend up north with her parents. He was so sure he had all the answers. He turned and walked away -- his young broad shoulders slumped in embarrassment and worry.

Several minutes later, Joggy, followed Danny from the field. After reaching the roadside he looked down the hill and even though his son was not visible, he was sure he was on the second half of the rising road but the stone bridge obscured his view. Joggy's anger still simmered. Fearing his own reaction if he saw his son again and the consequences that would ensue -- he was unprepared to go home just yet. He turned right.

He knocked on the door. "Hello, Nellie?" he called out as he opened it.

"Joggy," said Nellie, with a smile in her voice. "It's about time you called in to see your old Godmother."

Joggy gave her a kiss on the cheek and then sat on the same chair Danny had.

"I'm sorry I haven't been around lately. This Canavan thing is keeping me busy."

"How's that going for ya?"

"Ah you know lots of questions -- and not many answers."

Nellie studied his face in the glow of the flames from the turf fire. "Is something wrong, you look worried?"

"No, no, I'm fine, everything's fine."

"Your face is contradicting you."

Nellie sat up and reached out for Joggy's hands.

Joggy, pulled his hands out of her reach. "You know I don't believe in that stuff."

"I know you don't, but humour me anyway." Her smile was soft and warm and her hands were open waiting for his. Nellie said nothing more.

Joggy could feel his resolve weakening. After his mother's death when he didn't want to be held, Nellie had the uncanny knack of turning up at his most vulnerable moments with her beguiling smile and her open arms. And as much as he tried to resist, he always failed. Her arms had the power of magnets, drawing him into her: he felt safe there. "It won't do you any good. You won't learn anything from me."

"Let me be the judge of that."

Reluctantly, he placed his hands in hers.

She closed her eyes and began swaying gently from side to side. He felt the tingling heat first in his fingers. Then it began to move, thousands of heated pin pricks all marching forward in unison like soldiers on parade across his palms to his wrists and up his arms. Beneath her eyelids her eyes moved about at an alarming rate as if experiencing a nightmare. Joggy watched and was mesmerized. And even though he expected her eyes to open at any moment, it still gave him a start when they did.

She opened her hands and released him and then sank slowly back into her armchair. Several seconds of silence followed, which to Joggy, seemed longer "You've still not let go." Nellie said eventually

"Yes I have."

"Don't lie to me, Joggy. You know I hate being lied to."

"I'm sorry Nellie, but it's too late now."

"You've never shed one tear for your dad. Don't you think he deserved your tears -- your grief?"

"Of course he does, but too much time has gone by."

"Time doesn't matter. The prison of anger you've built around your grief is still there and one of these days you are going to have to break it down and set it free."

Joggy leaned forward, picked up a sod of turf and tossed it onto the fire. "I believe you were talking to Danny," he said changing the subject.

"A fine young man, he's the spitting image of your father."

"What'd you talk about?" he asked sheepishly.

"I didn't tell him anything other than what you should have told him -- his family history -- if that's what you want to know. I could have told him the truth but, I figured it wasn't my place."

"Thanks."

"Is that what ye fought about?"

Joggy, shot her a surprised glance. "He got the wrong end of the stick and," he looked back at the fire, "I sort of lost it with him." His words petered out.

"Nothing that can't be mended, I'm sure."

"I hope so." Joggy glanced at his watch. "It's getting late I'd better be heading home."

Nellie grasped one of Joggy's hands again. "Please, be careful," she said gravely. "I know you don't believe in my gift. But I've seen danger in your future and it comes from the sky. I saw something silvery with the sun gleaming of it, coming down fast from above. After that came darkness. Please, heed my warning, Joggy, don't turn your back on anyone you don't trust."

"Don't you be worrying about me, Nellie." He patted the back of her hand. "I never do. I'll be fine. Would you like me to make you a cup of tea before I go?"

"That would be lovely and if you don't mind, a couple of slices of Alice's currant cake"

# Chapter 23

Mc Neill turned up again at Heatherville House on Wednesday. It was close to one o' clock. The day was cloudy but dry and no rain was forecast. Joggy toiled away in the burgeoning garden, oblivious of McNeill's watchful gaze. Sunday's verbal spat had woken McNeill up, making him recognise his mistakes. Guile and emotional blackmail or -- emotional persuasion -- as McNeill like to refer to it, were the corner stone's of his investigative technique. Locating the soft or sore spot of his intended target and pressing it until he or she yielded the required information. Needless to say this did not make him popular with the local community. He had made the mistake of involving the local gossip, Spit Sweeny, in his petty squabble with Joggy. The information he had persuaded Spit to part with was rudimentary and was open to all kinds of interpretation. None of which he could use against Joggy. He had lost his focus and allowed his concentration to shift, letting Joggy Jackson's principles and motives cloud his judgment. He needed to get back on track. His initial perception of Joggy had also changed. The disdain he had originally held him in at the outset -- thinking he was dealing with an inferior -- someone he could exploit and use to achieve his own goals -- had now evolved into a grudging respect.

This time he did not hide in the internal shadows of the stone shed, Instead he made himself useful by setting up the foldaway card table and two chairs. When Joggy walked in, his tea was poured out and McNeill was sitting at one side of the table, safely out of view of the house.

"I didn't expect to see you so soon," he said, taking a seat.

"Nor did I, but I've done a bit of thinking since we last met and I may have let personal motives and feelings get in the way of the real reason we're doing this."

"Is that an apology?" Joggy asked more in jest than hope as he opened his biscuit tin lunch box and un-wrapped his corn beef sandwiches.

"No, just an explanation."

"Ok, explanation accepted. Have a sandwich."

"No thanks. I'd prefer if we got down to business."

"Fair enough, what do you want?"

"We need to do a recap of where we are in this investigation." He pulled out his pipe and began filling it with Plug tobacco. "To date, what do we know? Have we shed any doubt on Luke Baker's conviction?"

"Well we know we're looking for a man," said Joggy. "Canavan's skull was crushed with one blow and no woman that I know of anyway, is capable of that. But having said that… I wouldn't rule out a woman accomplice. We also now know that Luke was not the only one with a motive. There are at least three others. Two of them were been blackmailed and they were both in the area at the time. Rick Worrel and Jenny Roache for one and let's hope they've eloped and not escaped. The other, who'll remain nameless for the moment, I've already been to see and got nowhere. But I have a plan in mind that may unlock that particular secret."

Joggy expected some form of protest and was surprised when he got none. McNeill was calmness personified. "And who's the third suspect?"

"Fred Winter."

"Yeah, but he had no reason to kill him. They barely knew one another."

"That may be so. But I wouldn't rule him out of the equation just yet. He was after all the last person to see Canavan alive."

"You're beginning to think more like a cop every day."

Joggy ignored the flattering remark. He took a bite from his sandwich and a mouthful of tea and instead contemplated whether he should tell McNeill about Josie Tyrell. He figured he could not hold back everything. He had to give McNeill something to chew on. "I'm going to tell you some confidential information and I need your word that what I'm about to tell you will remain private and between us only."

"Go on." McNeill sighed. "You have my word."

"Josie Tyrell and in particular her daughter Hannah were the un-witting beneficiary's of Canavan's blackmail money."

McNeill sat straight up in his chair. His lips moved silently until finding the word he wanted to say. "Why?"

"Josie doesn't know why. He used to slide a brown envelope with between ten and twenty pound in it under the door at the end of every month. She eventually caught him. But he wouldn't give her a clear reason as to why he was doing it. He told her that even though she had caught him, he would continue doing it and he did, for close on five years. She's as much in the dark about it as we are."

The next few minutes were spent in silence. Joggy ate his sandwiches and drank tea while McNeill sat deep in thought, puffing on his pipe and staring at what he could see of the garden. "Guilt." He spoke out of the corner of his mouth, the pipe clenched firmly between his teeth.

"Guilt?"

"Yes guilt. I've seen it before. Someone who is not giving or charitable goes against type and suddenly starts to make donations to all sorts of things. I'd safely say that Canavan, was making reparation for something in his past."

"Maybe he felt bad about blackmailing people." Joggy drained another mouthful of tea.

"I doubt it. If he did he would have just stopped. No, it's something else."

Joggy stopped chewing as the thought hit him. "You know, if I remember correctly, the starting date in Canavan's, notebook was around the time Josie Tyrell began receiving the money."

"Right." McNeill, rubbed his hands together. "That gives us a time line. Whatever he felt guilty about happened in the preceding years. That gives me something to work on. What do you know of his past?"

"His father died when he was about eighteen. He fecked off to England when he was twenty-four. Ten years later he was back for his mother's funeral and stayed. To my knowledge he never worked."

"Why did he go to England?"

"To work I suppose."

"Yeah, but wouldn't you think that if someone was working for ten years in England, when he came home, would look for a job here?"

"Maybe, but then again he didn't need a lot. He wasn't married and he owned his own home. So the dole was probably enough to sustain him."

McNeill rose out of his chair. "Still, the clue is in his past and I'm going to find it. I'll be in touch shortly. Here seems a good safe spot to meet. Good luck with the other blackmail victim."

He disappeared out the back door of the stone shed.

* * * *

Joggy looked at his watch; it was eleven o' clock. It was turning out to be the perfect day to put his master-plan into operation. The incessant rain meant he could not work and that gave him some comfort. Under normal circumstances, he would not have been happy taking time off to go visit Edwin Barrett. He drove out of Dr Kelly's and turned for Kilpatrick. He knew as he passed Kilpatrick national school that Kevin Barrett always had his lunch there and would remain till after three. Time was important. The more time he had with Edwin, the better his chances were of discovering the secret.

Joggy had another stroke of luck when he reached Barrett's wooden gate -- it was open. Normally it was closed. Obviously because it was raining so hard, Kevin, after opening it that morning had decided to leave it open rather than risk getting soaked again. He pulled up in front of the house and cut the engine. Joggy sat back in the seat, took a couple of slow deep breaths and before his courage ran out, jumped from the car, moved swiftly to the front door and knocked.

"Joggy, how delightful to see you." Edwin, was dressed in paint a spattered white shirt. A pair of Canary yellow braces supported an equally spattered black trousers cut off just below the knees and on his feet, a pair of tatty open-toed brown leather sandals -- displaying painted toenails. "Excuse my appearance," he said. He stood aside to allow Joggy to enter. "I really wasn't expecting anyone to call."

"Ah, your fine Edwin, sure were both in working clothes."

"Yes, but yours are crisp and clean."

"That may be so, but you have the advantage of bright red toe nails."

"You're such a tease, Joggy. What are you here for?"

"To look at your paintings."

"You're interested in buying?"

"Hopefully. Its Alice's birthday shortly and I've been wracking my brain thinking of what to buy her. I wanted to get something completely different, something other than perfume, clothes vouchers, or nightwear and then you popped into my head."

"Mmm, I like that thought. I love a man with sensitivity, there's so few of them in the straight world."

Joggy gave a nervous half smile.

Edwin, noted the redness rising in Joggy's cheeks. "I'm sorry, I've embarrassed you. Maybe we should look at some paintings. Come let me show you into my Garrett," He opened the first door on the right in the hallway.

Edwin's "Garrett" was a ten- by- twelve- foot room littered with the discarded bric- a- brac of failed art -- canvases, some painted on both sides, empty paint cans their lids detached and among the debris, empty vodka bottles. A dirty green-formica topped table sat next to the easel in front of the only window -- strewn with the same bric- a- brac that was on the floor.

"The chaos of creativity." Edwin, hoped it was enough to explain the mess.

"Nothing imaginative was ever created out of an orderly mind.
"

"Perceptive as well as sensitive, you are surprising me."

"My understanding of a Garrett, Edwin… is an attic room?"

"Yes I know." His eyebrows lifted sharply, being pleasantly surprised that Joggy knew the meaning of the word. "But Garrett sounds so much more romantic, more exotic, than spare room. Don't you think?"

"Who am I to argue with your imagination?"

"Let me show you what I'm painting." Edwin said excitedly, as he led Joggy across the room, picking their steps between discarded paint tins, brushes and torn canvases. They stepped through a small space between the table on the left and the easel on the right. Sitting on the windowsill was a half empty bottle of scotch. "I like to paint in the morning when the rising light of the east is at its freshest."

He stood in front of Edwin's newest masterpiece -- a black canvas across which two uneven horizontal brush strokes had been painted: one orange, one red. The orange one had been allowed to bleed into the red one.

"I know it's not quiet finished yet, but what do you think?"

Edwin's breath reeked of alcohol. "What exactly will it be when you're finished with it?"

"It'll be whatever you or your wife wants it to be. That's the beauty of expressionism."

"Well I can't see my wife imagining a landscape or a pot of flowers in it. Have you any others? Finished ones I mean."

"Of course I have."

Edwin began sifting through a small pile of framed canvases that were standing on the bare concrete floor stacked against one wall. He sorted out five, cleared a space and laid them on the floor.

Joggy came from the front of the easel and stood close to Edwin. Four of the paintings were similar to the one on the easel -- vibrant colourful brush strokes of red, yellow and blue on neutral backgrounds. The fifth one was black.

"Why are you showing me that, it's not finished?"

"My paintings reflect my moods and feelings. People all over the world express how they feel in different ways, they shout, they cry, they hug and they love." Edwin turned. Joggy, could feel his eyes scrutinising him. "What do you think I'm trying to say here," he asked softly, his eyes never leaving Joggy's face.

Joggy gave Edwin a slight smile. "That you're depressed?" he joked.

"Close but no lollipop. I had been thinking on the meaning of death and what awaits us when we die."

"I don't know about you, Edwin," said Joggy jokingly, "but I'm going to be bitterly disappointed if I don't see a bit more light at the end of my tunnel."

Edwin took umbrage and began gathering up his paintings. "You're not really serious about buying a painting, Joggy, are you? What are you really here for?"

"Well actually I would like to buy a painting from you. Alice's birthday is coming up shortly. And she is very fond of your man Van Goff and that vase of yellow flowers he painted. If you could paint something on a similar line, I'd definitely buy it from you."

"It's pronounced Van Gogh," he said in exasperation, "and the painting is called "Sunflowers." It is one of the most famous paintings in the world."

"Oh, good, good, so you know what I'm talking then. By the way could you make them daffodils instead?"

"Are you taking the piss?" Edwin spluttered.

"No, no, I'm not. It's just that daffodils are her favourite flowers. I'll give you ten pounds to paint it."

Edwin's attitude suddenly brightened. "Really, ten pounds?"

Joggy knew his paintings did not sell, so ten pounds was a lot of money. It would keep him in paint and scotch for some considerable time.

"But I want something else as well."

"Name it," said Edwin, suddenly feeling accommodating.

"What has the quote - the love that dare not speak its name - got to do with Ann Dwyer and your brother?"

"Now we have it, this is what you're really after?"

"Yes, but I also want the painting. Tell me the truth and we will have a deal."

"I can't betray Kevin."

"I understand that Edwin, but let me try and allay your fears here. Think of me as a priest. If the information you give me proves to have nothing to do with John Canavan's death, then what you tell me will go no further. I will not even tell my wife."

"I don't know. How do I know I can trust you?"

"Ask anybody. They will all tell you, I'm not a gossipmonger."

Edwin seemed on the verge of folding but then seemed to find a second wind. "No, no, no, I can't. I just can't."

"Tell me Edwin, do you really think the parish priest, the school council and the parents would continue to employ Kevin to run their school if they somehow found out he was gay?"

Edwin looked horrified at Joggy. He was stunned into silence as the ramifications of everybody finding out seared through his brain. Kevin's beloved job would be gone and once the word was out, no one would employ him as a teacher again. They would have to move, but where to?

As Joggy waited on Edwin's answer, an observation from the last time he was at the house occurred to him. "The other evening," said Joggy, "I walked around this house looking for ye and noticed only one bed. Why is that?"

Edwin suddenly felt the crushing weight of helplessness bear down on his shoulders. He sat back heavily onto the windowsill, knocking over the half empty vodka bottle. It settled on its side. Drops of vodka began seeping out of the unfastened cap onto the floor. Edwin ignored it. He looked down at his hands; one clasped tightly to the other and knew he had no choice. "Kevin and I are lovers." He said it so softly, Joggy almost missed it.

"But you're brothers," Joggy exclaimed.

Edwin gave a little chuckle. "We're not brothers either. Our name is Barrett but we're not related. It's... just a happy coincidence."

"But why are ye telling everyone that you're brothers?"

"It makes life easier. Gay prejudice abounds and if they ever found out, they'd probably hang him from the nearest tree."

"So how did Canavan find out about ye?"

"He didn't. It wasn't Kevin he saw me fellating. It was someone else."

"Filleting... with a knife?"

"No, fellating. You know, a blow job, oral sex? My God, you are so, naive."

"I suppose I am. I just never heard it called that before. That someone else you were, fellating, wouldn't be Marcus Dwyer by any chance, would it?" Joggy was making an educated guess. He had two choices. There were only two people whom Ann Dwyer would pay hush money for -- the parish priest or her only son. Her husband was dead. Considering the parish priest was a man in his late seventies -- Marcus Dwyer seemed a more reasonable bet.

"Yes, Kevin and Ann paid him with one stipulation -- that our names were not to be written down anywhere."

"Edwin, I know it took courage to tell me all this, so I am assuring you again, I will not breath a word of what you just told me, that is unless I find out that you and Kevin had something to do with Canavan's death."

"You won't."

Edwin saw Joggy to the door. "By the way, I still want that painting. When can I hope to pick it up?"

"Give me two weeks." He closed the door.

# CHAPTER 24

Twelve days had passed since Danny last saw Victoria. He had not realised how much he needed her until she was not there. She had become like a drug to him. She excited him, challenged him, frightened him, she was wild to his calm. She had become his high, his weekend fix and the withdrawal symptoms had been painful. She was like no other he had known.

On Saturday morning he was in buoyant mood as he approached the backdoor of Fred Winters farmhouse. He was going to see Victoria. They locked eyes through the kitchen window. He gave her his best smile. Victoria looked impassively at him, as if she did not know him. She opened the back door.

"Oh Danny hi, I need".….said Victoria, in a flat unemotional voice, nodding in the direction of the kitchen to indicate Fred was still there, while at the same time giving Danny the kitchen's weekend's potato and vegetable needs. Twenty minutes later he returned with the required produce and met Fred in the farmyard. He gave Danny his orders for the day, climbed into his car and drove out of the yard. Danny's happiness shifted up a gear. With Fred temporarily out of the picture, he anticipated his first kiss in almost two weeks.

Victoria met him at the back door. She took the produce from him said, "Thanks." and closed the door.

For several seconds he stood there, stunned. First he thought she was just playing games with him. But the door did not open again. It was only when he heard water from the kitchen sink flowing down the waste pipe and into the shore, did he move. Through the kitchen window he could see her blonde head bent; her eyes down intent upon her work. He wanted to shout out her name, but was afraid he would be overheard. Reluctantly, he moved away to carry out Fred's instructions.

* * * *

On that same Saturday morning, Joggy with the daily paper spread across the steering wheel of his Morris Traveller, sat contented, close to the main entrance, in the supermarket car park. Alice was in doing the weekly shopping. A light drizzle was falling. The sport pages occupied his mind and in particular, a write- up on the hopes of his beloved county team, Offaly. They had won the All-Ireland football title for the previous two years and the sports Journalist's were speculating on their chances of a hat-trick.

The passenger door opened.

"That was quick," he said. Not lifting his eyes from the article.

"If anyone's quick, you are," said Kevin Barrett, as he slipped onto the passenger seat and closed the door.

"What do you want?" Joggy fought back the fear that what happened to Canavan was about to happen to him. Casually he pushed down the driver door lock with his elbow. He figured if this was a set-up at least Edwin was not going to be able to open the drivers-side and drag him out. Whatever danger came from within, he felt he could handle.

"Two of your children have passed through my classroom, and they have both been in the top five per cent," said Kevin, "and now I know why."

"I said... what do you want?"

Kevin did not answer directly, instead he continued on in the same vein. "Me and you, Joggy are in many ways similar. Under trying circumstances we have both carved out successful careers for ourselves: You, because of the loss of your parents at such a tender age and me, because of my sexuality."

"Don't be ridiculous, you had an education, a head start."

"Education has very little to do with my point, Joggy. You built a career and a reputation from hard work. Your clients are loyal, they trust you. That didn't happen overnight. No one questions your integrity or your ability to do the job. Likewise, I have worked hard to build trust in the people I work for and whom I work with. I have earned the respect of the parents, the pupils and my fellow teachers. My reputation is untarnished."

"You can't compare yourself to me," said Joggy, incredulously. "I'm not the one that's gay. I don't have sexual fantasies about boys."

"I'm not a fucking paedophile," Kevin shouted indignantly. "I've no sexual interest in children. I'm a gay man whose only sexual interest is in other gay men. By your yardstick I should be chasing young boys around the classroom and by the same yardstick heterosexual male teachers should be chasing young girls. But it doesn't happen, does it, why, because everyone sticks to their own."

"Alright, alright, I've got your point. Now what do you want?"

"What are you going to do with the information?"

"I don't know yet. I might give it to McNeill, the school council or maybe the other teachers and let them make the decision."

"You can't do that. Joggy, I'll be destroyed. I'll never be able to teach again."

"Yeah, and if something does happen, I'll have to live with the consequences of knowing and not doing anything about it."

"You have my solemn word, Joggy, nothing, will ever happen."

"Well that's just it, isn't it? Your word's been stretched to breaking point these days. The other day you gave me your word that Canavan, blackmailing you had nothing to do with his death, when all along you have the strongest motive of anyone to see him dead. You and Edwin probably saw him going into Luke's yard, followed him and whacked him. It was a simple matter then of lifting him into the car boot before tossing him over the bridge."

"That's a load of shite and you know it."

"That's just it, I don't know it. I know fucking nothing. Everyone is ducking and diving and giving me their word that they didn't do it. Well one of you has to have done it."

"Well what the fuck do you expect; you're nosing around in their dirty laundry. You don't expect them to come right out and tell you, do you?"

Joggy knew he was right but was not willing to say so. No one was going to reveal their innermost secrets, just because it was a good cause and you asked nicely. He had made the mistake of allowing his frustration to speak. It had sounded childish and naïve and now he was embarrassed. It was like he had let his family down, dropping them from the top five per cent to the bottom five per cent. "Get out. Go home."

"What are you going to do?" Barrett opened the passenger door.

"When I know, you'll know."

Kevin closed the door. In anger, Joggy crumpled the newspaper into an un-tidy ball and threw it as hard as he could into the back seat.

\* \* \* \*

Alice sensed almost immediately something was wrong. Not a word was said as they packed the back of the car with groceries. No word was spoken as they drove out of the car park and headed for home. If the silence set off tinkling bells, noticing that days newspaper crumpled up on the back seat, set them tolling.

She said nothing. She would wait till the children had gone to bed before broaching the subject.

\* \* \* \*

Ever since they had got together, they had secretively met twice a week -- Saturday and Sunday evenings. If it was dry, it was the Hazel-wood and if it was damp the old hay shed at the far end of Fred's yard -- In both they were well out of sight. Danny lived more in hope than expectation, as he made his way Saturday evening across the fields to the Hazel-wood. After the morning's events he was unsure whether Victoria would even turn up. He walked deep into the wood to the rendezvous point. Twenty yards short he stopped. Victoria was there by the fallen elm tree, walking in circles and by the trampled state of the bluebells and ferns had been there a while. She stopped when she saw him. They both looked at one another. A stand-off of confused minds had begun. Danny eventually moved forward. He feared the worst. He stood in front of her. Her breathing was short and sharp as if she had been running and her eyes looked at him with an indifference he could not fathom.

"Did ya miss me?" He asked in jest, forcing a nervous smile to his lips.

She slapped him across the left cheek, just hard enough to make it sting.

"I'll take that as a yes." He gave the wounded cheek a rub.

Again she slapped him, this time on the on the right cheek. He raised his hands to defend himself against further blows but Victoria turned from him.

"This was not supposed to happen. This was not supposed to happen." She repeated the same words over and over, like a mantra, as she continued walking in circles around the trampled bluebells and ferns. She suddenly stopped in front of a now totally bewildered Danny. "Fuck you -- this was not supposed to happen."

She reached out, pulled Danny towards her and kissed him, giving him the most passionate kiss he had ever received. Several seconds later, the surprise had dissipated enough for Danny to start thinking clearly again.

"What the fuck's going on?" He pushed her away from him. "One minute you're slapping me the next you're kissing me."

"You were supposed to be someone I could leave behind." Tears started rolling down her cheeks. "You were to be fun, someone to pass the time with, someone I could say goodbye to and not look back. I wasn't supposed to feel this way. I didn't want to feel this way again. At the end of the summer I've to go home and leave you behind," she said, as tears filled her eyes, "and I'll never see you again."

"You don't know that."

"Yes I do," she shouted. "You'll go your way and I'll go mine and it'll be like losing my best friend again."

Danny could not have loved her any more than he did at that moment. She had finally shown her soft side. She looked so beautiful and so vulnerable. "If it's any consolation…" He moved forward and engulfed her in his arms. "I'll be feeling the same way." He leaned back and held Victoria's tearful face between his hands. His thumbs gently wiped her tears away. "I'm in love with you too."

They walked and talked and when the urge overtook them, which was often, they kissed. Danny eventually got around to telling Victoria of his investigative pursuits and its disastrous consequences.

"Have you spoken to your father since?"

"No, I've been avoiding him. I don't know what to say to him."

"Sorry, is the mandatory response."

"I know, but it seems too small… too trivial. The apology needs to be more, bigger. I need to do something to get back in his good graces."

"Yeah, maybe, but I still think sorry will do the trick."

The route they took around the inner circumference of the Hazel-Wood brought them back to the fallen elm tree. They sat down.

"Was your weekend any less dramatic than mine?" Danny looped his arm around Victoria's slender waste.

"Well, I didn't have a blazing row with any of my parents, so I suppose by that standard the weekend was grand." Victoria paused and looked at Danny. Her face became thoughtful and dark. "Daddy did ask me to do something for him though."
She slipped her hand into her front denim jean pocket and produced a door key.
She displayed it in the palm of her hand. "I went for a walk with him and he gave me this."

Danny picked it up.

"You're holding the key to Fred's bedroom door. My father wants me to search it."

"How'd your father get it?"

"I don't know, he wouldn't tell me. Said it was better I didn't know."

"Why does he want it searched? I thought they were friends."

"They are, but it seems he wants to be sure of Fred's allegiance."

"His allegiance?"

"Maybe I should explain it the way my father explained it to me. As you know he recently became the Grand Master of his local Orange Lodge. It's a highly respected and sensitive position and he wants to be certain that his closest friend is above any and all suspicion. And that's where the problem is. Fred is a member of a secretive arm of the orange order called the Royal Black Perceptory. With all the sectarian killing that's been going on, he wants to be sure that Fred's hands are clean."

"Wow. What are you suppose to be looking for?"

"I've to take notes of anything that's out of the ordinary. "

"So when are we doing it?"

"I haven't made up my mind yet. And if I do it, I will be doing it alone."

"Ah come on, you can't do that."

"I can and I will. If Fred came back when we were searching his room, I'd have to get us both out of the room and you out of the house. It'd be too dangerous."

"No it won't, sure he'll be well and truly gone before we start searching. Come on Victoria," he pleaded. He slipped his long fingers inside the belt of her jeans, inside the elastic band of her knickers and inside her. "You know his room will only give you the creeps if I'm not there."

She groaned with pleasure. "All right, all right," she conceded. Her eyes now closed.   She leaned her head back and he covered her warm soft lips with his.

* * * *

The night was pleasant, so they sat on the front door step, cups of tea in hand, the night lights of Oldbridge glowing in the distance.

"You want to talk about it," Alice asked.

He had anticipated the question. It was only a matter of when. Keeping secrets from, Alice, was the one thing he was lousy at, also, the Barrett brothers had created a moral dilemma for him and he badly needed her opinion. "Do you remember what, Spit, said to us a few weeks back about secrets?"

"No."

"He said that secrets were like ugly children hidden in the dark... and until I started this thing I had no idea how many of them were hiding in Kilpatrick."

"You uncovered another secret?"

"I discovered the meaning of -The love that dare not speak its name - Knowing that Alice would never breath a word, he explained what had transpired, but left out the painting. He also explained what had happened in the car. "Now I don't know what to do. Should I take his word and hope nothing happens or should I tell somebody. Knowing what I know, I couldn't live with myself if something happened to one of the children. What do you think I should do?"

"You should talk to someone who would be knowledgeable about these things. Why don't you have a word with Doctor Kelly? You have an appointment coming up shortly."

# CHAPTER 25

The opportunity to search Fred Winter's bedroom took two weeks to arrive and it came by post. The letter addressed to all Macra Na Ferma delegates lay open, hidden under a pile of other papers on Fred's desk. It informed him of the venue, which was Stuarts Hotel in Clonmel, County Tipperary and the day was Saturday. The date on the letter was three weeks old. By nature, Fred was not into hoarding and had made a habit of destroying useless correspondence. Holding on to that particular letter, for Victoria, meant only one thing -- he would be attending. He was going and up to now had not said a word and it angered her. She was also certain she knew his reason -- by leaving it till the last minute he was preventing her from making any plans of her own.

It was after four when Fred arrived up from the yard. He rinsed his Wellingtons under an outside tap before taking them off and parking them against the scullery wall.

"Make us a ham sandwich and a mug of tea, Victoria? I'm going to have a wash and I'll be down in twenty minutes."

It suddenly dawned on her that Fred was travelling to Clonmel, that evening, obviously wanting to avoid the long one-day double trip. She made the ham sandwich, boiled the kettle and would wait until his feet were on the stairs again, before she made tea. While she waited, she debated the pro's and con's of helping her father. She wanted no part in his political scheme's -- she had told him that -- made it clear. He told her he understood her stance, that he was proud of her, that he loved her. He then slipped the key into her hand. Told her there was no pressure, he would stand by whatever decision she would make. The only reason, Victoria considered it at all, was because she loved him and he had never asked anything of her before.

The sudden bang of Fred's bedroom door closing crashed through her thoughts. She made the tea and poured two cups. Fred had his sitting at the end of the kitchen table while Victoria had hers leaning back against the towel rail of the Aga cooker. Fred had showered and changed into fresh clean clothes -- white shirt, brown cords and brown leather shoes -- his holdall was visible through the banister rails -- perched on the bottom step of the staircase.

"Going somewhere?" she asked, nonchalantly.

"Clonmel--Farmer's conference tomorrow. If I could get out of it I would. I'm representing the local boys. Unfortunately, someone else was to do it, but had to pull out at the last minute."

Victoria smiled at the lie. "I'm sure you'll do a great job."

"Thanks. I'm sorry I have to leave you alone on such short notice."

"Don't worry about me; I'm never alone when I have T. V. and a glass of brandy."

"They'll be no more brandy for you young lady," he said in a chastising manner.

"I didn't replace the last bottle. I have a responsibility to your father to keep you safe you know. I won't have it said that you turned into an alcoholic while you were here."

There and then she decided to search his room. "Keep your hair on, I was only teasing."

"Never- the- less, no more alcohol, you hear?"

"Loud and clear."

Message delivered, duty done, Fred picked up his hold-all. Earlier in the day he had washed the Wolseley and parked it in front of the house. He tossed his hold-all onto the front passenger seat, said goodbye and within seconds was gone, leaving a thinning cloud of gravel dust behind him.

A few minutes later, Victoria caught sight of Danny and Tomato Flynn coming up the yard. Danny had a half-day from school. She rushed to the back door.

"Danny," she called. "I need you to do a small job for me."

Tomato and Danny parted ways. Tomato headed home.

"He's gone," she whispered.

Danny wrinkled his brow.

"Don't look so stupid. Fred's gone to Clonmel, won't be back till tomorrow."

"How long is he gone?"

"About twenty minutes."

"Great, let's search his room."

"Not with those boots you're not. Take them off and leave them in the turf box. If anyone comes around the back, they won't see them."

He closed the lid and they both headed for Fred's bedroom. The key was a perfect copy. Victoria stopped in the doorway and took in the room. It was not very big. The window overlooking the back yard was directly in front of her. To her right was a teak wardrobe. The double-doors were solid on the bottom and slatted on top. On the floor was a well worn light blue carpet. Danny brushed passed her.

"Holy fuck." His jaw dropped in awe as he came and stood in front of Fred's bed. "Get a load of this, will ya. It's the sort of thing you'd see on T. V when some dignitary has died and they've laid him out in state."

An orange duvet, quartered by a thick black line covered the double bed and on the wall between two flags hanging at ease, flanking the bed -- the British flag on the right and the Ulster flag on the left -- was a large portrait of Queen Elizabeth.

In a corner beyond the bed was a headless mannequin, dressed in a purple shirt. Crisscrossing its chest were two sashes, one black and one orange.

Directly in front of the bed was a dressing table with one full mirror at the back. In a line underneath it were four small drawers. Victoria moved towards the dressing table. The room sent all the wrong messages to her brain -- she wanted to run out, lock the place and never go back again.

"Let's christen Fred's bed." Danny grabbed her and hauled her roughly onto it. "I bet it's a virgin."

"Danny, stop," she shrieked, and pushed him off her. She pushed so hard he fell off the bed. "I want nothing to do with this room. I just want to search it and get the hell out of here." She took out a small pocket notebook and began documenting everything she saw, while a chastened Danny smoothed out the imperfections on the bedcover. Finished, she slipped the note book into the rear pocket of her jeans.

"What's that?" said Victoria, standing as rigid as the mannequin, her hand still on the notebook. They listened intently.

"I think it's a car," said Danny. "Someone's coming down the driveway."

Alarmed, they rushed to the rear window, just in time to see Fred's Wolseley come to an abrupt halt. He jumped out.

"Shit." Victoria ran for the door. "Stay here and hide." She pulled the door closed and before Danny could react -- had locked it. He looked franticly about the room -- there were not many obvious places for a six foot two inch man to hide.

Victoria made her way as calmly as possible down the stairs. She met Fred in the kitchen, scurrying about like a headless chicken.

"What's wrong? I thought you'd be halfway to Clonmel by now."

"I should be." He stopped long enough to address her. "I pulled in to get petrol and realised I'd left my wallet behind. Did you see it?"

"No, I didn't. When was the last time you had it?"

"Yesterday evening in Oldbridge."

"What were you wearing?"

"My tweed jacket." He suddenly took off down the hall and up the stairs, taking them two at a time. He unlocked his bedroom door, made his way to the wardrobe and opened the first door. If he looked down he would have seen Danny's size twelve feet. In the split second of time he had to hide, it was the only obvious place. The bed was too low to the ground for him to climb under. In his ears, his heart was beating like a war drum. Drops of nervous perspiration ran down his forehead and into his eyes. They stung. He desperately wanted to rub them but couldn't move. He had pulled the clothes around him as best as he could and had curled up to make himself as small as possible, but Danny's gangling frame took up a lot of space. He could see Fred clearly through the spaces between the clothes.

He was sure Fred would hear his thumping heart, his short shallow breathing or his feet: he had to, how could he not? Downstairs, Victoria chewed her nails -- waiting for the uproar.

Fred was in a hurry. He had already lost valuable time coming back. His focus was on the tweed jacket, nothing else came into his range of vision. Wallet found, he slammed the wardrobe door closed. Through the slats, Danny watched him leave then Fred suddenly stopped, leaned down and picked something of the floor. He gave it a cursory glance and shoved it into his pocket. He locked the door. Within seconds, he was on his way again. Danny still did not move. The key was in the lock again. "Danny?" Victoria, stuck her head around the door.

Danny rolled out of the wardrobe, drained of all colour.

* * * *

The next morning, Victoria, rang her father. She read him her list of documented items.

"Thank you," he said. "I really appreciate what you've done. I know this wasn't easy for you."

"I only did it because I love you, Daddy."

"I love you too. Sweetheart, I'm looking down the list you just gave me. There are two items on it. One is a pearl-handled Swiss pocket knife and the other is a gold cigarette lighter. Do you remember seeing any initials on them?"

"No, but then I didn't lift them out of the drawer. Why, is that important?"

"It could be. Do you think you could run up and check them for me, please?"

"Ah Daddy, I've already been there. I was hoping I'd never have to see his room again."

"I wouldn't ask, sweetheart, only it's important. It'll only take a second. I'll hold on for you."

Victoria gave a heavy sigh. She dropped the receiver and ran up the stairs. Within seconds she was back. "The Swiss pocket knife has the initials, B. B.T, and the cigarette lighter has an inscription that reads, From Florrie with love, and if that's not enough, hard luck, because I'm not going back up again."

"No, that's perfect."

"Is Fred in trouble?"

"No, no, he's not. That just clears up a few outstanding matters -- that's all."

He thanked her again and put her mother on the line.

* * * *

The morning session of the farmer's conference was predictable, dull and uneventful. Lunch came as a welcome relief. With a little time to kill before the afternoon session, Fred went to the bar and ordered a Scotch. He dug his hand deep into his pocket and scooped out a handful of loose change. Among the silver and copper was the item he had picked up the previous day from his bedroom floor. He paid the barman then went and sat by a window and examined the item in a ray of sunshine. In an instant he recognised what it was. He closed his fingers tightly around it and squeezed, wanting to crush it, but instead the bronze, Our Lady of Lourdes, medallion cut into his skin and made him bleed.

# CHAPTER 26

Fred didn't wait for the afternoon session. He climbed into his car and gunned it for home He arrived back in his driveway just in time to catch Tomato, going home for the day. Fred skidded to a halt beside him

"Evening, Mister Winter," said Tomato, through the half opened window.

Fred rolled the window all the way down. "I thought you were loyal to my family, Tom?"

"I am. But I always quit this time every evening, Mister Winter."

"I'm not talking about when you quit, you stupid man," Fred shouted. "I'm talking about not keeping me informed about what goes on behind my back."

"I'm sorry, Mister Winter. I don't know what you're talking about." Tomato was totally confused.

"Right, let me enlighten you. Victoria, is she seeing someone?"

"Yes, yes, she is, she's seeing Danny Jackson. I saw them together awhile ago down in the Hazel-wood."

"And you didn't think of telling me this?"

"It wasn't important. It was a private thing and I didn't think it was my place to talk."

"How long have you worked for my family, Tom?"

"Just over thirty years."

"And you think working for us for that length of time, gives you the right to decide what is important and what is not. Is that how it is now?"

"No, of course not, Mister Winter; it was a mistake. I just presumed you already knew."

"Never presume, Tom, never, ever, presume."

"Yes, Mister Winter, I never will again."

"Do you know where they meet?"

"Not really. But I did see them one wet evening, going into the old hay barn at the end of the yard."

Fred stared straight down the avenue at the family home. He closed his eyes and sucked in his breath, slowly, deeply, and the rage that Tomato, had felt was sucked down with it, deep into the pit of his stomach. He opened his eyes again. The transformation had taken only seconds, but it was enough to unnerve Tomato. "What have you been doing since I left?" He did not look at Tomato.

He filled in his working day and when finished, Fred gunned the car.

"Good night, Mister Winter," said Tomato.

Fred did not answer. He took off leaving Tomato in a cloud of dust and deep apprehension.

* * * *

"You're back early," said Victoria.

"I'd made my contribution and what was on the afternoon agenda was of no interest to me, so I hit the road early."

"I've nothing cooked."

"Don't worry about it. I had a big dinner. Beans and toast will do us. Is that all right with you?"

"Yeah, fine." Victoria was delighted. It meant getting away quicker to see Danny. He had asked her earlier to meet him in the old hay shed at the end of the yard.

He had been excited about something, but would not tell her.

She opened a tin of beans, poured them into a small saucepan and placed them on the Aga hotplate. From the larder she took a newly baked loaf of brown bread and sliced it.

Fred sat in his usual seat at the head of the kitchen table, perusing his notes from the meeting, silently seething. He eyed her as she moved around the kitchen, never obvious, always circumspect. The long legs, the faded blue denim jeans stretched tight across her shapely round bottom. He allowed himself to become aroused, visualizing those long legs and round bottom, naked. Up to now -- after watching her standing topless in front of her window -- he had restricted his favourite fantasy of her for the bedroom or bathroom. But she had betrayed him and he no longer felt morally constricted. When she bent over and stuck her head in the fridge, he nearly jumped on her. He so wanted to wrap his forearm around her throat and tell her not to scream or he would break her scrawny neck. He would use his free hand to open the buttons of her jeans and push them down to her ankles, bend her over and then push hard into her. She would give a muffled scream, he would smile, his hands would hold her hips and he would pound her. She would cry, uncontrollably sobbing, but he would not care. The bitch deserved it. She had betrayed his side, gone over to the enemy, brought him into his home, his room, his inner sanctum and she had to pay. Ooh how she would pay, he would enjoy the feel of her hot trembling flesh beneath his finger tips and the smell of her fear as through gritted teeth he would pound her and pound her and pound her, the rhythmic slapping of skin against skin, music to his ears, until he had sated his revenge. But then he thought, she would talk, she would tell her father, and he could not have that. He would have to quieten her. Then that would bring huge trouble and shame on the family. For now, he needed to be more in control. He would wait.

He closed his eyes and sucked his breath deep and slow and like his rage his lust went down into the pit of his stomach.

"It's ready," said Victoria, and handed him a plate.

"Thanks." He was glad the solid table hid his lust.

They ate in silence.

"I'm going to lie down for a while," said Fred, when he finished his tea. "I didn't sleep well last night -- unfamiliar bed -- can't beat your own."

Victoria gave Fred a half-hour before slipping out the backdoor. In the semi-darkness of his room -- behind lace curtains -- Fred watched her leave. From where he stood he had an almost perfect view of the farmyard. He watched as she disappeared from view behind some stone sheds, only to reappear seconds later as she crossed the yard and slipped into the old hay barn. It stood alone away from the other sheds, its half round roof sheeted in galvanized corrugation. Flakes of red oxide paint clung grimly to the rusting metal. Victoria pulled the wooden door closed.

Holding the heat of the day, the air inside was stuffy. Danny was already there waiting for her. He kissed her. "Do you remember me telling you that I needed to do something big, by way of an apology for dad?

"Yeah."

Do you remember me telling you that dad was looking for John Canavan's bike?

"Yeah."

"Well, I know where there's one hidden."

"Where?"

"In this barn."

"Where?" She warily eyed the quarter full barn of hay.

"At the back wall, I remember seeing the handlebars of it last year when we were refilling it."

"But that means moving all the hay."

"No, we don't have to move all of it, just what's on this side." He pointed to the back left-hand corner. You feel like helping?" He removed his sweat shirt.

Victoria took a few seconds to decide. "Oh what the hell, let's do it."

They pulled them out one by one, re-stacking them into a wall behind them. So if anyone came in they wouldn't be seen and hopefully not notice anything out of place.    For a good ten minutes they worked hard, repeatedly wiping away sweat with their sleeves. Danny stopped. "I hear a tractor."

"It's not moving, it's just idling," said Victoria. They dived for cover behind the new hay wall. They held hands, listened and waited.

"What's he at?" Victoria whispered.

But before Danny could answer, the tractor engine revved and moved off. They did not move again until the sound faded into the distance.

Victoria let out a loud sigh of relief.

"That was close," said Danny.

"Too close for comfort. Let's get out of here before he comes back."

"We can't go yet, I haven't found the bike."

"You're only doing this to get back into your dad's good graces."

"Look you go if you want, but I'm staying 'till I find the bike."

"But you don't even know if the bike is Canavan's."

"Staying or going?" Danny stood with both hands on his hips.

"Alright, alright, but only for another ten minutes and if we haven't found it by then, were out of here."

"Thank you." Danny gave her a quick kiss.

They went back to work, feverishly shifting bale after bale. They were getting close. They could see the corrugated sheeting on the back wall. Another few minutes work and they would be there. Victoria abruptly stopped working.

"This is no time for a rest, we're nearly there," said Danny.

Victoria sniffed the air. "Do you smell smoke?"

Danny stopped and looked behind him.

"Oh Jesus." Smoke and flames were coming from the far side of the hay wall. They moved swiftly around the edge only to find their path cut off. The flames had swept easily through the loose hay creating a fiery barrier. It now spread rapidly in two directions. One side was closing in fast on the wooden door while the other was closing in fast on them.

"We can't get to the door," said Danny.

They looked frantically around for another way out but found none.

"This is an old shed with old galvanised sheeting, they have to give" said Danny. He aimed a kick at one. It did not move. The sheeting was secured to an iron frame. He tried again, this time harder, but with the same result. In desperation, he took several strides back and made a run and jump at it. His two feet came off the ground and crashed into the sheeting -- rebounding him back onto the ground -- knocking the wind out of him.

"Were going to die," said Victoria. She helped Danny to his feet.

He did not respond immediately, he was too busy getting air back in his lungs. Eventually he said through short intakes of breath, "We have to try and get to the door."

"How, the floor is on fire?"

"I'm going to try and beat a path." He grabbed his sweat shirt, folded it in two and began beating down the flames, but, instead of putting it out, it caused the fire to spread even more. By now the smoke was thicker and the flames were getting uncomfortably close. Seeing as he was not going to be able to beat a path to the door he tried to create a firebreak around them instead, by tossing bales aside and clearing an area with his feet while Victoria banged on the galvanised sheeting and screamed for help. But it was getting hotter and harder to breath and the smoke forced them to the floor. They found a nail hole and took it in turns to use it to breathe in what air they could.

* * * *

Tomato came to the open front door of his pebble-dashed cottage, cigarette in one hand and a cup of tea in the other. He leaned against the door jam, took a drag and slowly exhaled. He glanced across the fields at Winter's and thought he saw smoke. He waved the cigarette smoke away to be sure he was seeing what he was seeing. Then in one movement, dropped the cigarette and the cup on the gravel yard and hopped onto his bicycle. As he sped down the lane he had an awful premonition that something was wrong.

They huddled together on the floor, coughing and breathing in the thick smoke. Victoria stopped coughing and her body went limp in Danny's arms.

"Victoria, Victoria," he cried. "Don't give up, please, please, fight."

Tomato jumped off the bicycle while it was still moving and ran to the shed. He banged on the side. "Is anyone in there?" he shouted.

Danny banged back. "Hurry, get us out of here, Victoria's passed out."

Tomato ran to the door but it was on fire and he could not get near it. He looked around and saw the old T.V.O. tractor. The key was in it. He checked first that it was switched to petrol before climbing aboard. He prayed it still worked. Three long turns of the key and it spluttered into life. He jumped off the tractor and ran back to the shed. "Danny, I'm coming through the door, find cover and be ready to move."

He ran back, jumped on the tractor, revved her up and charged at the door. Under the momentum of the charge it collapsed it front of him, carrying him onwards into the burning bales.

"Get out, get out, now," he shouted.

The doors had slammed onto the flame-covered ground, sending a cloud of black charred embers and smoke ahead of it. Danny with Victoria already in his arms closed his eyes, held his breath and ran as fast as he could through the paused flames into the yard. Out in the cool air and safely away from the fire he placed Victoria on the ground and began C.P.R.

In the shed Tomato was having his own problems. Several burning bales had fallen on top of him. With one hand he tried pushing them away while with the other he endeavoured to find reverse gear.

Danny worked hard on Victoria and cried with relief when she finally coughed and threw up. It was the most beautiful vomit he had ever seen.

Tomato found reverse and came roaring backwards out of the inferno. His right arm engulfed in flame. Danny laid Victoria down gently and ran to help. He pulled Tomato off the tractor and together they sprinted for a nearby water trough and doused the flames.

The clamour of fire engines could be heard coming in the distance. Sounds of neighbour's cars coming up the driveway and the phut, phut, phut of Fred's tractor coming up the field filled their ears. Fred won the race, jumping off and running to them. "What on earth has happened? Is anyone hurt?"

"Tom needs an ambulance, his arm's badly burnt and Victoria is suffering from smoke inhalation," said Danny.

Victoria was up on her feet. But she was confused and walking unsteadily in small circles.

"How did this happen? Were you in the shed when it started?" Fred demanded.

"We both were. I don't know how it happened. One minute everything was fine, the next it was on fire and we couldn't get out, and only for Tom we'd be dead by now."

"One of you was smoking, was that it?"

"No."

The yard filled quickly with neighbours, all wanting to help, but there was nothing they could do -- it was out of control. The shed had become an inferno, its flames licking the sky.

"Right, let's get ye to hospital." Fred helped Tomato, to his feet. Danny helped Victoria.

Joggy drove in and parked in front of the farmhouse, out of the way of the fire engines. Fred was loading up the Wolseley when he came around the end of the house. He was helping Tomato, onto the front passenger seat, while Danny helped Victoria into the back.

"Danny," said Joggy, shocked at the state of his son's black face and singed hair.    "Are you alright?"

"I'm fine but Tom and Victoria are not," He slid in beside Victoria.

"Where do you think you're going?" growled Fred.

"I want to stay with Victoria."

"Out, you've caused enough trouble. I don't want to see you around my home or my family ever again. You're fired. "

"Where were you when the fire started?" Joggy noticed how smoke free Fred's clothes were.

"Not that it's any of your business, but I was down in the bottom field feeding the calves. I didn't know there was a fire until I heard the fire engines."

"How could you not see the flames -- you were not that far away?"

"The wood blocks my view of the house and yard. Otherwise I would have seen it earlier."

For several seconds they tried to stare one another down. Like Tomato, earlier, Joggy, became unnerved. Fred's eyes were dead, cold and unreadable.

"Can we get moving?" cried Tomato. "The pain's becoming unbearable."

Fred broke the standoff and opened the driver side. "Don't let me see you or your son in my yard again," he barked.

Fred drove out of the yard. Driving up the avenue he pulled into the grass margin to allow two fire engines to pass.

Danny and Joggy walked back towards the fire. At first the burning shed held their attention, astonished at the sheer heat it generated. Watching transfixed; lined up against the walls of the stone sheds were all the neighbours.

"Alright, what happened?" Joggy asked.

"We were in the hay shed when the fire started. It trapped us and we couldn't get out and only for Tom, we'd be dead."

"Don't try and palm me off with an outline, I want details," Joggy said, irritation in his voice. "What were ye doing in there in the first place?"

"It's all my fault. If I hadn't asked Victoria to help, she wouldn't have got hurt."

Joggy glared at his son.

Danny got the message. "Alright... I was searching for Canavan's, bike. It's buried behind the hay against the back wall."

"How do you know its Canavan's?"

"I saw the handlebars of it last year when we were restocking the shed."

"Again I ask... how do you know its Canavan's? It could be anybody's!"

"Who else's could it be? What other reason would Fred have for burying a bike under a shed of hay, unless he was hiding it?"

In his own mind, Joggy conceded, his son might be right and it excited him a little. He hoped, as the firemen battled the flames, that the fire would not damage it beyond all recognition. He turned his attention back to Danny. "How did the fire start?"

"I don't know."

"But surely you must have some idea: fires don't start by themselves. Were ye smoking?"

"No, I don't smoke. Victoria does, but she didn't light up. All I know is that it started after Mister Winter, left."

"Fred was there?"

"Yes and no. He was in the yard doing something, we could hear the tractor idling and after a while he moved off. We went back to our search and the next thing we knew, the place was on fire and we were trapped."

Danny and Joggy hung around and waited until the fire was out. The firemen began empting the shed, dragging the still smouldering bales out into the open. Last out was the bicycle. Joggy did not inspect it. From where he stood with Danny he could see it was not Canavan's. Again he glared up at his son.

"You risked your life, for a fucking woman's bicycle?"

Danny broke down and began to cry.

"It's alright, it's alright." Joggy wrapped his arms around him. "You weren't to know."

"I'm sorry dad; I was just trying to make it up to you. I said some horrible things and I just wanted to make amends, that's all."

"It's alright." He rubbed his sons back. "Next time, just say sorry, ok?"

# CHAPTER 27

It was dark by the time they got home. Joggy drove into the back yard and parked. Danny opened the passenger door. Joggy grabbed his son by the arm. "I think it's time we had a chat."

Danny closed the door and switched on the interior light. A silence ensued. He waited patiently while his father searched for a starting point. Joggy stared at his own reflection in the front windscreen and then at Danny's. "My father's death was the hardest thing I've ever had to deal with in my life," he said at last. "I was barely fifteen at the time and was just getting to really know him when he died. He had always been somewhat of a shadowy figure, flitting in and out of our lives. If he wasn't working, he was sleeping.

Years later, after I got married, relatives and friends began to open up to me. They spoke of how unhappy my father had been. They said he told them that he felt like he was a visiting relative and that his children were becoming strangers to him. I know he tried hard to play a part in our lives, but, often, we were in bed when he got home, and he was gone to work by the time we got up in the mornings. On the one Sunday in the month he had off, he'd spend all day with us, doing whatever we wanted. But by evening time he'd be so exhausted, the poor man would collapse into an armchair and fall asleep: the long hours and hard physical labour having caught up with him. As I got older, I'd stay awake and wait for him to come home and look in on us. In the darkness of the room, I'd watch him as he kissed each of us goodnight. He always looked tired and sad."

Another silence ensued and again Danny remained patient. Apart from Alice, Joggy, had not spoken of these matters to another living soul. He was touching depths of sensitivity that up to now, only his subconscious had visited.

"When my father died, my relatives tried to shield me from what really happened to him. They'd huddle together in twos and threes and talk about it, always in whispers, stopping when I came too close. But during the wake I found out. I overheard two old ladies talking. I stood close to them. They didn't know who I was and I didn't know them. That's when I found out how Waller, blaggarded my father."

Joggy paused again and looked at his son. His eyes held something that was not directly in front of him, seeing it as clearly and as sharply as the day it was described to him. "I still can't get the picture out of my mind….his still warm body covered with that dirty old sack….. it haunts my dreams." He paused once more, before snapping back to the present. "I swore then, I'd have my revenge. That evening after the funeral, I crossed the fields to Winter's barn. I stood in the doorway and struck match after match, letting them burn a little before throwing them into the hay. Then I walked down to the road and sat on his wall and watched. That's where Luke found me. I was laughing my head off, clapping hands and shouting, burn you bastard, burn. I think Luke thought I'd lost the plot and maybe he was right. I know I wasn't rational. Luke eventually talked me into leaving the area before someone saw me. But I didn't care. I was beyond caring. I just wanted everyone to know what I'd done. We walked across the fields away from the fire. Luke kept me out of sight until I'd calmed down. From a distance we watched it. It was beautiful – it looked like the sun was rising."

Through the back window of the kitchen Joggy, could see Alice pottering around. Every now and then she would stop and look out at them, then move away again.

"It was after I'd calmed down, that Luke began talking about the consequences of the fire. He was sure that they would come after me and put me in jail. And I wanted that. I wanted it to all come out in court. I wanted everyone there and all the newspapers to report what that bastard did to my father. I wanted him shamed. But Luke made me look at it in a different way. He said I was the oldest in the family and now had the responsibility to be the bread winner for my younger brother and sister.

I hadn't thought of it like that. I hadn't thought of them at all while I burnt down Waller's barn. Even if I did, I don't think I would have listened. That's when Luke said he'd take the rap. His argument was that no one would hire a criminal, or give a job to a known arsonist. He said it didn't matter if he went down, because he would never need a job -- the home farm was his to inherit. We argued over it for a long time. I still wanted the notoriety.

Eventually, Luke wore me down. We concocted the accidental fire story, thinking he'd get a slap on the wrist or at worst a couple of months. But unknown to us then, Waller, was pals with the judge and he wanted his pound of flesh. He gave him two years. And I have regretted my decision ever since."

He looked directly at Danny. "Now you know it all. They'll be no reason for you to go around getting into trouble again. Will that satisfy your curiosity?"

"Yes, thanks. I'm sorry for being such an asshole and putting you through that."

"You're a chip of the old asshole, who should have spoken to you sooner."

"Just one other thing dad before we go in. What happened to Waller and his farm?"

"O Neill's own it now. Waller was forced to sell up and move away. Once word got out about the way he had treated my father, no one would work for him… even the men who were working for him left. He was ostracised. The shops wouldn't serve him and people shunned him. He brought in some scab labourers but after a few of them were beaten up, he was left with no choice but to sell. At the auction, the protestant bidders were told in no uncertain manner, that the same fate awaited them if they tried to buy the farm. Last I heard he went to England and died there a few years later. Now let's go in." Joggy smiled mischievously. "I can't wait to see the look on your mothers face when she claps eyes on the state of you."

\* \* \* \*

Danny had a bath. As he lay back and soaked, he thought of Victoria and wondered how she was and whether he would ever see her again. He dried, wrapped a towel around his waist and came into the kitchen. "Any chance of some grub, mum, I'm starving?"

"Thanks be to God, you were not hurt," she said, repeating it for the umpteenth time that evening. She circled her son looking for marks or bruises. She checked his back and arms and then stopped in front of him. She fingered the silver chain around his neck. "Where's the Lady of Lourdes, medallion, your Aunt Frances brought home?" She raised up the empty chain from his bare chest, so he could see it was missing.

"Damn, must have lost it in the fire."

"Thanks be to God, it did its job. Our Lady saved you."

While Alice made Danny a sandwich, Joggy went out and sat on the porch step. Only one star was visible in the night sky and every now and then it would twinkle. He began to wonder was it really a star? Or was it a portal into the next life and what we mistook for twinkling was really the shadows of souls entering through it. He wondered also if his mother had come back through that same portal to collect his dad or had she just waited around for his time to be up. He began to have problems with his sight. It was like he was seeing it through the prism of a rain drop. Within seconds he could not see at all.

Alice heard a faint sobbing sound coming from the front step. She looked to see where her son was -- he was disappearing into his bedroom, wolfing his sandwich. She came and sat beside her husband whose elbows were on his knees and his hands held his head. The sobs were deep and heavy. He had held it back for over twenty five years, but once the tears started to roll, he could not stop them. They would take their own time -- they had waited long enough.

"I nearly lost him, Alice," he sniffled, his shoulders shuddering. "I nearly lost him.
I couldn't go through that again."

Alice was quiet, there was nothing more to say. She placed a hand on his shoulder and gently rubbed it -- that was all the comfort he needed. She had waited a long time for this moment, for the prison walls of his grief to crack and finally collapse. And now it all rushed forth.

Helen and Katie appeared in the kitchen doorway. Alice raised a finger to her lips indicating to Helen, silence -- and then with the same finger gestured for her to go back inside and to bring Katie with her. Joggy had taken refuge in the peacefulness of the front door step and having finally succumbed to grief, Alice, was determined to keep the world at bay until he was finished.

"Why is daddy crying?" asked Katie, as they went back to bed.

"Because daddy's sad."

"Why's he sad?"

Helen had not the answers her sister wanted and knowing Katie, the questions would continue to flow. She cringed at what she was about to say next, "Because that's the why."

# CHAPTER 28

McNeill walked smartly down the casualty ward corridor of Oldbridge hospital and then descended the polished stone steps to the ground floor. At the bottom he met two men ascending; Fred Winter and another man he did not know.

"I want a word, sergeant," said Fred. The other man also stopped. "Have you him in custody yet?"

"And who might he be?" asked McNeill.

"Danny Jackson, the young man who endangered my daughter's life," said the other man.

"Are you Victoria's father?"

"Yes."

"You haven't answered my question, sergeant," said Fred.

"No. I have not arrested him. What makes you think I should?"

"Well, who else could have done it?"

"That's what I'm trying to find out, Mister Winter."

"Have you spoken to Victoria?" her father asked.

"Yes I have."

"You've spoken to my daughter, without my permission?"

"I don't need your permission, Mister Clark. She's over eighteen -- an adult."

"Did she say how he started it?" asked Fred.

"I've taken a statement from her, if that's what you mean. The contents of which are private. What I will say, is that she's a bit hazy in her recollections -- which is not unusual in the circumstances, since she did pass out. Are you taking her home, Mister Clark?"

"Yes, have you any objections, sergeant?"

"No I don't. But I will need a telephone number, in case I need to talk to her again." McNeill wrote the number into his notebook.

"I want to see quick progress in this case, sergeant," said Fred, "My shed has been burnt to the ground, my hay destroyed and more importantly, my friend's daughter was nearly killed. Otherwise, sergeant, I will be forced to go above your head and have a chat with Inspector Murray."

"I can assure you Mister Winter that will not be necessary."

The two men started to climb again. A couple of steps later, Fred stopped and turned.

"Sergeant," he called.

McNeill turned to face him again.

"Like father like son," said Fred.

"Excuse me?" said McNeill.

"You do know sergeant that his father burnt down my uncles hay barn, don't you?"

"I'm sorry… whose hay barn are you talking about?"

"My uncle…George Waller. He employed Joggy Jackson's father on his land. Unfortunately, one day while working, the poor man collapsed and died from a heart attack. Joggy Jackson blamed my uncle for his father's death and took spiteful revenge by burning down the hay barn they had been working in at the time."

"Ah yes, I remember reading about that.  However, my recollection differs from yours, Mister Winter. Luke Baker was convicted for that crime and did two years."

"Don't be so naïve sergeant, every dog in the street knows Jackson did it."

"And you have proof of this, have you?"

"I don't need proof, I know."

"Well, Mister Winter, in my business, I don't have that luxury -- I need proof. And let me give you a little friendly advice -- be careful who you say that to, because I can assure you, slander is an expensive business."

"I know what I know sergeant." Winter started climbing the stairs again. "I know what I know," he repeated, over his shoulder.

Cars, like people have distinctive voices. In the silence of the kitchen Joggy, read his Sunday newspaper. His eyes focused on the print while his ears monitored the traffic for that one particular sound. When he heard it he raised his head slowly out of the paper and listened to the echo from the stone bridge as it passed under it -- the roar of the engine as it climbed the hill… then it slowed and parked and finally the squeak of the little gate at the bottom of the path and the heavy steady footsteps of hobnails on the concrete. The knock came on the open door. Joggy folded his paper and placed it on the seat he had just vacated. He removed his reading glasses and carefully put them back in their case and placed them with the paper. He stood in the doorway. "Come in," he said.

"No thanks, Joggy," said McNeill, "I prefer to do my business out here if you don't mind."

"Fair enough, I presume its Danny you want?"

McNeill nodded.

"Danny, can you come out here?" He was in his room. Joggy suspected McNeill might call. Alice had taking the two girls flower picking.

McNeill wandered across the front lawn forcing Joggy and Danny to follow.

The day was dry and the sky clear. A few wispy clouds gave feeble shelter from the beaming Sun. McNeill stopped and examined a yellow rose bush.

"Is this about last night?" Danny asked.

"What's your connection with Victoria Clark?" McNeill sniffed the rose.

"She's my girlfriend."

"And you have been seeing her for-- how long?"

"About six weeks."

McNeill turned his attention away from the flower and onto Danny. He fixed him with a hard stare and then took a step forward. "Were ye smoking?"

"No," said Danny, taking a step back.

"Were ye messing with matches; lighting wisps of hay and putting them out, only it got out of control? Is that what happened?" McNeill kept up the forward momentum.

Danny continued to back off. "No, it was nothing like that." He looked to his father for support, but his father seemed more interested in the progress of the plants around him than coming to his son's defence. Joggy knew the badgering was harmless. It was McNeill's game plan, attack and confuse, hoping Danny would make a mistake. If he was lying, he might trip himself up, and Joggy, needed to know that also.

McNeill stopped his advance. "Then what did happen, because, I'm curious to know how a fire could start without ye noticing it?"

Danny looked at his father, unsure of what he would want him to say.

"Tell him the truth," said Joggy.

"We were looking for what I thought might be John Canavan's bike. I thought I'd surprise dad with it. I'd seen the handlebars of it sticking out the summer before. We'd built a hay wall around us, in case anyone came in. We'd built it fairly high. That's why we didn't see the flames until it was too late."

"And did anyone come in?"

"No."

"And where was Mister Winter?"

"He was in the yard before the fire started. I could hear the tractor idling somewhere up around the main hay shed. Then he drove off."

"So how do you think it started then?"

"I honestly don't know."

"And the bike, was it Canavan's?"

"No, sergeant, it turned out to be a women's bike."

"It was most likely Missus Winters," said Joggy, "Fred, probably threw it into the shed after she died."

"Could have been his sisters either," Danny added.

"His sister?" said McNeill. "I never knew he had a sister."

"I'd forgotten about that," said Joggy, "She's died about twenty years ago."

"I think there was something wrong with her," said Danny.

"Wrong, how?" McNeill asked.

"In the family photo's that hang on their sitting room wall, she looks… I don't know, a bit funny in them, like maybe…. she was mentally retarded."

"I see. Well you're off the hook for the moment," said McNeill. "Your story tallies with that of Victoria's."

Danny's face lit up. "You saw Victoria. How was she?"

"She's recovering well. The hospital kept her in last night. I spoke to her father this morning; he had come to bring her home."

"Home, like, to the north, home?"

"Yes, I believe so."

Danny's face dropped as the weight of all his expectations came crashing down on him. Victoria was gone without as much as a goodbye and he would never see her again. He walked into the house and into his bedroom, closing the door behind him. Joggy watched his son go. He wanted to follow and console him, but McNeill temporarily put a stop to it.

"Are you making connections?" McNeill asked.

"I am."

"How come you didn't know that, Winter, had a mentally handicapped sister."

"We never saw her. We had only moved into this house a short while, when she died. There was never any talk about it after that."

"I was fascinated to learn this morning that there is another connection, between your family and Winter's, and in particular the burning down of hay sheds. A bit of a coincidence, don't you think?"

"I suppose so, but that's all it is, a coincidence. Who brought that up?"

"Winter, he was in the hospital with Victoria's father."

"I see," said Joggy, thoughtfully.

"He seems to think that you, not Luke Baker, burnt down his uncles barn."

"Does he now?" Joggy, smirked at the notion.

There and then McNeill guessed at the truth and the debt Joggy, owed Luke Baker. "He's pushing hard for Danny's arrest. Seems to think he set the fire."

"What do you think?"

"I've spoken to the fire officer and his view is the same as mine at the moment,: inconclusive. He has no idea how it started and neither do I. All he knows is that an accelerant wasn't used."

They began walking to the gate.

"Tell me something, if Fred Winter, believed so fervently, that you burnt down his uncles hay barn, why then would he turn around and hire Danny for Saturday work?"

"Because he could! He offered Danny the work and he jumped at it. I was dead set against him doing it. I knew Winter's reasons. But Danny's headstrong and he wouldn't listen. He went behind my back and took the job."

"What were they?"

"What were what?"

"Winter's reasons."

"It was his way of saying that after two generations -- our family had not risen above the level of farm labourers."

They walked in thoughtful silence down the concrete path. For McNeill, the temptation to say something about Joggy's debt to Luke Baker, hung like a juicy apple ready to be picked, and maybe if he had found out earlier, he would have. But their relationship had moved on to a new maturity, a new respect. It was enough now to know the truth and for Joggy to know that he knew.

"I did some digging into Canavan's past and in particular his time in England," said McNeill, when they reached the little wooden gate. "He took the boat in September of "fifty four". It seems he was a bar man for the first six months. After that he did a short stint on the buildings, but found the work to tough, before going back to bar work. And that's what he did for the remainder of his time there -- working in one bar or another."

"Why September, just when work is slowing down? If you go to England, you go in April or May, when there's plenty of work?"

"Maybe he was running, maybe he was fearful of something."

"Yeah, but from what?"

Joggy opened the small gate for McNeill and then closed it behind him. "I spoke to the other blackmail victim," he said. "And it turns out he also has a pretty powerful motive for wanting Canavan, dead. He also had opportunity. Unfortunately, like Rick Worrel, Jenny Roache and Fred Winter, there's not one scrap of evidence to tie them to the crime, and in Winters, case -- no motive."

"Yes, well let's just keep plugging away, something's got to give."

Joggy turned around when he heard laughter: the girls and Alice returning through the back fields, loaded down with wild flowers. They went inside.

"I'll be back in a minute," said Joggy. He trotted up the path and into the house. Within thirty seconds he was back. "Alice says it was May of "fifty five", when Margaret Winter died. She was about fourteen at the time. She was hospitalised in the north; some sort of virus. Women have better memories for these things."

"That rules her out," said McNeill, "Canavan, couldn't have done anything to her -- he was in England at the time."

Joggy pulled out his cigarettes and offered McNeill one.

"No thanks, I'm strictly a pipe man."

He lit his cigarette and flicked the burnt match into the road.

"You any thoughts on the other matter?" McNeill asked.

"Well," he said, then took a long drag on the cigarette before answering…."I look at it like this, there are only one of four people who could have started it; Danny, Victoria, Fred or God."

"God, what's he got to do with this?"

"You never heard of spontaneous combustion?"

"Of course I did -- it's right up there with the tooth fairy."

"That makes two of us, so that leaves three. I believe Danny and Victoria. If they were messing with matches or cigarettes, they would have got out before the fire trapped them. That leaves one."

"You're pointing the finger at Winter?"

"Have you a better suspect?" Joggy turned away. "Talk to you later," he said and ambled back up the path.

Joggy knocked on Danny's door and then opened it. Danny had closed the curtains. He was lying on top of the bed -- in the semi-darkness -- staring at the ceiling.

"You alright?" Joggy asked.

"I'm fine."

"If you want to talk," he suspected it probably was the last thing Danny wanted at the moment, "you know where I am."

"Thanks." Danny turned his back and assumed the foetal position. "I just want to be left alone."

Joggy closed the door and went back to his paper.

After reading the same article three times, he gave up. He couldn't concentrate. McNeill had used the word fearful and it had triggered a reaction in Joggy's brain. It was now like the melody of a song that he did not particularly like, but for some reason it was stuck in his head and it would not stop.

Alice and the girls were at the kitchen table busily arranging the wild flowers into three vases. They started playfully arguing over who had the best arrangement. "I'm going for a walk," he said.

He lit a cigarette at the gate, slipped his left hand into his trousers pocket and began walking slowly down the hill, head down, looking at the ground. He got as far as the grey stone bridge, paused underneath for a few minutes, then turned around sharply and started walking at speed back up the hill, head up. He burst through the open doorway, over to the dresser and opened the bottom right-hand door. He lifted out Canavan's, manuscripts and

215

peeled off the last one. Alice and the girls stared at him in stunned silence. Joggy flicked through the pages until he found what he had remembered.

"I thought you were finished with those?" said Alice.

"Listen to this, Alice" he said, "and tell me what you think it means."

*My Game.*
*Her mind, so inviting and so trusting.*
*Her innocence, so playful and so obliging.*
*My guilt, so sleepless and so fearful*
*My heart, so heavy and so tearful*
*My punishment, so slow and so deserving.*

"It sounds like someone has done something to a child and afterwards is wracked with guilt."

"Exactly. When's my check up with Doctor Kelly?"

"Wednesday evening. What's going on?"

"I don't know yet, but I hope to know more after Wednesday."

# CHAPTER 29

Joggy's last job on Wednesday evening for Doctor Kelly was to cut the front lawn. When he finished, he cleaned down the lawnmower and put it away. He washed his hands and waited in the surgery waiting room. A small man with a hat was ahead of him. They exchanged greetings and talked about the weather. Joggy was not in a chatty mood, so he picked up a well thumbed copy of Woman's Own magazine and perused it. He didn't read any of the stories his mind was too preoccupied with what he had to ask the Doc.

Dr Kelly stuck his head out of the surgery door. "I can see you now, Joggy," he said softly,

He followed the Doctor into the surgery.

"Take your shirt off," he said.

He then took his blood pressure and listened to his heart and lungs.

"Everything seems to be in good working order, Joggy. And If you can avoid getting beaten up in the future, it'll probably stay that way."

"I'll do my best. Do you have a few minutes to spare -- there are a couple of other things I'd like to discuss with you?"

"Fire away, there's no one else waiting."

"How would I go about seeing the medical records of someone who died in "nineteen fifty five" -- in a Northern Ireland hospital?"

"I'd imagine with great difficulty, Joggy. They won't open them up for just anybody who walks in off the street. Is this related to John Canavan?"

"Yes, and it's vital I find out what is written in those records."

"Can you be a bit more specific with your information?"

"I don't know the name of the hospital, but her name was Margaret Winter." He also gave the date of her death and the area her family lived in.

"I still have a couple of friends I went to medical school with who are working in hospitals up there. I could if you want, ring them for you. There's no guarantee they'll be able to help, but it's a shot."

"That would be brilliant, but I don't want you to do it, if it places you in an awkward position."

"No, no." Dr Kelly waved away his protest with a gentle wave of his hand. "There'll be no trouble."

"Well, thanks then, that's very generous of you."

"That's one, what was the other?"

"The other one is of a sexual nature." Joggy put back on his shirt. He was embarrassed to have to ask, so he kept his head down and tried to look busy buttoning it up. "Again this cropped up during my search. I have a good idea of what the answer is, but for official clarification, I have to ask. What's the difference between a paedophile and a homosexual?"

"A paedophile is someone who is sexually aroused by children, while a homosexual is aroused by adult males or in a lesbian's case, by adult women."

"Is a homosexual a danger to children?" Still keeping his head down, he pushed the shirt tails into his trousers.

"Not usually-- but a paedophile is. Do you know a paedophile, Joggy? If you do and he's in contact with children -- I would need to know."

"No, thankfully -- I don't know any paedophiles?" He lifted his head and smiled. "But I do know a gay person who has contact with children and your definition has eased my mind. Getting back to the other matter -- when do you think you could have word for me?"

"If they can't do anything for me, I'll know in a couple of hours. And if they can, it could take a week or more."

"Again, Doctor, I'd like to thank you for your help. What do I owe you?"

"I don't charge friends, Joggy." He placed a hand on Joggy's shoulder and escorted him to the door. "Just think of it as one the perks of the job."

\* \* \* \*

The weatherman had forecast heavy intermittent showers for Friday -- clearing by evening time. A heavy shower had just passed over and the evening Sun was now out. It was now five days since Victoria went home. Danny had spent the entire time, either in his room with the curtains closed or sitting somewhere quietly, staring into space.

Joggy appeared in front of him. "Let's go for a walk."

"No thanks, I prefer to stay where I am."

"Well, I was hoping you'd come with me, there are a few things I want to talk to you about."

"I don't feel up to talking about my love life, dad."

"I don't want to talk about your love life either. This is something entirely different."

Danny hesitated. He eyed his father with a look that was a mixture of suspicion and doubt. "Okay, but I'm turning around if you start on my love life."

"Scouts honour." He gave him a mock salute.

They ambled in silence down the hill and under the stone bridge. Along the length of the road, as far as they could see -- Vapour clouds rose up, like spirits ascending from the wet road. They turned left over the bridge fording the slow moving stream and onto a side road that ran parallel with the river. It's rippling and tinkling waters rolled along soothing and comforting those who walked along with it.

Joggy decided the silence, while nice, had gone on long enough. He gave a soft cough. "So, you've been inside Winter's?"

"Yeah."

"Was Fred there?"

"No, God no, he was away for the weekend."

"So how did you get in?"

"Victoria invited me."

"I see. When was that?"

"That was the night I came home drunk, remember." Danny gave a fleeting smile. "We drank all his Brandy."

"And did he find out?"

"Victoria told him that she'd drunk it all over two nights."

"And he believed her?"

Danny cracked a gentle smile. "She can be quiet convincing."

"What's the place like?"

"A big disappointment really. I thought by the way he didn't allow anyone into the house, was because he was house proud or something, but it's no different from a lot of other farmhouses I've seen. Most of the furniture is old and badly worn and with the exception of the new Aga cooker, the whole place needs to be done up."

The road was narrow with a thin strip of grass running down the middle. They stopped by a rock pool.

"There's pinkeen's down there," said Joggy. They gazed down at the tiny silver fish. "Katie's favourites."

"Pity we don't have a jam jar," said Danny. He kneeled down for a closer look. "We could have brought her home some."

After a few minutes, they turned and began walking back. They reached the little bridge that forded the stream. Danny sat on one wall while his father sat facing him on the other.

"I want to ask you something Danny," said Joggy, finally getting around to the real reason for the walk. "On the night of the fire, is there any way that Fred Winter could have known that you and Victoria were in the hay shed?"

"I don't know, but, the more I think about it, the more I think he might have. Winters, bedroom is always kept locked. Victoria was not even allowed to clean it. He was very secretive about it and always kept the key with him. And that made us curious. Then Victoria acquired a copy key. On the evening before the fire, Winter took off for a farmer's conference in Clonmel. We opened his bedroom and found it festooned with British and Ulster flags and he had a big portrait of the Queen above his bed. But then he came back -- he'd forgotten his wallet. I couldn't get out so Victoria locked me in and I had to hide in the wardrobe. He came into the room, opened the wardrobe and took his wallet from a jacket pocket. Thankfully he didn't see me. But when he was leaving he picked something off the floor and put it in his pocket. I think it might have been the, Our Lady of Lourdes, medallion that Aunty brought back."

"How did it get on the floor?"

"I was messing with Victoria. I threw her onto the bed and she pushed me off it. I landed where Mister Winter, picked something off the floor. So if it was the medallion, then he probable knew we had been in his room. He could have followed Victoria, the evening after."

Having absorbed the information, Joggy stood up and crossed the bridge to where Danny sat.

"Do you think Mister Winter, set the fire, dad?"

"I'm leaning that way, but I can't work out why. Because he found out that ye were in his bedroom? He shook his head. "It doesn't seem reason enough." He stared down at where Canavan's body once lay, blessed himself, said a quick prayer, then blessed himself again.

Recalling the scene photos, he looked up and studied the overhanging whitethorn and once again pondered on how the straw became entangled in the high branches. No clear answer came. But like the steam rising from the road, the confusion surrounding his thoughts had begun to evaporate and a clearer more defined picture of what really happened was beginning to emerge. All he needed now was for Dr Kelly to come back with what he suspected. It excited him and at the same time sent a shiver down his spine.

"Let's go home," he said to Danny. "Tell me about Victoria?" he asked as they sauntered down the hill.

"I thought we weren't talking about my love life, dad?"

"Were not, I just wanted to know a little bit about her -- that's all."

"What you want to know?"

"Well, is she a good kisser and did those long legs of hers really go all the way up to her armpits?"

"Dad," exclaimed Danny. He laughed and gave his father a friendly thump on the shoulder.

"Hey, go easy, I'm an old man." Joggy smiled.

The good humour died down and Danny's mood became reflective. Joggy could see the far off look in his son's eyes. He hated seeing him like this. He reached across and like Alice had done on so many occasions with him -- he gave his son's back a comforting stroke.

Danny looked at his father, his eyes glistening. "I miss her, dad. Why does love have to hurt so much?"

"Love doesn't hurt. If it did, none of us would want anything to do with it. Being in love is the most wonderful feeling in the world. It's been apart that hurts. It's because you can't be with her right now that's painful. Why don't you write to her?"

"And what," he sniffled, "become pen pals? A pen's no substitute for her hand."

"There's an old saying, Danny, if it's meant to be, love will find a way."

When they reached the little gate leading up to the house, Joggy, gave Danny, a slap on the back. "There now Son, I told you I wouldn't talk about your love life."

"But you did."

"No son, you did."

* * * *

There was lightness to Joggy's step on Wednesday morning and a not-a-care-in the-world smile was plastered on his face. He waved and smiled at everyone. Those he came face to face with, he greeted as if they were his dearest friends.

As he worked in the vegetable garden of Heatherville house that morning, he could not help noticing that somehow the air smelt fresher and the birdsong sounded sweeter. He whistled while he worked.

When he came in for his lunch, McNeill was sitting, waiting by the card table.

"Well," said McNeill. "I was really intrigued by your telephone call yesterday evening. So tell me, what's this news, as you put it, that's going to blow my socks off?"

Joggy did not respond. He sat down and opened his biscuit tin lunch box. He then unscrewed the cap from the thermos flask and poured tea into the plastic thermos cap. He poured in some milk, then un-wrapped the tin foil from around his sandwiches, peeled one back to inspect the contents, then smiled, it was ham and egg.

McNeill waited patiently. He figured that whatever information Joggy, had was gold or he would not have called this meeting. So, if he wanted to drag out the tension a little until he was ready to speak, then he would play along.

Joggy took a bite of his sandwich and a mouthful of tea. "I know who killed John Canavan," he said, before taking another bite and a mouthful of tea.

"I'm listening."

"Fred Winter."

"What makes you think that?"

"I discovered his motive."

"Which was?"

"Canavan killed Margaret Winter. Not directly, but indirectly."

"You're not making any sense. Canavan, was in England, remember."

"Not in September of-fifty four-he wasn't. That's when he raped her."

"Rape?"

"As far as I can make out, he didn't force himself on her or hold her down. It was more a kind of a game he played with her. Probable something like, mothers and fathers or husband and wives. Got her to play along and in the course of the game duped her into having sex with him."

"How do you know this?"

"It was in his journal."

"I thought you said there was nothing in them."

"There was nothing. That is until we discovered that Winter, had a mentally handicapped sister, and the fact that he was running from something, plus, you used the word fearful the other day. That word rang a bell. Then I remembered a poem he had written." He extracted a copy of it from his pocket and passed it to McNeill. "I got someone to check on her hospital records and guess what we discovered?"

"Go on."

"She didn't die from a virus, like we were all told. The poor girl died in childbirth."

"Jesus. How'd you find that out?"

Joggy smirked. "You're not the only one that knows people."

"That's one hell of a motive all right. And the child, what happened to that?"

"Orphaned: The family refused to have anything to do with it." Joggy sipped his tea and then returned to his theory. "Anyway, as I was saying, Canavan must have flagged Winter down that day." Joggy said excitedly -- the story fresh in his mind. It was all he could think about since Doctor Kelly came through with the news. He had knitted the story together and now he could not get it out fast enough to McNeill. "Probably told him he had something to tell him about his sister. Winter would have thrown his bike into the trailer and then on the way back in the car Canavan more than likely confessed to what he did to his sister and probable said how sorry and repentant he was. My guess is they drove down into the farm yard and while Canavan was unloading his bike, Winter bashed in his skull with the pipe."

"Ok, suppose it happened that way --- where did Winter get the pipe?"

"They were just after putting in a new A.G.A cooker. The old piping was probable lying around afterwards."

McNeill sat back, pulled out his pipe and lit it. Joggy continued with his lunch.

"Right," said McNeill, after several minutes of uninterrupted thought. "You think, because Canavan was dying and feeling remorseful, he confessed to Winter?

"Yep."

"That's one brave confession."

Having finished the last of his sandwiches Joggy sat back and sipped the remains of his tea.

"Ok, next question. How did the body end up in the river?" McNeill asked.

"That Saturday evening, Winter, waited until it was getting dark. He was due to bring the boar up to Tom Bakers sows for their annual servicing. He threw the body in with the boar and covered it up with straw and when he reached the bridge, tossed it over the side. Up in Tom's yard, with no one around, he unloaded the boar into the sty, tossed out the bloodied straw and after wiping the pipe clean, dropped it in the yard."

"All-right, two more questions. You told me that Jenny Roache said, that the sound of the iron cart wheels never stopped."

"Yeah."

"So how did he get Canavan, into the river if the cart never stopped moving? The creels on that thing are at least five foot high"

"I don't know. It's possible that Jenny was mistaken and that he did stop for a few seconds."

"Also, how could he be sure that Luke and not Tom would pick up the pipe?"

"I don't know that either. I don't have all the answers. But I do know we have our man. All the rest of the pieces fit. He had a powerful motive, he had opportunity and he had a way of getting rid of the body and planting the evidence. It's him, I know it's him. What are you going to do about it?"

"Nothing, at the moment all we have is a good story."

"We have more than a story. We have motive, opportunity and he had access to the murder weapon."

"Yes and they all fit into the story very well, but, we have no hard evidence. If we knew this when the original investigation was ongoing, the outcome could have been very different. But now, we need more. We need to place the bicycle or the book of Robert Frost poems in his hands. Without that, the case will not be reviewed."

"If you knew this at the start, why didn't you say something?"

"Because, if I'm to be honest, I didn't think you'd get anywhere. And the fact that we have achieved so much is down to your dedication and hard work."

"A fat lot of good that turned out to be, I might as well have done nothing." Joggy was crestfallen. He suddenly felt tired. Like a vampire had sucked all the energy out of him.

McNeill stood up and began making his exit. He stopped and turned. "If it's any consolation to you, Joggy, I too, believe we have the right man."

But it was of no consolation. The right man was slipping between his fingers and there was not a damn thing he could do about it.

* * * *

McNeill could not wait until the following Monday to ring Inspector Murray. He took a chance and rang him that evening, eight o' clock, sharp.

"This better be important," said Murray, who was a John Wayne fan and had been watching a western on T.V.

"It is, sir. I've discovered the identity of Canavan's real killer. His name is Fred Winter."

"The farmer who's shed was recently burnt down?"

"Yes sir."

"What have you got on him?"

"My big stumbling block, sir, was a motive. There seemed to be no connection between Canavan and Winter. Then during my questioning of Danny Jackson over the barn fire, I found out that he had seen a photo of a mentally retarded child in Winter's house. It turned out to be Winter's sister, who had died in a hospital in

Northern Ireland in May of 1955. Canavan, as you know had been donating twenty pounds a month for the upkeep of a mentally retarded child. When I was investigating Canavan's background recently I discovered he'd left for England in September of 1954. I figured for him to be going over that late in the season that he was probable running from something. I then noticed that nine months was the distance between September and May. It got me thinking. I made a few calls to a doctor friend of mine in the North. He got access to the records and discovered that Winter's sister had died in Childbirth. It seems Canavan raped her and that's why he ran. When he found out he was dying he confessed to Winter and then Winter killed him."

"And what hand had Jackson, in this discovery?"

"None sir, it came together solely from my interview with Danny Jackson and Canavan's, background check."

"Good work, sergeant. We could do with a man of your experience around here."

"Thank you, sir. What's your next step, sir?"

"Next step?"

"Yes sir, for the case to stand up in court, we need to retrieve Canavan's bicycle."

"And how do you suggest we go about that?"

"A search warrant, sir."

"Do you know precisely, where the bicycle is?"

"No, sir, not precisely."

"Are you off your rocker, sergeant? I've no intention of wasting scarce departmental monies on a wild goose chase. Winter has over two hundred acres and at least a dozen sheds all full of hay, straw and God knows what else. He may or may not have the bicycle and until I know for certain he has, I have no intention of making myself or this force look stupid. Remember Sergeant, this is not an official case. Don't get me wrong, I want to see Baker's name cleared. But it has to be by the book. If you can physically put your hands on the bike, then we might have something. But until that happens, I'm afraid Sergeant we have nothing.

"But I know in my bones he has it."

"Well then, sergeant, you go and find it. But remember, probable cause, without it, you have no reason to be on his land. Have you, probable cause sergeant?

"No sir." McNeill responded, feeling as downbeat as Joggy did earlier.

"Then this case is over and so is this conversation."

CHAPTER 30


Kilpatrick sports day was an annual event and the highlight of the local social year. In the weeks leading up to it, it was all people could talk about. It was held on the village green every August bank holiday Monday. In the centre of the green was a handball alley and around it a track was cut out. People came long distances to participate in the numerous open cycling, field and athletic events. Everyone betted with the bookies and every year people hoped for a local winner. But there was one event in which the bookies did very little business and that was the Winter Cup. This was its sixteenth year and there had ever only being two winners; Luke Baker won it for the first twelve and Fred Winter for the last three. On the less serious side was the carnival, with its swing boats, bumper cars and amusement stalls. Around the edge of the green, the hucksters came and set up shop. They sold everything from hand tools to shoes to clothes to cheap plastic toys. Fast food was also available, and anyone who wanted something a little more wholesome, entered the I.C A (The Irish country women's association.) marquee. There, you could have tea, homemade scones, apple or rhubarb tart, brown bread, currant cake and other delicacies. During the afternoon the ladies culinary skills would be judged. The competition would be fierce -- bragging rights for the following year were jealously coveted. The events started at two o' clock sharp with the much lauded cycling races and the day would finish somewhere between six and seven that evening. Everyone prayed for a fine dry day and the weather God's did not disappoint them.

The Jackson family arrived just before the first race. The children, as soon as they set foot on the green, took off, as if they had been under the starter pistol for the carnival. Alice made a bee line for the huckster stalls and Joggy, with his hands in his trousers pockets, wandered aimlessly about.

He had spent the last five weeks searching under the cover of darkness every nook and cranny of Winter's farm by guided torchlight. This was achieved by taping a cardboard tube to the torch head. It minimized the chance of Winter spotting him. Nevertheless, Winter had surprised him and had nearly caught him on a couple of occasions, but he managed to hide just in time. He had to hold his breath while Winter passed within feet. He thought he had been seen, but it turned out that he was just checking everything was alright before going to bed. There were two sheds Joggy could not search successfully, one contained hay the other barley straw, and for all he knew Canavan's bike could be buried under either one.

"You've done your best. Luke would be happy with that." Alice had said when he came into the kitchen, disconsolate, after his last night of searching.

He tried hard not to think about it, but like his shadow it stayed with him.

Out of the corner of his eye he spotted the tall blonde head of Fred Winter, walking along the edge of the grass track, making his way to the area where the bale tossing was to be held. The first round was due to start shortly.

Joggy left the green and walked solemnly up the hill towards the graveyard. He slipped over the sty and made his way along the gravel path to Luke's graveside.
For several minutes he stood there reading and re-reading the inscription.

In loving memory.
Luke Albert Baker
1930----1973
Rest in Peace.

"Rest in Peace my arse." Joggy spun around and lashed out at some loose stones, sending them flying in all directions -- a couple of them pinged off a nearby headstone. "How can you rest knowing that bastard's walking around free." He then looked around to see if anyone had seen or heard him, but luckily everyone was at the sports day. He turned back to Luke's headstone. "I'm sorry, Luke, I've let you down. He's down there on the Green swaning around, without a care in the world. I know the truth and its burns me up inside to know that I can't say a word about him. You know Luke, truths a funny thing -- without proof it's slander. He's getting away with murder and all I can do is watch."

The sounds coming from the Green carried clearly to the graveyard. Joggy peered down the hill, over the headstones, and even though a stand of Elm trees blocked his view of the Green; in his minds eye he could imagine the excitement. Around him, he could feel the air bristling with the magic of it all. Wonderful sounds like that of the carnival music, the screams of the children on the swing boats, the calls of the hawkers trading their wares and the oohs and aahs of the people cheering on the track and field events. It lifted his mood. He grinned mischievously at Luke's headstone. "Any chance you could do something from your side of the fence? No, probable not." He sighed. "Just thought I'd ask. I have to go. Talk to you later."

He first went to the carnival and checked on the children: they were having too good a time to notice him. He then went in search of Alice and found her bargaining with a shoe hawker. The poor man looked shell-shocked. Alice was tenacious, she loved to barter, and had the man backed into a corner. They eventually slapped hands on a pair of men's brown patented leather shoes.

"Do you want to get a cup of tea?" Joggy enquired.

"I'd love one. Me mouths dry from talking. I got some great bargains. I'm having a great time haggling with these people." She glanced around to make sure no one could hear her then whispered, "It's nearly as good as sex."

She squeezed her husband's hand and they both laughed.

From the doorway of the marquee, with a cup in one hand and slice of apple tart in the other, Joggy watched the concluding stages of the bale tossing contest. Winter was winning hands down. While everyone else grimaced and groaned with their efforts, Winter, took it all in his stride -- slinging the bale over the bar with nonchalant ease. He would then turn away with a barely concealed look of contempt on his face.

"Pity Luke, God rest his soul, wasn't here to put him in his place." said an elderly gentleman, who had come to watch. He stood beside Joggy, supporting himself with a walking cane.

"Yeah." Joggy smiled at the memory. "Winter could never get the better of him."

"I'd say there's a bit of an animal lost somewhere in that fellow." He pointed his walking cane in Winter's direction.

"Strong as an ox," agreed Joggy.

"Strong enough I'd say to throw a man over that bar, let alone a bale of hay."

Joggy stopped chewing, looked sharply at the elderly gentleman and then at Winter. He realised then that Jenny Roache had been right, when she said that the thunderous roll of the Winter's cart wheels had not stopped -- he had not needed to stop. The Wooden creels were only high on three sides. The driver's side was much lower. Which meant that Winter lined up the horse with the right hand side of the bridge and as they drew close, climbed into the back, lifted Canavan, above his head and when they were level with the bridge, tossed him over the creel, over the parapet and into the river and the loose straw on the body floated and became entangled in the high branches of the whitethorn tree. Because it was dusk, no one could see anything and the noise of the iron wheels covered the sound of the body hitting the water.

"You know, you're right," responded Joggy. "I do believe he could throw a man over that bar if he wanted to."

Refreshed, Alice returned to her bargain hunting, while Joggy, wandered around again. He checked on the children and then watched the Kilpatrick mile and along with everyone else, cheered a local into finishing third. All the shouting gave him a thirst, so he made his way to O Meara's. He ordered a pint and spoke to several locals before spotting Tomato Flynn, sitting alone in a corner. Joggy bought a second pint and placed it in front of Tomato.

"Get that inside ya," he said.

"Thanks, that's very kind of you" said Tomato.

"Do you mind if I join ya?"

"I'd be offended if you didn't." Tomato moved up and Joggy slid in beside him. Tomato's right arm and hand was swathed in gauze and bandages and was suspended in a sling.

"How's the recovery coming along?"

"Slowly. It's only painful when they change the bandages, other than that, its fine."

"Good, good."

"Listen, I want to thank you and your good wife for everything you've being doing for me over the past few weeks. All that cooking and cleaning -- it's too much."

"Nonsense, it's the least we could do for you after what you did for Danny."

"Anyone would have done the same."

"I don't know about that," said Joggy, dismissively. "I don't think Winter would have done what you did. That took guts."

Tomato stared at his pint. His hand paused on the glass, as if he wanted to say something but then he picked it up and drank.

"Did the doctors give you any idea as to when you'll be able to get back to work?"

Tomato did not answer. He kept his head down and gently ran his fingers over his injured hand.

"You all right, Tom?" Joggy was concerned that he might have upset him.

"You know, I've lost my three middle fingers?"

"Yeah I know. But I wouldn't worry about that, you'll adapt. You'll still be able to grip things with the other two. It won't stop you from driving a tractor."

"Winter, didn't think so." There was a note of anger in his voice. "He let me go."

"The ungrateful bastard," said Joggy. "And you after risking your life for Victoria."

Tomato fell silent again. Joggy caught the bar mans eye. He lifted up two fingers.

"So what are you going to do now?"

"The dole I suppose. After thirty years...I don't think his father would have done that to me." He was barely concealing his anger.

Two pints arrived and Joggy paid.

"It's my round Joggy, I should pay for this."

"Nonsense."

"I don't want you treating me as a charity case," he snapped. "I can still pay my way."

"I know you can. It's only because I feel beholden to you. I feel I can never repay you."

"Well I'm buying the next one, whether your beholden to me or not." Tomato took another drink, leaned back against the leather seat and sighed deeply. He fell silent for a short while. Then he started -- the anger in his voice not much louder than a whisper. "I've been loyal to that family through thick and thin."

Joggy could read in his face, the battle that was going on in Tomato's head. The sense of anger and betrayal after giving so many years of loyal service was eating away inside him.

He looked at Joggy, a steely look in his eye. "Do you remember the summer we had two years ago?"

"God I do. It was long and hot and I was never as glad when it eventually rained."

"That long hot period dried up Winter's, slurry pit." He paused to take another gulp from his pint. Joggy began to wonder why he was telling him this.

"With all the piss dried up," he continued, "what was left was hard dried shit and stuck in the middle of that was a man's bike. At the time, I thought it a bit unusual. The only member of the Winter family who ever had a bike was young Margaret. I never remembered anyone else with one. It could be Canavan's.... then again, it might not."

"Is it still there?"

"It could be, but I can't be sure -- Winter could have moved it."

While the information was useful, it was also useless. Because Winter would never allow him to drain the slurry pit, let alone to set foot on the farm.

"You know Winter treats his land and his house like they belong to Great Britain?"

"It's not gone unnoticed."

"In all of thirty years, I have never been in the kitchen and I've never been offered tea. He likes playing the lord of the Manor, but behind the front he puts up, is something totally different." Tomato shook his head. "There's something about that man that's not right."

"What do you mean?"

"It's hard to explain. A few years ago, he reclaimed some land from the Hazel-wood. The grass was slow to grow there. He blamed it on the thin top soil. He's been keeping calves down there for the last month, feeding them regularly to make up for the shortage of grass."

"That's the field he said he was in when the fire broke out."

"Right. Except, when I was going home that evening I ran into him in the driveway. He had found out that Danny and Victoria were seeing one another and he was not happy. Then something strange happened. His mood changed almost immediately from anger to something more controlled, more….sinister. I don't know how else to explain it."

Tomato took another drink. He started again. "Anyway. Why I'm saying this is because I think Winter, set fire to the hay shed."

"What makes you think that?"

"Because, I had already fed the calves that evening. I told Winter that when I met him in the driveway. The only reason he used that excuse, was because he knew I wouldn't say anything… and I still wouldn't have if he hadn't let me go."

A rage in Joggy began to burn. He now had proof that Winter had tried to kill his son. The more he thought about it the hotter his rage burned. He finished his pint. "The old man was right," he said. "It's time he was put in his place." Joggy pushed his way through the crowded pub and out into the street. He was now like a man possessed. He asked several people if they had seen Fred Winter, but no one had.

His frantic search pattern however was not going unnoticed. From the height of the presentation platform, McNeill watched with keen interest.

Joggy suddenly heard a familiar sound. He turned towards the street in time to see Winter's Wolseley pull out of its parking space and drive slowly away. He ran towards his own car. He drove into the street and caught a glimpse through the crowds of the Wolseley, already turning O Meara's corner for home. Like Winter before him, he could only move slowly. Eventually he too turned the corner, pushed hard on the accelerator and gave chase. Tomato, watched from the footpath. As the speed built up, trees, gateways and houses began to flash past. His mind buzzed with questions that had no answers. "Was he getting back at me? Was that why he tried to kill Danny?" Around every turn he hoped to catch a glimpse of him. He ignored the speedometer. "But even that did not make sense" He floated over Greig Hill -- his work tools made an almighty racket as they clattered of the boot floor. At the other end of the strait that followed, he caught sight of the Wolseley. "Because what reason would he have for harming his housekeeper?" He accelerated harder. He still had no idea what he was going to say to Winter, when he caught up with him. Baker's yard flashed by. Seconds later he floated over the river bridge, zoomed down under the grey railway bridge and past his home. When he rounded the next bend, Winter's Wolseley was turning in his own driveway. Winter pulled up and got out with the bale tossing trophy in his arms. He turned to see Joggy, come to a screeching halt behind him.

"Come to congratulate me on my successful defence, have you?" he asked with an air of arrogance.

Afterwards, Joggy could not recall exactly what happened next. The only reminder he had was the pain coming from the bruised knuckles of his right hand and Winter on his back on the gravel yard, still holding the silver cup. "You bastard," Joggy shouted. "You tried to kill Danny. On the night of the fire you told me the reason you didn't see the blaze was because you were feeding calves in the field behind the wood."

"That's right, I was." Winter wiped the corner of his mouth with the back of his free hand and then inspected the blood smear.

"You're a fucking liar. Those calves had already been fed by Tomato."

Winter sat up and let out a derisory laugh. "Tomato is a disgruntled former employee. He'd say anything to make me look bad."

"I would take his word before yours. He also told me something else very interesting. He said you had Canavan's bike hidden in the slurry pit."

"I've had enough of this. You come into my yard and assault me and now you're calling me a liar. I can prove here and now that Tomato is the liar. There's a grappling hook in the tool shed. I use it to un-earth tree stumps. I'll give you a half-hour to scour the slurry pit. That should prove who's telling the truth."

Joggy, delighted with the turn of events, accepted Winter's offer. He started down the yard. He had only gone a few yards when he heard the gravel crunch behind him. He glanced over his shoulder and suddenly remembered Nellie Roe's warning, "Never turn your back on anyone you don't trust". The last thing he saw was the sun gleaming off the Silver trophy as it descended rapidly from the sky. Then all was dark.

# CHAPTER 31

Acidic vapours drew him from the darkness. They burnt his nostrils. As his senses revived, he realised he could not move. His chest and face lay on something hard and painful, while his hands and legs seemed to be tied to one another behind his back. He opened his eyes, lifted his aching head and found himself perched precariously, chest down, on a six inch solid block wall. On one side was the stone yard, overlaid with loose straw, dried cow dung and baked mud. On the other was the slurry pit.

"Ah, you're awake." Winter leaned down and peered into Joggy's face.

"Let me go," he demanded. He squirmed about, trying to fall onto the yard, but Winter had a solid grip of the rope that bound his hands and feet.

"Patience, Joggy, patience, I'll let you go in a minute."

"What are you going to do with me?"

"I thought that was painfully obvious. You wanted to know if Canavan's, bicycle is in this slurry pit, well, you're now going to find out first hand. And afterwards, when you're chatting to him, tell him I hope he burns in hell."

Joggy realized that his only hope was to keep the man talking and trust that someone or something would turn up. Then he suddenly realised that nobody knew he was here. He had left without telling anybody. They were all still at the sports day. Now at last he began to panic. "It was immoral -- what Canavan did to your mentally handicapped sister," he said quickly, trying to appease Winter. "Taking sexual advantage of a fourteen-year-old innocent was unpardonable."

"She was not mentally handicapped, she was mildly retarded," Winter said sharply. "What else do you know about Margaret?"

"I know she died in childbirth."

"How'd you find that out?" He pulled up the rope.

"It doesn't matter how I found out." Joggy winced at the sudden stab of pain in his shoulders. "Did you know that he was dying of cancer and had only a few weeks left to live?"

"No, and it wouldn't have made any difference if I did. I wouldn't have denied myself the pleasure of taking his sorry life. Do you know he flagged me down that Saturday? Said he had something important to tell me. Then as we drove along he describes how he took advantage of my baby sister. He's crying and asking for forgiveness, the fucking prick -- thought that if he said sorry, that that was going to be enough to satisfy my family's honour -- he had another thing coming to him. So when he went to get his bike from the trailer, I picked up a pipe and crushed his fucking skull. Oooh, that felt so good." His eyes closed, reliving the moment. "Now it's your turn, Joggy."

"Wait, wait, why did you set up Luke?"

Winter laughed. "Good ploy, Joggy, keep me talking, delay the inevitable. I suppose if I was in your position, I'd do the same."

"Come on Fred, the least you can do is to tell me why you set up Luke?"

Winter laughed again. "I didn't. That was a piece of good fortune. I was just trying to deflect the blame away from myself. It didn't matter to me whether Tom or Luke picked it up -- the fact that Luke was the one who did -- was sweet. I could eventually win my mother's trophy. No more coming second. The day Luke got sent down -- that was a good day. I was free. That was until you started nosing around and causing trouble."

"Is that why I'm tied up and about to drown?"

"Not entirely. It's also because you trespassed on the Queen's land, when you were told never to set foot on it again and of course you assaulted me, one of her subjects."

"What on earth are you on about? This is Ireland, not England."

"You don't get it, do you, Joggy? I'm an Orangeman, a Williamite and the Queen's loyal subject. My land is the Queen's land and I am its guardian and high protector and in her Majesty's absence, I am the law, judge and executioner."

Joggy swallowed hard as he suddenly realised he was dealing with a deranged human being. "Why'd you try and kill Danny and Victoria?"

"You're putting off the inevitable, Joggy." He pulled on the rope again.

"Just answer me before I go," he gasped.

Winter sighed. "Because one was a spy and the other a traitor -- they both had to die. Now it's your turn."

"You're not going to get away with this, Fred. People know I'm here."

"You're such a bullshitter. You came after me in a blind rage and I'm betting you told nobody. He pulled sharply on the restraints. "Talking's over Joggy, it's time for you to take your last breath."

Joggy winced as a bolt of hot pain seared through joints and muscles. It felt as if his arms were been ripped from their sockets. "Fuck you, you miserable piece of shit."

"Joggy, such language, I'm surprised at you, and you about to meet your maker."

"They'll find me and they'll know it was you," he shouted.

"You'll never be found," he said with sadistic joy. "I guarantee it. Take your last breath," he sneered, "it has to last you a lifetime." Winter leaned closer to his face. "Goodbye Joggy, be sure to pass on my regards to Luke." With a rough push, he was rolled of the narrow wall.

McNeill turned the corner just in time to see what was happening. "Stop," he yelled, but it was too late Joggy was already in the pit.

Surprised, Winter turned sharply. He was completely off-guard. He really thought Joggy had told no-body where he was going. "Ah, so the lone ranger has turned up to save the day," he said humorously as he tried to regain composure.

"I have you, Fred," said McNeill as he Jogged to the pit. "You'll not get away with murder this time."

"Now, that's where you're wrong, Sergeant, within a couple of days I'll be in the North. My friends there will hide me."

"But you'll have to get past me and out of this yard first. I can't see how you're going achieve that."

Winter gave a derisive laugh. "Very easily, you're going to let me. You have a choice now…. try and arrest me, which I know you don't have the required strength to do and by the time you figure that out, little auld Joggy here will really have been murdered. Or you can decide to save Joggy first, unfortunately, by the time you do that, I'll be well gone. Time to choose, Sergeant.

Tick tock, tick tock," Winter waved a hand from side to side like a pendulum.

The biggest prize of his life was in front of him, capture him and instant promotion was assured. For a split second McNeill froze, caught in two minds. "Fuck it," he swore, under his breath, as he stripped off his tunic. He moved swiftly past Winter and leaped over the sty wall. He sank until the slurry was chest high. He then dipped his arms in up to his shoulders and walked and groped around the area he figured Joggy was in --his nose inch's from the putrid mire. It was as thick as peanut butter and the more he moved the more the slurry was agitated and the stronger and more rancid became the smell. He held his breath aware he was also stirring up methane gas. He was on the verge of retching when his foot came to rest on something solid. It moved under his foot. He felt it with his foot and realised it was a leg. His arms were not long enough to reach him. He cursed Jackson as he leaned his head back and took a deep breath, then dived below the surface and grabbed hold of Joggy by the shoulders and with every ounce of strength he had, hauled him to the surface.

They both gasped and spat to rid the bitter taste but it remained in their mouths. McNeill then pinned Joggy to the slurry wall while he fumbled in his trousers pocket for his penknife. He cut the rope and then grabbed one of Joggy's legs and boosted him out off the pit and on to the stone yard. McNeill collapsed over the wall and landed beside him. Joggy lay on his back, hyperventilating, suddenly he turned on his side and vomited. McNeill lay on his back beside him.

"Thanks," Joggy gasped. He lifted his hand to wipe his mouth but when he saw the state of it, changed his mind. "I thought I was a gonner."

"By jaysus, you're going to owe me big time for that, Jackson."

"I owe you a couple of pints in McNamara's," he gasped again. "But other than that, I owe you fuck all."

"Two fucking pints, I don't think so. You're beholding to me now, Jackson. I dived into shit to save your miserable hide."

"Beholding my arse, McNeill, you were working and duty bound to save me. Anyway...he was about to insult him by saying, that he thought all pigs were happy in shit, but thought better of it... "again... thanks."

McNeill was fuming, but for the present he had to let it go; Winter had to be captured.

They found an outside tap and washed the sludge of their hands and faces.

When they got back to the house, Winter, true to his word, was gone and the police car radio was smashed. Three of its four tyres had also been knifed. Joggy checked his car and found that the keys were still in the ignition but the tyres had met the same fate as McNeill's.

McNeill kicked in Winter's back door and found the house phone; it was in bits on the floor. He then went to the nearest houses, the ones at the head of Winter's avenue, but no-one was home. They were all still at the Kilpatrick sports day. Winter had bought himself valuable time. When McNeill did eventually flag down a car and get in contact with the station, an hour and a half had elapsed.

Inspector Murray arrived along with a search team. "I have roadblocks set up between here and the border Sergeant; we'll have him before nightfall."

Joggy watched as the team drained the slurry pit and recovered the bicycle. They also recovered the remains of a small dog with a brick around its neck. Sandy was on the name tag. Murray allowed Joggy to pull off the perished rubber handgrip. The initials J.C. were still visible. Up in Winter's bedroom, under his pillow, they found the book of Robert Frost poems with the corner of the initials scratched off.

"You're a lucky man. Mister Jackson," said Murray, "that Sergeant McNeill was looking out for you or my team could have been pulling your body out of that slurry pit. Now tell me, how on God's earth did you get yourself into this mess in the first place?"

"It's a long story, Inspector."

"I have time."

"I know all the relevant facts, Sir," said McNeill, trying to keep the rising panic out of his voice, afraid of what Joggy might say, "it will all be explained in my report."

"I'm sure you do, Sergeant, and I'm really looking forward to reading it, but, Mister Jackson is here now and I would like to hear it first-hand."

Joggy started with the letter. He then related a version of the story that kept McNeill out of trouble, saying that he approached McNeill for help. Ed, incredulous with disbelief, stood open-mouthed, as Joggy, even gave him credit for his part in the investigation and finished off with how he had saved him from the slurry pit.

Murray now had two versions of the same investigation, McNeill's selfish one and Joggy's. But he wasn't born yesterday and reckoned that neither told the whole truth, but reasoned that Joggy's was probably the nearest to it.

"So, yes Inspector, I was very lucky." Joggy smiled benignly at McNeill. "And Ed already knows how grateful I am. I meant to ask you Ed, how did you know I was here?"

"Tomato told me. He was worried for your safety."

"It looks like I owe him a pint as well."

"I've arranged for a car Joggy, to pick your wife and children up from Kilpatrick," said Murray. "They should be home shortly. Garda Fleming over there," he said, glancing at a guard who was covering the passenger seat of his patrol car in duet sacks, "will take you home. It looks like he has it just ready"

Joggy thanked both men again and then moved towards his lift home.

# CHAPTER 32

"This is why I don't trust you, Sergeant," said Murray in a muted snarl. "You would not know how to tell the truth if your very life depended on it. That man came within seconds of losing his life today and it's all down to your cowboy attitude to law enforcement. Fortunately for you right now, you're the hero of the hour. I should by rights be kicking your sorry arse out of the force, but that would raise to many questions. From now on you'd better do everything by the book, because, I will be watching you very closely." Murray moved towards the house. He had only gone a few yards when he paused and looked back at McNeill who was still in the same spot looking miserable with yellow urine and the disgusting remnants of solid matter adhering to his clothes. He did not think he had been unfair to McNeill, but felt he needed to say something else. After all he knew McNeill's reasons for doing what he did. "You performed heroically today, Sergeant. Now all we need is to get our hands on Winter, and you'd never know what the future might hold."

"Thank you, sir," said McNeill with a straight face that hid a huge smile of relief.

Murray moved towards the house.

Garda Fleming's car pulled up beside McNeill. All four windows were fully rolled down.

Joggy leaned out through the passenger window and held his hand out. McNeill took it. "Thanks again," said Joggy with a broad smile. "Now were even."

As he watched them drive away, McNeill knew what he meant. Joggy had paid his debt: A policeman's career for a gardener's life.

* * * *

Joggy arrived home shortly after the Garda car had dropped off Alice and the children.

Garda Fleming jumped from the driver seat, came around and pulled open the passenger door. He wanted Joggy and his stench out of his car as quickly as possible.

From the doorway Alice glowered down the length of the path at him. When he opened the gate she turned and went inside. He knew what lay ahead, cold shoulder and silent tongue for a week, but not until, in the privacy of their bedroom, she would give him an earful. He was prepared for his punishment. When he entered the kitchen, Alice was standing with her back to him at the kitchen table. The children were seated around it. She turned to face him. Her eyes were red from crying and her face was white with rage. She raised a trembling right index finger and pointed it at him. "I don't want to hear a word." She shook with anger. "Not one fucking word."

Arguing in front of the children was something they did not normally do, but Alice at this point was beyond caring. "I went looking for you, but you and the car were gone and nobody knew where. And then this guard turns up." Her eyes watered up and tears began to flow once more. She shook them angrily away. "I stood there frozen to the spot, fearing the worst. Everyone was looking at me. But then he told me what had happened and I was so relieved I burst out crying. I cried all the way home.

"I'm sorry," he said.

"You chased after a murderous maniac," she screamed. "You Left us behind and told nobody. What were you thinking? You could have been killed. A few seconds more and

\* \* \* \*

"I'm sorry, I wasn't thinking." It was all he could say. He knew no amount of excuses could cover his foolhardiness.

Danny, Helen and Katie watched, riveted to their seats. They had never heard their mother use bad language or seen their parents openly fighting before. Danny began to feel uncomfortable, as if he should not be there. He contemplated taking the girls and himself into one of the bedrooms, but then changed his mind; this was a rarity, this was just too good to miss.

By now Alice was in meltdown. She ignored her husband's protestations. She simple did not want to hear them. "You didn't give one fucking thought to us, did you? If you'd been killed, what would I have done then? I'd have no husband and the children would have no father."

"I'm really sorry," he said again.

But it was swallowed up in Alice's non-stop attack. The questions rained down on him. She barely paused to take a breath between each one -- leaving no room for him to answer. She did not want him to answer. She knew his answer. "He didn't think." There was a course to run and she could not stop until she had run it. When she finished, she ordered him out of the house, followed by. "I don't want to see you for the rest of the evening."

He stood there and looked at her like a chastened child.

"What are you waiting for?" she screamed.

"Can I get cleaned up first and change my clothes."

Alice did not respond. She turned away from him, opened the top lid of the range and tossed in some turf.

\* \* \* \*

Joggy washed and changed into fresh clothes and then went for a walk. In his heart he knew that Alice was right; what he did was reckless. He began to think of the--what ifs. What would have happened lf McNeill had not shown up. What if Winter had gotten away with it. Would I have ever been found? What would have happened to my family? His muscles twitched nervously as the possible consequences of his actions hit home.

He had not gone far when he heard footsteps running up behind him.

"Do you mind if I tag along?" said Danny.

"Not if you don't mind been seen with an outcast?" he said, half smiling.

"That was some ear bashing you got, dad."

"I deserved it. Your mother was right. I took a stupid risk and nearly lost everything. I have no qualms with that. But I suppose on the plus side, Luke's name was cleared today."

"But they haven't caught Winter, yet?"

"It doesn't matter if they find him or not. Luke didn't care one way or the other if his name was cleared in a court of law, so long as his friends and neighbours knew the truth, that's all he wanted, and by now, everybody knows. He can rest easy now"

As he strolled along with Danny by his side, he realised Alice would never forget what he did, but she would eventually forgive him. He would wait patiently for the signal -- when she would dish up his favourite meal.

"Dad, there's something I wanted to ask you."

"Yeah."

A cheeky grin creased Danny's face. "What does slurry taste like?"

"Vanilla," said Joggy smiling. "It tasted just like vanilla ice cream."

# CHAPTER 33

Three days later Winter's burnt out car was found in an isolated wooded area outside of Belturbet in County Cavan.

"The tip-off was correct sir. The car's burnt out. There are two sets of car tracks. It looks like he was met." The investigating officer said down the phone line to Inspector Murray. "And by now, he's surely been shepherded over the border."

"What's your relationship with the RUC like," Murray asked.

"Pretty good at the moment, sir. I wouldn't lose faith just yet. We have friends in the RUC and the army. They're keeping an eye out for him."

\* \* \* \*

That night, on a lonely mountain road, the car in which Fred Winter was travelling, came to a halt at a paramilitary checkpoint. The front seat passenger got out and opened the rear passenger door. With a side-ways movement of his head he gestured for Winter to get out. They then walked in the same way they had driven -- in silence -- for about a mile into the woods until they came upon a deserted cottage. As they approached, one of the men gave a signal -- an owl hoot -- three times. Two men with rifles stood outside the door and watched them approach. Without uttering a word, one of them opened it and ushered Winter into a vacant room. They closed the door and left. The only piece of furniture in the room was a chair.

The two men resumed sentry duty outside the door, while the front-seat passenger guarded the window. After pacing the room for a while Winter sat on the chair and waited. It was after midnight when the room door opened again and three men walked in. Two were armed with hand guns. They closed the door and took up sentry duty -- one each side of the door. One looked to be in his twenties, while the second was touching the mid-forties.

"About bloody time," said Fred, when he saw the smiling face of the third man, his good friend, Terry Clarke. He gave a short high-pitched nervous laugh. "I was beginning to fear that the other side had got me."

"You're safe, we have you now." They shook hands. "You're now among people who want to take care of you."

"I didn't know you were involved…"

"I'm not. But there are a lot of things you don't know about me, Fred. Like my connections, they come in useful from time to time."

"These are our people, aren't they?" he asked, nodding in the direction of the two sentries. He was feeling a little uneasy and could not put his finger on the exact reason for it.

"They're my people, and I have a good working relationship with them."

Terry's answers were not helping Fred's uneasiness. "What's with all the silence? No one has spoken one word to me since I was picked up."

"Security. You know how it is."

Even though he did not understand fully, Winter still nodded acceptance.

* * * *

Terry walked slowly to the window. Beyond the dusty and cobwebbed glass the night was black and impenetrable. The light from the primus lamp that hung from a hook in the ceiling was reflected in the window. Winter moved about underneath it. He was getting edgy. Something was off. The hairs standing on the back of his neck told him so. He scrutinized the two sentries for several seconds, before returning his attention to his friend. "What's really going on Terry?"

Terry stared into the darkness in thoughtful silence for several seconds more before wiping the dust from the window-sill with his hand. He then turned around and sat on it.    "Sit down, we need to talk," he said solemnly.

Fred obeyed and sat on the front edge of the chair.

"There's something I have to discuss with you before we leave here. As you can appreciate Fred, my status in the community here places me in a delicate position." His tone was measured. "It will not allow me to have friends who could embarrass me with their hidden pasts. I and everyone I'm closely associated with have to be above reproach. My task as Grandmaster of the local order is an onerous one and one I take very seriously. So when I took on this job, I took it upon myself to investigate everyone who was close to me -- and that included you, Fred.  Because if there was any shit coming down the pipe to me -- I needed to be forewarned. So is there anything you want to tell me?"

"You're supposed to be my friend, not my interrogator."

"I am your friend. But the question is what kind of friend are you to me?"

"What? What are you talking about?"

"Do you remember the name of the young catholic lad that was mentioned in my father's diary, the one found tied to a tree in Blackfield woods?"

"Can't say I do."

"Of course not. Why would you want to remember his name? All you were interested in at the time was smashing in his skull with an iron bar."

"Now you're talking shite."

"Do you remember your grandparents' next door neighbour, Charlie Wright?"

"Of course I do. You think I killed him as well?"

"Did you not think I would find out?"

"There's nothing to find out, I didn't kill them."

"Let me refresh your memory. It was the night your sister Margaret died. You were distraught. Charlie Wright was in the hospital with your parents. He volunteered to take you home. But on the way back he took a detour to Blackfield woods. He parked the car and told you to wait, while he attended to a little business. Curiosity got the better of you. So you followed and watched as he slipped on a balaclava and joined a small group of hooded men who were administering a punishment beating to a young man by the name of Rory Donovan. They were shouting abuse at him, calling him a catholic bastard and since you were looking for someone on whom to take revenge for your sister's death, a catholic -- here was your opportunity tied to a tree. You ran in to where the men were standing. Grabbed the iron bar out of Charlie Wright's hands and screaming like a banshee, you smashed it into his skull -- killing him instantly. They didn't know you and apart from Charlie, you didn't know them. Charlie reassured them that it was alright. That you were only after losing your sister and that he would take care of it. On the way back to your grandparents, Charlie's words played on your mind. You got nervous. You didn't know what he meant by, he would take care of it. So you decided to strike first. Later that night you sneaked out and tampered with the brakes on Charlie's car. The next morning they failed going down Forkhill, and he was killed."

Fred clapped. "That's some story, Terry. What work of fiction did you extract that from?"

"I don't do fiction, I prefer reality. In fact, I'm willing to bet that in your house you have in your possession two incriminating items. Let me correct that. They were in your possession. The Gardai have them now. One is a gold cigarette lighter -- given to Charlie Wright, on the occasion of their fortieth wedding anniversary -- as a present from his wife. The inscription reads, "From Florrie with love." The other is a pearl handled Swiss pocket knife. Remember, you picked it up off the ground after you killed Rory -- it had the initials B. B. T. You kept them as souvenirs."

Fred's penetrating gaze bore into Terry. All he knew about his friend was being turned on its head. The one person in the world he trusted; was making him very nervous. "How did you find out all of this?"

"I have my sources."

Terry reached into his jacket pocket and extracted a pearl handled Swiss pocket knife. "Rory had my knife and I had his. The initials on this one are B. B. R. The initials on the one you had were, B. B T."

"What the fuck is going on here? I thought you were supposed to be helping me disappear?"

"That will happen later, but first we have to deal with this."

"Deal with what, he was a fucking Catholic -- one less to worry about. So I killed a Catholic and an old man who would have turned me in. Now you know the truth, are you proud of yourself?"

"No I can't say I am." He stood up again, turned and for a few reflective seconds stared into the darkness. "He was my best friend -- my blood brother -- that's what the B.B. stood for -- and you killed him," he said, his voice tinged with emotion. "We were like Abbott and Costello. I was the serious one and he was the joker. He knew how to make me laugh. Religious differences had nothing to do with us. We were just two best friends who loved spending time together. I couldn't even go to the funeral proper. I watched, hiding in the trees, outside the walls of the graveyard as they buried him. I had to wait till everyone was gone to stand at his graveside. There and then I swore on his grave, that I would avenge his death. The funny thing is -- I don't think he would have wanted me to -- but I wanted to. And I didn't care how long it took. It wasn't 'till years later I found out that my father was behind it. He wasn't part of the group that night. But he was the instigator. He organised the beating. Like you, he hated Catholics. But dad wouldn't leave it alone. He was always trying to separate us. They threatened him first and when that didn't work they kidnapped him, tied him to a tree and broke every bone in his body. He might have lived." Terry, turned back to face Fred. "But thanks to you, he never got that chance."

Fred stood up as the truth slowly dawned on him. He glanced at the two sentries before focusing his attention fully on Terry. "The only people who knew what you know now are dead -- and they were killed by the I.R.A."

"Yes they were."

Fred sprang forward, wrapped his hands around Terry's throat and lifted him off his feet. "Who the fuck are you?" he roared. His fingers tightened around his throat and his thumbs crushed his windpipe.

"Let him go," shouted the younger sentry, pressing the muzzle of his gun hard against Winter's skull. "If you don't I'll blow your fucking brains out where you stand."

Reluctantly, Winter released his grip.

"Now sit in that chair and don't get up again. If you do I'll fucking knee-cap ya."

Terry coughed, stretched and massaged his neck. He sat back into the window.

"You bastard, you're the traitor," growled Winter. "Because of you a lot of good men have died."

"Yes and because of you, I had to sell my soul. I've had to pay a heavy price."

Winter glanced at the two sentries. One of them had his gun trained on him.

"Did you kill your father?"

"I told them about his weak heart and they worried him to an early grave. I didn't want him to die quick like the others. I wanted him to die slowly, thinking about what he did."

"So really you're no better than me?" sneered Winter.

"In a way, I suppose not. The only difference is I don't take innocent lives."

"Being friends -- that, I suppose, was just to keep me close?"

"Yes, well you know what they say."

"So what happens now? You going to shoot me?"

"No. I've never killed anyone."

A flicker of relief crossed Winter's face.

Terry stood up and walked to the door. He placed his hand on the shoulder of the forty-something sentry. "He's going to shoot you."

"What's so special about him?"

"He's been waiting a long time to do it and his name is the last one you'll ever hear: Michael Donovan; Rory's brother. But don't fret about it, it'll be quick. You'll be dead before you know you're dead: Which is more than you gave Rory."

"What are you talking about, he died quick."

"He died in terror." For the first time his voice rose above the measured tone. "What must he have felt, his last seconds of life, unable to defend himself, writhing in agony, and just as he thought it was over -- in you come screaming like some fucking demented demon. Quick, I don't think so. They must have been the longest seconds of his life?"

"My conscience is clear."

"How does it feel, Fred, knowing you're about to lose everything? Was it really worth it?"

"I might die for Queen and Country tonight but I'll die in the knowledge that my land is safely out of Catholic hands. It will be safeguarded. I have family who will gladly take it over."

"By family, you mean second cousins, no one... closer?"

"What are you talking about? What do you know?"

"I said, everything, Fred. Your family really should have been more careful about what they threw away all those years ago."

"I said, what do you know?"

"Think on it Fred, they say one man's rubbish is another man's gold." Terry walked out of the cottage and into a wall of darkness. His head was swimming and there was no joy in his heart. For years he had dreamt of this moment, acting it out in his head, how it would go and the elation he would feel. He had not bargained on this weight of sadness.

Winter's head was also swimming as he sat on the wooden chair. One question was doing laps. "What was thrown away in his families past that could now take his farm away?"

"Kneel." The older sentry commanded.

"Fuck you. I'll kneel for no fucking catholic. You can shoot me where I sit."

With the cold steel barrel pressed hard against his skull, the answer came. His eyes widened as the realization hit him. "Clarke, you bastard you…." The bullet entered his brain and trapped forever the answer in his throat.

# EPILOGUE

Inspector Murray rang Sergeant McNeill the next morning. McNeill was sitting at his desk finishing the last of his tea.

"I'm sorry to have to tell you sergeant, but Fred Winters body was found this morning in Northern Ireland, dumped on the side of a mountain road. He was shot once at close range through the head. I'm afraid any hopes you had of promotion will have to be put on the long finger. Because without Winter, we won't get a conviction and without a conviction.... well you know how it goes."

"Any idea how long I'll have to wait, Sir?" he asked.

"Indefinitely."

Murray hung up. McNeill gazed for several seconds into the half-empty cup – his future now as murky as the tea. He smashed it against the far wall of the station house.

\* \* \* \*

The following Sunday after mass, Joggy, sent his family ahead of him to O Meara's, while he paid a quick visit to the graveyard. He stood in front of Luke Baker's grave. In the distance he could see his parents' headstone. He paused and smiled lightly before returning his attention to Luke.

"I'm not John Canavan, Luke, but, as John would have said - in the words of that great Negro spiritual leader, Martin Luther King – *'free at last, free at last, God almighty, we're free at last'."*

He turned and headed for O Meara's.

May 1974.

It was a Saturday morning. Joggy knocked on Danny's bedroom door and entered. "Are you awake?"

"I am now." Danny wiped the sleep from his eyes.

"How's college?"

"Please tell me you didn't wake me up to ask that?"

"No I didn't. You still want to earn money?"

"Do you have to ask? What have you in mind?"

"There's a chance of Saturday work down on Winter's, farm. I hear new owners have moved in during the week. Why don't you try them?"

"Great, I will… later."

Danny went back to sleep. He eventually arose in the afternoon, had something to eat and went for a walk. He climbed the steps and knocked on Winter's front door. A slim middle-aged lady answered.

"Yes, young man, how can I help you?" She had a northern accent.

"I believe you've just taken over the farm. I'm looking for part-time work and I was wondering if you needed anyone on Saturdays?"

She became a little flustered. "Hold on… I'll get the boss."

Danny turned on the doorstep and looked out across the flat green fields -- their hedgerows in full bloom.

"Are you still kissing your sister?" He spun around in instant recognition -- the shock sucking the breath from his body. Confusion reigned for several seconds, then he smiled; a huge beaming smile.

"Nah, moved on to me mother -- needed more experience."
They laughed.

"How long are you staying for this time?"

"For good I hope" said Victoria. She smiled, moved forward and wrapped her arms around his neck. "I inherited the place.

The End

If you have enjoyed what you have just read…there are two short
stories on my Blog site

-    www eldoda.simplesite.com

Email – hughpflanagan@gmail.com

Many thanks for purchasing my first novel.

Hugh

Made in the USA
Charleston, SC
15 September 2013